50p

Wuthering Heights

Emily Brontë

Wuthering
Heights

A shortened version
prepared by

H. OLDFIELD BOX

London: HODDER & STOUGHTON, Limited

First published 1846

This shortened version
First printed February 1952

Printed in Great Britain for Hodder and Stoughton,
Limited, by Richard Clay and Company, Ltd.,
Bungay, Suffolk

INTRODUCTION

By H. Oldfield Box

THE story of Emily Brontë is not her story alone. It is the story of a family of geniuses. And it is one that has never ceased to fascinate, filled though it is with suffering, and overcast by the shadow of death.

In the West Riding of Yorkshire, close to the borders of Lancashire, lies Haworth, an ugly and even repellent village, little changed in the last hundred years. The town of Keighley, four miles away, straggles almost into it. The village, which like the neighbouring town, derives its living mainly from the manufacture of worsteds, is set on a steep hill. At the top of this hill, just off the main street, are the church, an overcrowded graveyard, and finally the old parsonage. A two-storied dwelling, built of grey stone, it is the last house of the village. Beyond are the moors.

Here in February, 1820, came the Rev. Patrick Brontë, with his wife and six little children. Maria, the eldest, was not yet seven. Charlotte, the third in age, was not four. Emily herself was a baby of two. Their mother, stricken with an internal cancer, was soon a dying woman. They were seldom allowed to enter her room. Mr. Brontë, when not out walking, was largely shut up in his study. He took his meals apart. The children, " grave and silent beyond their years ", spent most of their time alone, in a little room on the first floor, called, not the nursery, but the children's study. This alone is indicative of their characters. " You would not have known there was a child in the house," Mrs. Gaskell was told by a

woman who came to nurse Mrs. Brontë during her illness,
" they were such still, noiseless, good little creatures.
Maria would shut herself up in the children's study with a
newspaper, and be able to tell one everything when she
came out; debates in parliament, and I don't know what
else. She was as good as a mother to her brothers and
sisters. But there never were such good children. I used
to think them spiritless, they were so different to any
other children I have ever seen." The same woman told
Mrs. Gaskell how " the six little creatures used to walk
out alone, hand in hand, on to the wild glorious moors
(which in after days they loved so passionately), the elder
ones taking thoughtful care of the wee toddling things."
This is an unforgettable, heartrending picture. How
vividly one can imagine this pale-faced little chain, so
devoted to each other, already, in effect, motherless.

They were soon to be motherless in fact. In 1821,
Mrs. Brontë died. A year later one of her sisters came
from Cornwall, to look after the family. She taught her
nieces needlework, and saw that they learned to be useful
about the house. Otherwise she exercised little influence
on them; their general habits remained unaltered.
Divided from other children—and not even desiring their
company—they were driven increasingly within themselves. They read—adult books from their father's
library. (" Long before Maria died at the age of eleven,
her father used to say he could converse with her on any
of the leading topics of the day with as much freedom
and pleasure as with any grown-up person.") They
acted plays of their own devising; to amuse themselves,
they began to write. Apart from the brief unhappy inter-
lude of Cowan's Bridge, a seminary for the daughters of
clergy to which Maria, Elizabeth, Charlotte and Emily
were all sent for a short period, none but Charlotte ever
went to school, and *she* was not sent until she was nearly

fifteen. They lived in books, in their own imaginations, and in each others' company.

A family such as this, so highly aware, so different from ordinary people, could never adapt themselves to the conditions of life in the outside world. The two eldest, Maria and Elizabeth, were mercifully spared the struggle, both dying of consumption in early childhood. The remaining four lived to grow up. Charlotte, Emily and Anne made repeated attempts to earn their living by governessing, but their efforts were always defeated, not by incompetence or lack of courage, but by the bruising their experiences inflicted on their sensitive souls, and the consequent effect on their health. They were intensely attached to their home and the moors, and only there could they know any measure of peace. Their brother, the brilliant Bramwell, was by nature more sociable than his sisters, but possessing insufficient strength of character to match his gifts, he became a drunkard and a drug addict, and quickly degenerated.

Then, one by one, their brief candles guttered and went out. Bramwell died at thirty, of delirium tremens (September 1848). In December of the same year Emily, a strong, fiercely independent spirit, followed him to the grave, a victim of the same disease as her elder sisters. She was twenty-nine. *Wuthering Heights*, her only novel, had been published a year before, but time was to pass before its genius was recognised. The gentle, patient, enduring Anne (author of *Agnes Grey* and *The Tenant of Wildfell Hall*) was carried off the following May, aged twenty-seven.

Thus Mr. Brontë was deprived of all his children but Charlotte; and she died seven years later (also of consumption), at the age of thirty-nine; to be followed at last, after another six years, by the old clergyman himself.

Of all this remarkable family Charlotte is perhaps the

best known, as she is certainly the most widely read. Her novel, *Jane Eyre*, was an immediate and sensational best-seller, which still retains its popularity. And her three others—*Shirley*, *Villette* and *The Professor*—are all (and especially *Villette*) remarkable books. After the death of Maria, Charlotte became, and remained, the little mother of her sisters and brother. And, in a sense, their father too; for the Rev. Patrick Brontë, living his own detached life, was hardly an adequate parent. It was Charlotte who initiated all the enterprises—literary and tutorial—of this strange and tragic group. And as far as such lives as theirs could be managed, she managed them. The tale of this little woman, half-blind, struggling against her own natural reserve and shyness, to fight, not only her own battles, but the battles of all the rest of her family, and to find for them all the means of earning a living, is moving and heroic indeed.

But the great genius of the family was Emily; and next to Bramwell, she was Charlotte's greatest problem. In Emily's composition there was no weakness of character as in her brother's. But hers was the soul of the greatest sensitivity, and with this went fierce detachment and reserve. In a family of suffering introverts, she was the introvert supreme. The wild lonely moorland which lay beyond Haworth Parsonage had become an integral part of her being; and for her to be exiled from it was an agony so great as to be beyond bearing. Yet, in her own way, she possessed the most indomitable spirit of them all. To the casual visitor to Haworth Parsonage she would have seemed the most self-sufficient member of the family. She went about her household tasks with an almost robust readiness, and insisted on carrying on with them as long as, and even after, sufficient strength remained to her. And so strong was her will that her family dared not oppose her. Throughout her illness she refused to see a doctor, and on the very day of her death she dressed and came downstairs as usual. But she could not share Charlotte's determination to carve a way into life. To her the external world was a thing of no importance; the life of the spirit was everything.

" Emily's self ", writes Charles Morgan, " was set apart from these things " (i.e. the tasks and drudgery of every-day life).—" She communicated it in her art because being an artist who drew from the distillations of her spirit . . . she could not do otherwise, but she was reluctant that her art should confess herself to the world. She was angry when Charlotte dragged out her poems."

But for Charlotte, Emily's poems (some of which place her among the great) might easily have been destroyed without ever seeing the light of day. And had it not been for Charlotte's scheme—after the failure of their collected poems to sell—that she and Emily and Anne should each set to work on a novel, *Wuthering Heights* would never have been written. Emily had no craving for public success and approbation.

Wuthering Heights is a strange, brutal and terrifying book. In the whole story there is barely a handful of sane and normal characters. It is badly constructed, and abounds in inconsistencies. And yet it is a novel of a strange compelling beauty; every page grips; and because it is the work of a unique mind, tortured by a vision of pure ecstasy, it is haunting and unforgettable. Here there is Hell in Heaven, and Heaven in Hell; and we know not if love is from God or from the Devil.

CHAPTER I

1801.—I have just returned from a visit to my landlord—
the solitary neighbour I shall be troubled with. This is
certainly a beautiful country. In all England I could not
have fixed upon a neighbourhood so completely removed
from the stir of society—a perfect misanthropist's heaven;
and Mr. Heathcliff and I are such a suitable pair to divide
the desolation between us. A capital fellow! He little
imagined how my heart warmed towards him when I
beheld his black eyes withdraw so suspiciously under
those brows as I rode up to his bleak, wind-swept dwelling,
and announced my name.

" Mr. Heathcliff? " I said.

A nod was the answer.

" Mr. Lockwood, your new tenant, sir. I do myself
the honour of calling on you as soon as possible after my
arrival, to express the hope that I have not inconvenienced
you by my perseverance in soliciting the occupation of
Thrushcross Grange."

" Thrushcross Grange is my own, sir," he interrupted,
wincing. " I should not allow anyone to inconvenience
me, if I could hinder it. Walk in ! "

The " walk in " was uttered with closed teeth, and
expressed the sentiment, " Go to the devil," and I think
it was that circumstance which determined me to accept
the invitation. I felt interested in a man who seemed
more exaggeratedly reserved than myself. I unmounted.

" Joseph, take Mr. Lockwood's horse, and bring some
wine," he called as, with a very ill grace, he turned and
preceded me up the causeway to the door of Wuthering
Heights. An old man, sour and ill-visaged, appeared in
answer to his summons, and relieved me of my horse.

" Here we have the whole establishment of domestics, I suppose," was the reflection suggested by his master's compound order. " No wonder the grass grows between the flags, and cattle are the only hedge-cutters."

Before passing the threshold, I paused to admire a quantity of grotesque carving about the front, and over the door I detected the date " 1550 ", and the name " Hareton Earnshaw ".

One step brought us into the family living-room— beyond which, from the kitchen, I distinguished a chatter of tongues, and a clatter of culinary utensils. (So there were other occupants.) Above the huge fireplace were sundry villainous old guns, and a couple of horse-pistols; and, by way of ornament, three gaudily painted canisters disposed along the ledge. The floor was of smooth, white stone; the chairs, high-backed, primitive structures painted green, one or two heavy black ones lurking in the shade. In an arch under the dresser reposed a huge, liver-covered bitch pointer, surrounded by a swarm of squealing puppies, and other dogs haunted other recesses.

The apartment would have been nothing as belonging to a homely, northern farmer. But Mr. Heathcliff forms a singular contrast to his abode and style of living. He is a dark-skinned gipsy in aspect, in dress and manners a gentleman—that is, as much a gentleman as many a country squire; rather slovenly, perhaps, yet not looking amiss with his negligence, because he has an erect, hand-some figure; and rather morose. Some people might suspect him of a degree of under-bred pride; I have a sympathetic chord within that tells me it is nothing of the sort. I know by instinct that his reserve springs from an aversion to showy displays of feeling, to manifestations of mutual kindness. He'll hate or love equally under cover, and esteem it a species of impertinence to be hated or loved again.—No, I am running on too fast. I bestow my own attributes over liberally on him. Mr. Heathcliff may have entirely dissimilar reasons from myself for keeping his hand out of the way when he meets a would-be acquaint-ance. Let me hope my constitution is almost peculiar. My dear mother used to say I should never have a com-fortable home, and only last summer I proved myself perfectly unworthy of one.

While enjoying a month of fine weather at the sea coast I was thrown into the company of a most fascinating creature. I never told my love vocally; still, if looks have language, the merest idiot might have guessed that I was over head and ears. She understood me at last, and looked in return—the sweetest of all imaginable looks. And what did I do? I shrank icily into myself, till finally the poor innocent was led to doubt her own senses, and overwhelmed with confusion, persuaded her mamma to decamp. Such is my unfortunate disposition, by which I have gained a reputation of deliberate heartlessness; how undeserved I alone can appreciate.

I took a seat at the hearthstone opposite my host, and filled up an interval of silence by attempting to caress the canine mother. My caress provoked only a long, guttural snarl.

" You'd better let that dog alone," growled Mr. Heath-cliff, checking further demonstrations with a punch of his foot. " She's not accustomed to be spoiled." Then, striding to a side door, he shouted again, " Joseph ! "

Joseph mumbled indistinctly in the depths of the cellar, but gave no intimation of ascending; so his master dived down to him, leaving me *vis-à-vis* the ruffianly bitch and a pair of sheep-dogs, who shared a jealous guardianship over all my movements. Not wishing to come in contact with their fangs, I sat still, but, imagining they would not understand tacit insults, I unfortunately indulged in making faces at the trio—which so irritated madam that she suddenly broke into a fury and leapt on my knees. I flung her back, and hastened to interpose the table between us. This proceeding roused the whole hive. Half a dozen four-footed fiends of various sizes leaped at me from hidden dens, and I was constrained to shout for assistance.

Mr. Heathcliff and his man climbed from the cellar in obvious phlegm, but without haste. Happily an inhabitant of the kitchen made more dispatch. A lusty dame, with tucked-up gown, bare arms, and fire-flushed cheeks, rushed into the midst of us with a frying-pan, and used that weapon and her tongue to such effect that the storm had subsided before Heathcliff entered.

" What the devil's the matter ? "

" What the devil, indeed," I muttered. " You might as well leave a stranger with a brood of tigers."

" They won't meddle with persons who touch nothing," he remarked, putting the bottle before me. " The dogs do right to be vigilant. Take a glass of wine."

" No, thank you."

" Not bitten, are you ? "

" If I had been, I would have set my signet on the biter." Heathcliff's countenance relaxed into a grin.

" Come, come," he said; " you are flurried, Mr. Lockwood. Here, take a little wine. Guests are so rare in this house, that I and my dogs, I own, hardly know how to receive them. Your health, sir."

I bowed and returned the pledge, beginning to perceive that it would be foolish to sit sulking for the misbehaviour of a pack of curs. I found him very intelligent on the topics we touched; and before I went home I was encouraged so far as to volunteer another visit tomorrow. He evidently wished no repetition of my intrusion. I shall go, notwithstanding. It is astonishing how sociable I feel myself, compared with him.

CHAPTER II

YESTERDAY afternoon set in misty and cold. I had half a mind to spend it by my study fire, instead of wading through heath and mud to Wuthering Heights. On coming up after dinner, however (N.B.—I dine between twelve and one o'clock), I saw a servant-girl on her knees, surrounded by brushes and coal-scuttles, and raising an infernal dust as she extinguished the flames with the heaps of cinders. This spectacle drove me back immediately. I took my hat, and after a four miles walk, arrived at Heathcliff's garden gate just in time to escape the first feathery flakes of a snow-shower.

On that bleak hill-top the earth was hard with a black frost. Being unable to remove the chain, I jumped over the gate, and running up the flagged causeway, knocked vainly for admittance, till my knuckles tingled and the dogs howled.

"Wretched inhospitable inmates!" I ejaculated. "But I will get in!" So resolved, I grasped the latch and shook it vehemently. Vinegar-faced Joseph projected his head from a round window of the barn.

"What are ye for?" he shouted. "T' maister's down i't' fowld. Go round by th' end ot' laith, if ye went to spake to him."

"Is there nobody inside to open the door?"

"There's nobbut t' missis, and shoo'll not oppen't an ye mak yer flaysome dins till neeght."

"Why? Cannot you tell her who I am, eh, Joseph?"

"Nor-ne me! I'll hae no hand wi't," muttered the head, vanishing.

The snow began to drive thickly. I seized the handle to essay another trial, when a young man without a coat, and shouldering a pitch-fork, appeared in the yard behind. He hailed me to follow him; and, after making through a wash-house, and across a paved area, we at length arrived in the huge, warm, cheerful apartment where I was formerly received. And near the table, laid for a plentiful evening meal, I was pleased to observe " the missis ", an individual whose existence I had never previously suspected. I bowed, thinking she would bid me take a seat. She looked at me, leaning back in her chair, motionless and mute.

" Rough weather, Mrs. Heathcliff," I remarked.

She never opened her mouth. I stared—she stared also—in a cool, regardless manner, exceedingly embarrassing and disagreeable.

" Sit down," said the young man gruffly. " He'll be in soon."

I obeyed, and hemmed, and called the villainous bitch Juno, who deigned, on this second interview, to move the extreme tip of her tail.

" A beautiful animal ! " I commenced again. " Do you intend to parting with the little ones, madam ? "

" They are not mine," said the amiable hostess, more repellingly than Heathcliff himself would have replied.

I hemmed once more, drew closer to the hearth, and repeated my comment on the wildness of the evening.

" You should not have come out," she said, rising and reaching from the chimney-piece two of the painted canisters.

I now had a distinct view of her whole figure and countenance. She was slender, scarcely past girlhood, and possessed the most exquisite little face I have ever had the pleasure of beholding : small features, very fair ; golden ringlets hanging loose on her delicate neck ; and eyes that, had they been agreeable in expression, would have been irresistible. The canisters were almost out of her reach. I made a motion to help her. She turned on me as a miser might if anyone attempted to assist him in counting his gold.

" I don't want your help," she snapped. " I can get them for myself."

" I beg your pardon."

" Were you asked to tea? " she demanded, standing with a spoonful of the leaf poised over the pot.

" I shall be glad of a cup," I answered.

" Were you asked? " she repeated.

" No," I said, half smiling. " You are the proper person to ask me."

She flung the tea back, and resumed her chair in a pet. Her forehead corrugated, and her red under-lip pushed out, like a child's ready to cry.

Meanwhile the young man had slung on his person a decidedly shabby upper garment, and, erecting himself before the blazing fire, looked down on me for all the world as though there were some mortal feud unavenged between us. I began to doubt whether he were servant or not. His dress and speech were rude; his thick brown curls rough and uncultivated, and his hands embrowned like those of a common labourer. Still his bearing was free and haughty, and he showed none of a servant's assiduity in attending upon the lady of the house.

After five minutes the entrance of Heathcliff relieved me in some measure from my uncomfortable state.

" You see, sir, I am come, according to promise," I exclaimed with affected cheerfulness.

" So I perceive. But I wonder you should choose a thick snowstorm to trouble about it. Do you not know that you run a risk of being lost in the marshes on your return journey? Even those familiar with these moors often miss their road on such evenings; and there is no chance of the storm abating at present."

" Perhaps you could spare one of your lads to act as guide, and stay at the Grange till morning."

" No, I could not."

" Oh indeed ! Then I must trust to my own sagacity."

" Are you going to make th' tea ? " demanded he of the shabby coat, shifting his ferocious gaze from me to the young lady.

" Is *he* to have any ? " she asked, appealing to Heathcliff.

" Get it ready, will you ? " was the answer, uttered so savagely that I started. The tone in which the words were uttered revealed a genuine bad nature. I no longer felt inclined to call Heathcliff a capital fellow.

" Now, sir, bring forward your chair," said he, when the preparation was finished. We all drew round the table, an austere silence prevailing while we set about the meal.

I thought, if I had caused the cloud, it was my duty to try and dispel it.

" It is strange," I began, " how custom can mould our tastes. Many could not imagine the existence of happiness in a life of such complete exile from the world as you spend, Mr. Heathcliff. And yet I'll venture to say that you, with your amiable lady as the presiding genius of your home and heart—— "

" My amiable lady ! " he interrupted, with an almost diabolical sneer. " Where is she—my amiable lady ? "

" Mrs. Heathcliff, your wife, I mean."

" Oh, you would intimate that her spirit has taken the post of ministering angel, and guards the fortunes of Wuthering Heights even when her body is gone ? "

Perceiving myself in a blunder, I endeavoured to correct it. I might have seen that the disparity in age was too great. Heathcliff was about forty. The girl did not look seventeen.

Then it flashed upon me.—" The uncouth young clown

at my elbow may be her husband—Heathcliff, junior, of course. She has thrown herself away on that boor! A sad pity. I must beware how *I* cause her to regret her choice." My last reflection may seem conceited. But I knew, through experience, that I was tolerably attractive. My neighbour struck me as bordering on repulsive.

"Mrs. Heathcliff is my daughter-in-law," said Heathcliff, seeming to corroborate my surmise.

"Ah, I see now. You are the favoured possessor of the beneficent fairy," I remarked, turning to my neighbour.

This was worse than before. The youth grew crimson, and clenched his fist, with every appearance of premeditated assault.

"Unhappy in your conjectures, sir," observed my host. "Her mate—my son—is dead."

"And this young man is—— "

"Not my son, assuredly." Heathcliff smiled as if it were rather too bold a jest to attribute the paternity of that bear to him.

"My name is Hareton Earnshaw," growled the other; "and I'd counsel you to respect it."

"I've shown no disrespect," was my reply, laughing internally at the dignity with which he announced himself. But I began to feel unmistakably out of place in that pleasant family circle, and anxious to quit it.

The business of eating over, I approached a window. A sorrowful sight I saw—dark night coming down prematurely, and sky and hills mingled in one bitter whirl of wind and suffocating snow.

"I don't think it possible for me to get home without a guide now," I could not help exclaiming. "The roads will be buried already. How must I do?"

My question was ignored; and looking round, I saw that Heathcliff and Earnshaw had left the room. Joseph was bringing in a pail of porridge for the dogs, and Mrs.

Heathcliff leaning over the fire. The former, when he had deposited his burden, grated out—

" Aw wonder how yah can faishion to stand thear i' idleness un war, when all on 'em's goan out ! Bud yah're a nowt. Yah'll goa raight to t' devil, like yer mother afore ye ! "

I imagined for a moment that this piece of eloquence was addressed to me, and, sufficiently enraged, stepped towards the aged rascal with an intention of kicking him out of the door. Mrs. Heathcliff, however, checked me by her answer.

" You scandalous old hypocrite ! " she replied. " Are you not afraid of being carried away bodily, whenever you mention the devil's name ? I warn you to refrain from provoking me, or I'll ask your abduction as a special favour. Stop ! Look here, Joseph," she continued, taking a long dark book from a shelf, " I'll show you how far I've progressed in the black art. I shall soon be competent to make a clear house of it. The red cow didn't die by chance, and your rheumatism can hardly be reckoned among providential visitations."

" Oh, wicked, wicked ! " gasped the elder; " may the Lord deliver us from evil ! "

" No, reprobate; you are a castaway. Be off, or I'll have you modelled in wax and clay; and the first who passes the limits I fix shall—I'll not say what he shall be done to, but you'll see. Go ! I'm looking at you."

The little witch put such a mock malignity into her beautiful eyes, that Joseph, trembling with sincere horror, hurried out, praying and ejaculating. Now that she and I were alone, I endeavoured to interest her in my plight.

" Mrs. Heathcliff," I said earnestly, " with that face, I'm sure you cannot help being good-hearted. Do point out some landmarks by which I may find my way home."

"Take the road you came," she answered briefly, ensconcing herself in a chair. "I cannot escort you."

"*You!* I should be sorry to ask you to cross the threshold on such a night as this. I want you to *tell* me my way, not to *show* it;—or else persuade Mr. Heathcliff to give me a guide."

"Who? There is himself, Earnshaw, Zillah, Joseph, and I. None of *them* will go, and there is no one else."

"Then, it follows that I must stay the night."

"I hope it will be a lesson to you to make no more rash journeys on these hills," cried Heathcliff's stern voice from the kitchen entrance. "As to staying here, I don't keep accommodation for visitors. You must share a bed with Hareton or Joseph, if you do."

"I can sleep on a chair in this room," I replied.

"No, no. I will not allow a stranger the range of the place when I am off my guard!" said the unmannerly wretch.

With this insult my patience was at an end. I uttered an expression of disgust, and pushed past him into the yard, running into Earnshaw in my haste. It was so dark, I stumbled about, unable to find the means of exit.

"I'll go with him as far as the park," I heard Earnshaw exclaim.

"You'll go with him to hell! Who is to look after the horses?"

"A man's life is of more consequence than one evening's neglect of the horses. Somebody must go," murmured Mrs. Heathcliff, more kindly than I expected.

"Not at your command!" retorted Hareton. "If you set store on him, you'd better be quiet."

"Then I hope his ghost will haunt you; and I hope Mr. Heathcliff will never get another tenant till the Grange is a ruin!" she answered sharply.

I now distinguished Joseph, milking the cows by the

light of a lantern, which I seized unceremoniously, and calling out that I would send it back on the morrow, rushed to the nearest postern. But in a trice Joseph was after me, calling out that I was stealing the lantern, and exhorting the dogs to hold me. Two hairy monsters flew at my throat, bearing me down and extinguishing the lantern; while a mingled guffaw from Heathcliff and Hareton put the copestone on my rage and humiliation. Fortunately, the beasts seemed more bent on stretching their paws and flourishing their tails than devouring me alive; but they would suffer no resurrection. The vehemence of my agitation brought on a copious bleeding at the nose; and still Heathcliff laughed and I scolded. I don't know what would have concluded the scene had there not been one person at hand more benevolent than my entertainer. This was Zillah, the stout housewife, who at length issued forth, and put the dogs to flight by throwing a bucket of icy water over us. She pulled me into the kitchen, where I lay, feeling exceedingly dizzy and faint.

I was thus compelled perforce to accept lodgings under Heathcliff's roof. He ordered Zillah to give me a glass of brandy, and then passed on to the inner room. And when the spirits had somewhat revived me, the woman brought a candle and bade me follow her upstairs.

CHAPTER III

WHILE leading the way, she recommended that I should hide the candle, and not make a noise, for her master had an odd notion about the room I was occupying, and never let anyone lodge there willingly. I asked the reason. She did not know, she answered. She had lived at Wuthering Heights only a year or two; and they had so many queer goings on, she could not begin to be curious.

Too stupefied to be curious myself, I fastened my door the moment I was alone, and glanced round for the bed. The whole furniture consisted of a chair, a clothes press, and a large oak case, with squares cut out near the top resembling coach windows. This structure turned out to be a singular sort of old-fashioned couch, forming in fact a little closet; and the ledge of a window which it enclosed served as a table. I slid back the panelled sides, got in with my light, pulled them together again, and felt secure against the vigilance of Heathcliff and everyone else.

The ledge where I placed my candle had a few mildewed books piled up in one corner, and it was covered with writing scratched on the paint. This writing, however, was nothing but a name repeated in all kinds of characters, large and small—*Catherine Earnshaw*, here and there varied to *Catherine Heathcliff*, and then again to *Catherine Linton*.

In vapid listlessness I continued spelling over Catherine Earnshaw—Heathcliff—Linton, till my eyes closed. But they had not rested five minutes when a glare of white letters started from the dark as vivid as spectres—the air swarmed with Catherines. Rousing myself to dispel the obtrusive name, I discovered my candle-wick reclining on one of the antique volumes, and perfuming the place with an odour of roasted calf-skin. I snuffed it off, sat up, and spread the injured tome on my knees. It was a Testament, dreadfully musty. A fly-leaf bore the inscription, " Catherine Earnshaw, her book," and a date some quarter of a century back. I shut it, and examined the other books. Catherine's library was select, and its state of dilapidation proved it to have been well-used, though not altogether for a legitimate purpose. Every fly-leaf and every margin space had been written upon. Some of the writing consisted of detached sentences; other parts took the form of a regular diary, scrawled in a childish hand. At the top of one page I was amazed to see an excellent caricature of my friend Joseph. An immediate interest kindled within me for the unknown Catherine, and I began forthwith to decipher her hieroglyphics.

" An awful Sunday ! " commenced the paragraph beneath. " I wish my father were back again. Hindley is a detestable substitute—his conduct to Heathcliff is atrocious. H. and I are going to rebel—we took the first step this evening.

" All day had been flooding with rain. We could not go to church so Joseph must needs get up a congregation in the garret; and while Hindley and his wife basked downstairs before a comfortable fire, Heathcliff, myself, and the unhappy plough-boy were commanded to take our prayer-books and mount. We were ranged on a sack of corn, groaning and shivering, and hoping that Joseph would shiver too, so that he might give us a short homily for his own sake. Vain idea ! The service lasted precisely three hours; and yet my tyrant brother had the face to exclaim, when he saw us descending, ' What ! done already ? '—and added, ' I'll demolish the first who puts me out of temper ! I insist on perfect sobriety and silence. O boy ! was that you ?—Frances darling, pull his hair as you go by ! ' Frances pulled Heathcliff's hair thoroughly, and then went and seated herself on her husband's knee; and there they were, like two babies, kissing and talking nonsense by the hour. We made ourselves as snug as our means allowed in the arch of the dresser. I had just fastened our pinafores, and hung them up for a curtain, when in comes Joseph on an errand from the stables. He tears down my handiwork, boxes my ears and croaks—

"'T' maister nobbut just buried, and Sabbath no o'ered, and t' sound o' t' gospel still i' yer lugs, and ye darr be laiking! Shame on ye! Sit ye down, ill childer, an' think o' yer sowls. There's good books enough, if ye'll read 'em.'

"Saying this, he compelled us to square our positions that we might receive from the far-off fire a dull ray to show us the text of the lumber he thrust upon us. I could not bear the employment. I hurled my dingy volume into the dog-kennel, vowing I hated a good book. Heathcliff kicked his off to the same place. There was a hubbub.

"'Maister Hindley!' shouted our chaplain, 'coom hither! Miss Cathy's riven th' back off "Th' Helmet o' Salvation," un Heathcliff's pawsed his fit into t' first part o' "T' Brooad Way to Destruction!" It's fair flaysome that ye let 'em go on this gait. Ech! the' owd man wad ha' laced 'em properly; but he's goan!'

"Hindley hurried up from his paradise on the hearth, and hurled us both into the kitchen; and there left us. I reached this book, and have got the time on with writing for twenty minutes; but my companion is impatient, and proposes we should have a scamper on the moors. A pleasant suggestion. We cannot be damper or colder on the moors than we are here."

. . . . .

I suppose Catherine fulfilled her project, for the next sentence reads—

"How little did I dream that Hindley would ever make me cry so. My head aches till I cannot keep it on the pillow. Poor Heathcliff! Hindley calls him a vagabond, and won't let him sit or eat with us any more; and he says he and I must not play together, and threatens to turn him out of the house if we break his orders. He has been blaming my father (how dared he?) for treating H. too liberally, and swears he will reduce him to his right place!"

.   .   .   .   .

I began to nod over the dim page, sank into bed, and fell asleep. Alas for the effect of bad tea and bad temper! What else could it be that made me pass such a terrible night?

I began to dream, almost before I ceased to be sensible of my locality. I thought it was morning, and that I had set out for home, with Joseph as guide. The snow lay yards deep on our road; and as we floundered on, my companion wearied me with constant reproaches that I had not brought a pilgrim's staff. For a moment I considered it absurd that I should need such a weapon to gain admittance to my own residence. Then a new idea flashed across me. We were not going there. We were going to hear the famous Jabes Branderham preach in the chapel.

We reached the building, lying in a hollow between two hills, near a swamp. Jabes had a full and attentive congregation, and he preached—good God! what a sermon, divided into *four hundred and ninety* parts, and each discussing a separate sin—odd transgressions, many of them, that I had never imagined.

Oh, how weary I grew! How I writhed and yawned! Finally I could bear it no longer, and I rose in my seat and denounced the preacher as the sinner of the sin that no Christian need pardon.

Exhorted by Jabes, the whole assembly, exalting their pilgrim's staves, rushed upon me. But the blows aimed at my head fell on other sconces. Presently the whole chapel resounded with rappings and counter rappings. Every man's hand was against his neighbour. And Jabes

Branderham, unwilling to remain idle, poured forth his zeal in a shower of loud taps on the boards of the pulpit, which responded so sharply that at last, to my unspeakable relief, they woke me. And what had suggested this tremendous tumult? Merely the branch of a fir-tree that touched the lattice as the blast went by, and rattled its dry cones against the panes.

Soon I dozed and dreamt again—if possible, still more disagreeably than before. This time I was lying in the oak closet. I heard the fir-branch repeat its teasing sound, and determined to silence it. And, in my dream, I rose and endeavoured to unhasp the casement. But the hook was soldered into a staple—a circumstance observed by me when awake, but forgotten. Breaking the glass with my knuckles, I stretched out my arm to seize the importunate branch; instead of which my fingers closed on the fingers of a little, ice-cold hand. The intense horror of nightmare came over me. I tried to draw back my arm, but the hand clung to it, and a most melancholy voice sobbed, "Let me in—let me in!" "Who are you?" I asked, struggling to disengage myself. "Catherine Linton," it replied shiveringly. (Why did I think of *Linton*? I had read *Earnshaw* twenty times for Linton.) "I'm come home. I'd lost my way on the moor." As it spoke, I discerned, obscurely, a child's face looking through the window. Terror made me cruel; and finding it useless to attempt shaking the creature off, I pulled its wrist on to the broken pane, and rubbed it to and fro till the blood ran down and soaked the bedclothes. Still it wailed, "Let me in!" and maintained its tenacious gripe, almost maddening me with fear. "How can I?" I said at length. "Let *me* go, if you want me to let you in!" The fingers relaxed; I snatched mine through the hole, hurriedly piled the books up in a pyramid against it, and stopped my ears to exclude the lamentable prayer.

I seemed to keep them closed above a quarter of an hour; yet the instant I listened again, there was the doleful cry moaning on! "Begone!" I shouted; "I'll never let you in—not if you beg for twenty years." "It is twenty years," mourned the voice—"twenty years. I've been a waif for twenty years!" Thereat began a feeble scratching outside, and the pile of books moved as if thrust forward. I tried to jump up, but could not stir a limb, and so yelled aloud in a frenzy of fright. To my confusion, I discovered the yell was not ideal. Hasty footsteps approached my door; and as I sat up shuddering and perspiring, it was pushed open, and a light glimmered through the squares at the top of my bed. The intruder appeared to hesitate, and muttered to himself. At last he said in a half-whisper, plainly not expecting an answer, "Is anyone here?" Recognising Heathcliff's accents, I considered it best to confess my presence. I turned and opened the panels. I shall not forget the effect it produced.

Heathcliff stood near the entrance, a candle dripping over his fingers, and his face as white as the wall behind him. The first creak of the oak startled him like an electric shock. The light leaped from his hand to a distance of some feet, and his agitation was so extreme that he could hardly pick it up.

"It is only your guest, sir," I called out, desirous to spare him the humiliation of exposing his cowardice further. "I had the misfortune to scream in my sleep owing to a frightful nightmare. I'm sorry I disturbed you."

"Oh, God confound you, Mr. Lockwood! Who showed you up to this room? Who was it? I've a good mind to turn them out of the house this moment."

"It was your servant Zillah," I replied, flinging myself on to the floor, and rapidly resuming my garments. "I should not care if you did, Mr. Heathcliff; she richly deserves it. I suppose she wanted to get another proof that the place was haunted, at my expense. You have reason in shutting it up, I assure you."

"What do you mean?" asked Heathcliff; "and what are you doing? Lie down and finish the night, since you *are* here; but for heaven's sake don't repeat that horrid noise. Nothing could excuse it, unless you were having your throat cut!"

"No, I have had enough of it," I returned. "If that little fiend had got in at the window, she would probably have strangled me. She must have been a changeling—wicked little soul! She told me she had been walking the earth these twenty years—a just punishment for her mortal transgressions, I've no doubt—Catherine Linton, or Earnshaw, or however she was called."

Scarcely were these words uttered, when I recollected the association of Heathcliff's with Catherine's name in the book. I blushed at my inconsideration, and hastened to add by way of explanation, "The truth is, sir, I passed the first part of the night in spelling over the name scratched on that window-ledge—a monotonous occupation, calculated to set me asleep, like counting, or——"

"What *can* you mean by talking in this way to *me*?" thundered Heathcliff. "How dare you, under my roof? —God, he's mad to speak so!" And he struck his forehead with rage.

I did not know whether to resent this language or pursue my explanation; but he seemed so powerfully affected that I took pity and proceeded with my dreams, affirming I had never heard the appellation of "Catherine Linton" before, but reading it often over produced an impression which personified itself when I had no longer my imagination under control. Heathcliff gradually fell back into the shelter of the bed as I spoke, finally sitting down almost concealed behind it. I guessed, however, by his irregular breathing, that he struggled to vanquish an excess of violent emotion. Not liking to show him that I had heard the conflict, I continued my toilet rather noisily, looked at my watch, and soliloquised on the length of the night : " Not three o'clock yet ! I could have taken oath it had been six. Time stagnates here. We must surely have retired to rest at eight ! "

" Always at nine in winter, and rise at four," said my host, suppressing a groan, and, as I fancied, by the motion of his arm's shadow, dashing a tear from his eyes. " Mr. Lockwood," he added, " you may go into my room. You'll only be in the way, coming downstairs so early ; and your childish outcry has sent sleep to the devil for me."

" And for me too," I replied. " I'll walk in the yard till daylight, and then I'll be off ; and you need not dread a repetition of my intrusion. I'm now quite cured of seeking pleasure in society, be it country or town. A sensible man ought to find sufficient company in himself."

" Delightful company ! " muttered Heathcliff. " Take the candle, and go where you please. I shall join you directly. Keep out of the yard, though—the dogs are unchained ; and the house—Juno mounts sentinel there, and—nay, you can only ramble about the steps and passages. But away with you ! I'll come in two minutes ! "

I obeyed, so far as to quit the chamber ; when, ignorant where the narrow lobbies led, I stood still, and was witness, involuntarily, to a piece of superstition on the part of my landlord, which belied oddly his apparent sense. He got on to the bed and wrenched open the lattice, bursting, as he pulled at it, into an uncontrollable passion of tears. " Come in ! come in ! " he sobbed. " Cathy, do come ! Oh, do—*once* more ! Oh, my heart's darling ! hear me *this* time, Catherine, at last ! " The spectre showed a spectre's ordinary caprice. It gave no sign of being; but the snow and wind whirled wildly through, even reaching my station, and blowing out the light.

There was such anguish in the gush of grief that accompanied this raving that my compassion made me overlook its folly, and I drew off, half angry to have listened at all, and vexed at having related my ridiculous nightmare, since it produced that agony; though *why* was beyond my comprehension. I descended cautiously to the lower regions, and landed in the back kitchen, where a gleam of fire, raked compactly together, enabled me to rekindle my candle. Nothing was stirring except a brindled, grey cat, which crept from the ashes, and saluted me with a querulous mew.

Two benches, shaped in sections of a circle, nearly enclosed the hearth. On one of these I stretched myself, and was nodding ere anyone invaded my retreat. Then it was Joseph, shuffling down a wooden ladder that vanished in the roof, through a trap—the ascent to his garret, I suppose. He cast a sinister look at the little flame which I had enticed to play between the ribs, and, sitting down on the vacant bench, began to stuff a three-inch pipe with tobacco. My presence in his sanctum was evidently esteemed a piece of impudence too shameful for remark. He finished his pipe in silence, and heaving a profound sigh, got up and departed as solemnly as he came.

A more elastic footstep entered next; and now I opened my mouth for a " good morning ", but closed it again, the salutation unachieved, for Hareton Earnshaw was performing his orisons, *sotto voce*, in a series of curses directed against every object he touched, while he rummaged in a corner for a shovel to dig through the snow-drifts. He glanced at me, dilating his nostrils, and obviously with no intention of exchanging civilities. I rose from my hard couch, and made to follow him out.

He noticed this, and thrust at an inner door with the end of his spade, intimating by an inarticulate sound that there was the place I must go if I changed my locality.

It opened into the house, where the females were already astir—Zillah urging flakes of flame up the chimney with a colossal bellows; and Mrs. Heathcliff, kneeling on the hearth, reading a book by the aid of the blaze. I was surprised to see Heathcliff there also. He stood by the fire, his back towards me, just finishing a stormy scene to poor Zillah, who ever and anon interrupted her labour to pluck up the corner of her apron and heave an indignant groan.

"And you, you worthless—— " he broke out as I entered, turning to his daughter-in-law; "there you are at your idle tricks again. Put your trash away, and earn your bread like the rest of them. Do you hear, damnable jade?"

Heathcliff lifted his hand, and the speaker sprang to a safer distance, obviously acquainted with its weight. I stepped forward briskly, and, perceiving me, each had enough decorum to suspend further hostilities during the remainder of my stay. This was not long. I declined joining their breakfast, and at the first gleam of dawn took an opportunity of escaping into the free air.

The snow had ceased to fall, but it lay thick on the ground. Fortunately my landlord hallooed me to stop ere I reached the bottom of the garden, and accompanied me across the moor. It was well he did, or I should assuredly have fallen into a concealed quarry, or lost myself in the swamps.

We exchanged little conversation, and he halted at the entrance of Thrushcross Park, saying I could make no error there. Our adieus were limited to a hasty bow. The distance from the Park gate to Thrushcross Grange is two miles; I believe I managed to make it four; and, what with losing myself among the trees, and sinking up to the neck in snow, it was twelve o'clock before I entered my own door.

Mrs. Dean, my housekeeper, and her satellites rushed to welcome me, exclaiming tumultuously that they had given me up. Conjecturing that I had perished in the night, they were wondering how they must set about the search for my remains.   I bid them be quiet, and dragged myself upstairs ; whence, after putting on dry clothes, I adjourned to my study, feeble as a kitten—almost too much so to enjoy the cheerful fire and the smoking coffee which the servant had prepared for my refreshment.

CHAPTER IV

WHAT vain weathercocks we are ! I, who had determined to hold myself independent of all social intercourse—I, weak wretch, after maintaining till dusk a struggle with low spirits and solitude, was finally compelled to strike my colours ; and, under pretence of ascertaining the necessities of my establishment, I desired Mrs. Dean, when she brought in my supper, to sit down while I ate it, hoping sincerely she would prove a regular gossip.

" You have lived in this house a considerable time ? " I commenced.

" Eighteen years, sir. I came when the mistress was first married ; after she died, the master retained me as his housekeeper."

There ensued a pause. She was not a gossip, I feared. But at length, after an interval of meditation, she ejaculated—

B

" Ah, times have greatly changed since then ! "

" Yes," I remarked, " you've seen a good many alterations, I suppose ? "

" I have ; and troubles too," she said.

" Oh, I'll turn the talk on my landlord's family ! " I thought to myself. " A good subject to start with. And that pretty girl-widow, I should like to know her history." With this intention I asked Mrs. Dean why Heathcliff let Thrushcross Grange, and preferred living in a residence so much inferior. " Is he not rich enough to keep the estate in good order ? " I enquired.

" Rich, sir ! " she returned. " He has nobody knows what money, and every year it increases. But he's very close-handed."

" He had a son, it seems ? That young woman, Mrs. Heathcliff, is his widow ? "

" Yes."

" Where did she come from originally ? "

" Why, sir, she was my late master's daughter. Catherine Linton was her maiden name. I nursed her, poor thing ! I did wish Mr. Heathcliff would remove here, and then we might have been together again."

" What ! Catherine Linton ? " I exclaimed, astonished. But a minute's reflection convinced me that it was not my ghostly Catherine.

" Then," I continued, " my predecessor's name was Linton ? "

" It was."

" And who is that Earnshaw—Hareton Earnshaw ? Is he related to Mr. Heathcliff ? "

" No ; he's the late Mr. Linton's nephew."

" The young lady's cousin, then ? "

" Yes ; and her husband was her cousin also—one on the mother's side ; the other on the father's side. Heathcliff married Mr. Linton's sister."

"I see the house at Wuthering Heights has 'Earnshaw' carved over the front door. Are they an old family?"

"Very old, sir; and Hareton is the last of them, as our Miss Cathy is of us—I mean of the Lintons. Have you been to Wuthering Heights? I beg pardon for asking; but I should like to hear how she is."

"Mrs. Heathcliff? She looked very well, and very handsome; yet, I think, not very happy."

"O, dear, I don't wonder! And how did you like the master?"

"A rough fellow, rather, Mrs. Dean. Is not that his character?"

"Rough as a saw-edge, and hard as whinstone. The less you meddle with him the better."

"He must have had some ups and downs to make him such a churl. Do you know anything of his history?"

"It's a cuckoo's, sir. I know all about it—except where he was born, and who were his parents, and how he got his money at first. And Hareton has been cast out like an unfledged dunnock! The unfortunate lad is the only one in all this parish that does not guess how he has been cheated."

"Well, Mrs. Dean, it will be a charitable deed to tell me something of my neighbours. I feel I shall not rest if I go to bed, so be good enough to sit and chat with me an hour."

Thus encouraged, the worthy woman bustled off, to fetch some sewing, evidently pleased to find me so companionable.

. . . . .

Before I came to live here, she commenced (when she had again settled herself beside the fire), I was almost always at Wuthering Heights, because my mother had nursed Mr. Hindley Earnshaw—that was Hareton's father—and I got used to playing with the children. I ran errands, too, and did anything about the farm that was required of me. One summer morning, at the beginning of harvest, Mr. Earnshaw, the old master, came downstairs, dressed for a journey; and after he had told Joseph what was to be done for the day, he turned to Hindley, and Cathy, and me—for I sat eating my porridge with them—and he said, speaking to his son, " Now, my bonny man, I'm going to Liverpool today; what shall I bring you ? Only make it small, for I shall walk there and back : sixty miles each way." Hindley named a fiddle; and then he asked Miss Cathy. She was hardly six, but she could ride any horse in the stables, and she chose a whip. He promised to bring me a pocketful of apples and pears; and then he kissed his children good-bye and set off.

He was away for three days, and it seemed a long time to us all. It was after dark—eleven o'clock—when he returned. The children had got tired of running down to the gate to look for his coming when he stepped in. He threw himself into a chair, laughing and groaning, and bid them all stand off, for he was nearly killed. He would not have another such walk for the three kingdoms.

" And at the end of it to be frighted to death ! " he said, opening his greatcoat, which he held bundled up in his arms. " See here, wife ! I was never so beaten with anything in my life; but you must e'en take it as a gift of God, though it's as dark almost as if it came from the devil."

We crowded round, and over Miss Cathy's head I had a peep at a dirty, ragged, black-haired child, big enough both to walk and talk. Yet when it was set on its feet it only stared round, and repeated over and over again some gibberish that nobody could understand. I was frightened, and Mrs. Earnshaw was ready to fling it out of doors. She asked what he meant to do with it, and whether he were mad. The master tried to explain the matter; but he was really half dead with fatigue, and all I could make out, amongst her scolding, was a tale of his seeing it starving and homeless in the streets of Liverpool. Not a soul knew to whom it belonged; and his money and time both being limited, he thought he had better take it home with him, because he was determined he would not leave it as he found it. Well, the conclusion was that Mrs. Earnshaw grumbled herself calm; and my master bid me to wash it, and give it clean things, and let it sleep with the children.

But Hindley's fiddle had been crushed to morsels in the greatcoat, and Cathy's whip had been lost in attending on the stranger. They entirely refused to have " the stupid little thing " in bed with them, or even in their room; and I had no more sense, so I put it on the landing by the stairs hoping it might be gone on the morrow. By chance it crept to Mr. Earnshaw's door, and there he found it on quitting his chamber. In recompense for my cowardice and inhumanity, I was sent out of the house.

This was Heathcliff's first introduction to the family. For, on coming back a few days afterwards (I did not consider my banishment perpetual), I found they had thus christened him. It was the name of a son who had died in childhood, and it has served him ever since, both for Christian and surname. Miss Cathy and he were very thick; but Hindley—then a boy of fourteen—hated him, and, to say the truth, I did the same. We plagued him shamefully, and the mistress never put in a word on his behalf when she saw him wronged.

He seemed a sullen, patient child—hardened, perhaps, to ill-treatment. He would stand Hindley's blows and my pinches without shedding a tear. But old Earnshaw was furious when he discovered his son persecuting the poor fatherless child, as he called him. He took to Heath-

cliff strangely, and petted him far away above Cathy, who
was too mischievous for a favourite.

So from the very beginning he bred a bad feeling about
the house; and at Mrs. Earnshaw's death, which happened less than two years after, the young master had
learned to regard his father as an oppressor, and Heathcliff
as a usurper of his privileges. I sympathised a while; but
when the children fell ill of the measles, and I had to
tend them, and take on me the cares of a woman at once,
I changed my ideas. Cathy and her brother harassed me
terribly; but Heathcliff, although dangerously sick, was
the quietest child I ever watched over. It was hardness,
however, not gentleness, which made him give so little
trouble.

He got through, and the doctor praised me for my care—
which caused me to soften towards the being by whose
means I had earned them. And thus Hindley lost his last
ally. Still I could not dote on Heathcliff, and I often
wondered what my master saw to admire so much in the
sullen boy, who never, to my recollection, repaid his
indulgence by any sign of gratitude. He was not insolent
to his benefactor; he was simply insensible—though
knowing perfectly well the hold he had on his heart, and
conscious he had only to speak and all the house would
be obliged to bend to his wishes. No wonder Hindley was
filled with hatred and resentment against the intruder.

§

In the course of time Mr. Earnshaw began to fail. He
had been active and healthy, yet his strength left him
suddenly, and when he was confined to the chimney-
corner he grew grievously irritable. This was especially
to be remarked if anyone attempted to impose or domineer
over his favourite. Twice or thrice Hindley's manifestations of scorn while his father was near roused the old

man to a fury. He seized his stick to strike him, and shook with rage that he could not do it.

At last our curate (we had a curate then, who made a living by teaching the little Lintons and Earnshaws and farming a bit of land himself) advised that the young man should be sent to college; and Mr. Earnshaw agreed, though with a heavy spirit, for he said Hindley was naught and would never thrive.

I hoped heartily we should have peace now. It hurt me that the master should be made uncomfortable by his own good deed. And, indeed, we might have got on tolerably, but for two people—Miss Cathy and Joseph the servant. Then, as now, Joseph was the wearisomest, most self-righteous Pharisee that ever ransacked a Bible to rake the promises to himself and fling the curses to his neighbours. By his knack of sermonising he contrived to make a great impression on Mr. Earnshaw, and the more feeble my master became, the more influence he gained. He was relentless in worrying him about his soul's concerns, and about ruling his children rigidly. He encouraged him to regard Hindley as a reprobate; and night after night he grumbled out a long string of tales against Heathcliff and Catherine, always minding to flatter Earnshaw's weakness by heaping the heaviest blame on the latter.

Certainly she had ways with her such as I never saw a child take up before. We had not a minute's security that she would not be in mischief. Her spirits were always at high-water mark, her tongue always going. A wild, wicked slip she was; but she had the bonniest eye, the sweetest smile, and the lightest foot in the parish. And, after all, I believe she meant no harm; for when once she had made you cry, it seldom happened she did not keep you company, and oblige you to keep quiet, that you might comfort her. She was much too fond of

Heathcliff. The greatest punishment we could invent for her was to keep her separate from him.

She did not understand why her father should be crosser and less patient in his ailing condition than he was in his prime. His peevish reproofs wakened in her a naughty delight to provoke him. She was never so happy as when we were all scolding at once, and she defying us with her bold, saucy look, and her ready words, and doing just what her father hated most—showing him that her insolence had more power over Heathcliff than all his kindness. After behaving as badly as possible all day, she sometimes came fondling to make it up at night. "Nay, Cathy," the old man would say, "I cannot love thee; thou'rt worse than thy brother. Go say thy prayers, child, and ask God's pardon."

But the hour came at last that ended Mr. Earnshaw's troubles on earth. He died quietly in his chair one windy October evening. We were all together. Cathy had been sick, and that made her still. She leant against her father's knee, and Heathcliff was lying on the floor with his head in her lap. I remember the master, before he fell into a doze, stroking her bonny hair, and saying, "Why canst thee not always be a good lass, Cathy?" And she turned her face up to his, and laughed, and answered, "Why cannot you always be a good man, father?" But as soon as she saw him vexed again, she kissed his hand, and said she would sing him to sleep. She began singing very low, till his fingers dropped from hers, and his head fell on his breast. We all kept as quiet as mice for a full half-hour, till Joseph said he must rouse the master for prayers and bed. He stepped forward, and called him by name, and touched his shoulder; but he would not move, so he took the candle and looked at him. I thought there was something wrong as he set down the light, and seizing the children by the arm, whispered to them to " frame upstairs, and make little din."

" I shall bid my father good-night first," said Catherine, putting her arms round his neck before we could stop her. The poor thing discovered her loss immediately. She screamed out, " Oh, he's dead, Heathcliff—he's dead ! " And they both set up a heartbreaking cry.

CHAPTER V

MR. HINDLEY came home to the funeral; and—a thing that amazed us all—he brought a wife with him. What she was, and where she was born, he never informed us. Probably she had neither money nor name to recommend her, or he would scarcely have kept the union from his father.

She was not one that would have disturbed the house much on her own account. Every object she saw, every circumstance that took place about her from the moment she crossed the threshold seemed to delight her—saving only the preparations for the burial. I thought she was half silly, from her behaviour while that went on. She made me come with her into her chamber, though I should have been dressing the children, and there she sat shivering and crying, and asking repeatedly " Are they gone yet ? " When I asked her what was the matter, she answered that she did not know, but she felt so afraid of dying. I imagined her as little likely to die as myself. She was rather thin; but fresh complexioned, and her eyes sparkled as bright as diamonds; though I did notice that mounting the stairs made her breathe quick, and that she coughed troublesomely sometimes.

Young Earnshaw was altered considerably in the three years of his absence. He had grown sparer, and lost his colour, and spoke and dressed quite differently; and on the very day of his return he told Joseph and me that we must quarter ourselves in the kitchen in future. Indeed he would have carpeted and papered a small spare room for a parlour; but his wife, to whom he was devoted, expressed such pleasure at the common sitting-room that he thought it unnecessary for her comfort and dropped the intention.

At the beginning, too, she showed much affection for Catherine. This soon tired, however, and when she grew peevish, Hindley became tyrannical. A few words from her, evincing a dislike to Heathcliff, were enough to rouse all his old hatred of the boy. He drove him from their company to the servants, deprived him of the instruction of the curate, and compelled him to labour out of doors, as hard as any other lad on the farm.

Heathcliff bore his degradation pretty well at first, because Cathy taught him what she learned, and worked or played with him in the fields. They both promised fair to grow up as rude as savages, the young master being entirely negligent how they behaved. It was one of their favourite amusements to run away to the moors in the morning and remain there all day, and the after-punishment grew a thing to laugh at. The curate might set as many chapters as he pleased for Catherine to learn by heart, and Joseph might thrash Heathcliff till his arm ached; they forgot everything the minute they might be together again, and contrive some naughty plan of revenge. One Sunday evening it chanced that they were banished from the sitting-room for some light offence which I cannot remember, and when I went to call them to

supper I could discover them nowhere. At last Hindley
in a passion told us to bolt the doors, and swore that no
one should let them in that night. The household went to
bed; and I, too anxious to lie down, opened my lattice
and put my head out to hearken, though it rained. In a
while I distinguished steps coming up the road. I threw
a shawl over my head, and ran to prevent them from
waking Mr. Earnshaw by knocking. There was Heathcliff, by himself.

"Where is Miss Catherine?" I cried anxiously. "At
Thrushcross Grange," he answered; "and I would have
been there too, but they had not the manners to ask me to
stay." "Well, you will catch it," I said. "What in the
world led you wandering to Thrushcross Grange?"
"Let me out of my wet clothes, and I'll tell you all about
it, Nelly," he replied. And while he undressed, he told
me that he and Cathy had escaped from the wash-house
to have a ramble at liberty. Getting a glimpse of the
Grange lights, they thought they would go and see how
the Lintons passed their Sunday evenings. They crept
through a broken hedge, and groped their way up to the
drawing-room window. The shutters had not been put
up, and the curtains were only half closed. Both, by
standing on the basement and clinging to the ledge, were
able to see into the room. And a beautiful place it was,
said Heathcliff,—crimson carpet, crimson-covered chairs
and tables, and a pure white ceiling bordered by gold.
Old Mr. and Mrs. Linton were not there; Edgar and his
sister, Isabella, had it entirely to themselves. But
instead of enjoying this heaven, Isabella lay screaming at
the further end of the room, while Edgar stood on the
hearth weeping silently. In the middle of the table sat a
little dog, shaking its paw and yelping. From their
mutual accusations it appeared that they had nearly
pulled the poor creature in two between them. "The

idiots ! " said Heathcliff, concluding his account. " That was their pleasure—to quarrel who should hold a heap of warm hair. We laughed outright at the petted things. We did despise them. Would you catch me wishing to have what Catherine wanted; or find us by ourselves yelling and sobbing? I'd not exchange for a thousand lives my condition here for Edgar Linton's at Thrushcross Grange—not if I might have the privilege of flinging Joseph off the highest gable, and painting the house-front with Hindley's blood ! "

" Hush, hush ! " I interrupted. " Speak low, or you will wake them. You have still not told me why Catherine is left behind."

The Lintons, it appeared, had heard them laughing, and, frightened out of their wits, had called for their papa and mamma. Catherine and Heathcliff had made frightful noises to terrify them still more; but then, hearing that someone was drawing the bars, they had dropped from the ledge and made off. But Cathy had fallen, and a bull-dog which had been let loose after them seized her by the ankle. " She did not yell out," Heathcliff continued; " no, she would have scorned to do it had she been spitted on the horns of a mad cow. I did though. I vociferated curses enough to annihilate any fiend in Christendom; and I got a stone and thrust it between the creature's jaws. A servant came up; the dog was throttled off; and Catherine, now unconscious, was carried into the house. I followed, grumbling execretions and vengeance. ' What prey, Robert ? ' hallooed Linton from the entrance. ' Skulker has caught a little girl, sir,' replied the man; ' and there's a lad here,' he added, making a clutch at me, ' who looks an out-and-outer. Very like, the robbers were for putting them through the window to open the doors to the gang after all were asleep, that they might murder us at their ease. He shall go to the gallows for this ! ' I was pulled into the drawing-room; Mrs. Linton raised her hands in horror. The cowardly children crept nearer also, Isabella lisping, ' Frightful thing ! Put him in the cellar, papa. He's exactly like the son of the fortune-teller that stole my tame pheasant. Isn't he, Edgar ? '

" While they examined me Cathy came round. She heard the last speech and laughed. Edgar Linton, after an inquisitive stare, collected sufficient wit to recognise her. They see us at church, you know, though we seldom meet elsewhere. ' That's Miss Earnshaw ! ' he whispered to his mother; ' and look how Skulker has bitten her— how her foot bleeds ! '

" ' Miss Earnshaw ? Nonsense ! ' cried the dame; ' Miss Earnshaw scouring the country with a gipsy !—And yet, my dear, the child is in mourning. Surely it is. And she may be lamed for life.'

" ' What culpable carelessness in her brother ! ' exclaimed Mr. Linton. ' I've understood from Shielders, the curate, that he lets her grow up in absolute heathenism.—But where did she pick up this companion ? Oho ! I declare he's that strange acquisition my neighbour made on his journey to Liverpool—a little Lascar, or some other castaway.'

" ' A wicked boy, at all events,' remarked the old lady, ' and quite unfit for a decent house ! Did you notice his language, Linton ? I'm shocked that my children should have heard it.'

" I recommenced cursing, and the servant was ordered to take me off. I refused to go without Cathy. They dragged me into the garden, and secured the door on me. But I resumed my station at the window, intending, if Cathy wished to return, to shatter the great glass panes to a million fragments, unless they let her out. She sat on the sofa quietly, Mrs. Linton gently expostulating with her. She was a young lady, and they made a distinction between her treatment and mine. Warm water was brought, and her wound bathed. She was given negus and cakes, and generally fussed over, while Edgar stood gaping at a respectful distance. I saw they were full of stupid admiration, she is so immeasurably superior to them—to everybody on earth, is she not, Nelly?"

"There will be more come of this business than you reckon on," I answered, covering him up and extinguishing the light. "You are incurable, Heathcliff; and Mr. Hindley will have to proceed to extremities—see if he won't." My words came truer than I desired. The luckless adventure made Earnshaw furious. And then Mr. Linton paid him a visit himself on the morrow, and read him such a lecture on the way he guided his family that he was stirred to look about him in earnest. Heathcliff was told that the first word he spoke to Catherine should ensure a dismissal; and Mrs. Earnshaw undertook to keep her sister-in-law in due restraint when she came home, employing art, not force. With force she would have found it impossible.

CHAPTER VI

CATHY stayed at Thrushcross Grange five weeks. By that time her ankle was thoroughly cured and her manners much improved. The mistress meanwhile had commenced her plan of reform by trying to raise her self-respect with fine clothes and flattery, which she took readily. So that, instead of a wild, hatless, little savage, there returned on a handsome black pony a very dignified person. "Why, Cathy," exclaimed her brother delightedly, as he lifted her down, "you are quite a beauty. You look a lady now. Isabella Linton is not to be compared with her, is she, Frances?"

Her eyes sparkled when the dogs came bounding up to welcome her, but she hardly dare touch them, lest they should fawn upon her splendid garments or disarrange her brown ringlets. She kissed me gently, and then she looked round for Heathcliff. Mr. and Mrs. Earnshaw watched anxiously for their meeting, thinking that it would enable them to judge, in some measure, what grounds they had for hoping to succeed in separating the two friends.

Heathcliff was hard to discover at first. If he were careless and uncared for before Catherine's absence, he had been ten times more since. Dirty and ill-clothed as he was, he might well skulk behind the sofa on beholding such a bright graceful damsel enter the house, instead of a rough-headed counterpart of himself. "Is Heathcliff not here?" she demanded, pulling off her gloves, and displaying fingers wonderfully whitened.

"Heathcliff, you may come forward," cried Mr. Hindley, enjoying his discomfiture; "you may come and bid Miss Cathy welcome, like the other servants."

Cathy, catching a glimpse of her friend in his concealment, flew to embrace him. She bestowed seven or eight kisses on his cheek in a moment, and then drew back, exclaiming, "Why, how very black and cross you look! But that's because I'm used to Edgar and Isabella Linton. Well, Heathcliff, have you forgotten me?" She had some reason to ask the question, for shame and pride threw a double gloom over his countenance, and kept him immovable.

"Shake hands, Heathcliff," said Mr. Earnshaw, condescendingly; "once in a way that is permitted."

" I shall not. I shall not stand here to be laughed at. I shall not bear it." And he would have broken from the circle, but Miss Cathy seized him.

" I did not mean to laugh at you," she said, " I could not hinder myself. Heathcliff, shake hands at least. What are you sulky for ? It was only that you looked so odd and dirty. If you wash yourself you will be all right."

She gazed concernedly at the dusky fingers she held in her own. But he snatched his hand away, crying, " I shall be as dirty as I please; and I like to be dirty, and I will be dirty." And with that he dashed from the room, to the merriment of the master and mistress, and the serious disturbance of Catherine.

After playing lady's-maid to the new-comer, and making the house and kitchen cheerful with great fires, as befitted Christmas Eve, I prepared to sit and amuse myself by singing Christmas carols all alone; Joseph had returned to private prayer in his chamber, and Mr. and Mrs. Earnshaw were engaging Missy's attention by sundry gay trifles bought for her to present to the little Lintons, as an acknowledgement of their kindness. They had invited them to spend the morrow at Wuthering Heights, an invitation which Mrs. Linton had accepted on one condition—that her darlings might be kept carefully apart from that " naughty swearing boy ".

Under these circumstances I remained solitary in the scoured, shining kitchen. I remembered how old Earn-shaw used to come in, and, praising me for my good work and tidiness, slip a shilling into my hand for a Christmas-box. And from that I went on to think of his fondness for Heathcliff, and the boy's sadly changed condition; and anxious to cheer him, I went into the court to seek him. I found him smoothing the glossy coat of the new pony in the stable, and feeding the others, according to custom.

"Make haste, Heathcliff!" I said; "the kitchen is so comfortable, and Joseph is upstairs. Make haste and let me dress you before Miss Cathy comes out, and then you can sit together, with the whole hearth to yourselves, and have a long chatter till bedtime."

He proceeded with his task, and never turned his head towards me.

"Come; are you coming?" I continued. "There's a little cake for each of you, nearly enough."

I waited five minutes, but getting no answer, left him: Cathy supped with her brother and sister-in-law. Joseph and I joined them at an unsociable meal, seasoned with reproofs on one side and sauciness on the other. Heathcliff's cake and cheese remained all night for the fairies. He managed to continue work till nine o'clock, and then marched up dumb and dour to his chamber. Cathy sat up late, having a world of things to order for her new friends. She came into the kitchen once to speak to her old one, but he was gone, and she stayed only to ask what was the matter with him, and then went back. In the morning he rose early; and, as it was a holiday, he carried his ill-humour off to the moors. When he returned, fasting and reflection seemed to have brought him to a better spirit.

"Nelly, make me decent; I'm going to be good."

"High time, Heathcliff," I said; "you have grieved Catherine. She's sorry she ever came home, I dare say. It looks as if you envied her."

The notion of *envying* Catherine was incomprehensible to him, but the notion of grieving her he understood well enough. He promised to ask her pardon for his surliness when she came in. "You must go up and offer to kiss her," I continued, "and say—you know best what to say; only do it heartily, and not as if you thought her converted into a lady by her grand dress. And now, though I have to get dinner ready, I'll steal time to arrange that Edgar Linton shall look quite like a doll beside you. You are eleven, a year younger than he is, but you are so much taller and stronger you could knock him down in a twinkling."

"But, Nelly, if I knocked him down twenty times, that wouldn't make him less handsome, or me more so. I wish *I* had a fair skin, and was dressed and behaved as well, and had a chance of being as rich as he will be."

"And cried for mamma at every turn," I added, "and sat at home all day for a shower of rain. Oh, Heathcliff, you are showing poor spirit! Learn to smooth away those surly wrinkles on your forehead and to raise your eyelids frankly, and you'll have nothing to fear from him where looks are concerned."

"In other words I must wish for Edgar Linton's great blue eyes and even brow," he replied. "I do, and that won't help me to them."

"A good heart will help you to a bonny face, my lad," I retorted, "if you were a regular black. And now that we've done washing, and combing, and sulking, come to the mirror. Don't you think yourself rather handsome? I'll tell you, I do. Who knows but your father was Emperor of China and your mother an Indian queen, each of them able to buy up, with one week's income, Wuthering Heights and Thrushcross Grange together."

So I chattered on; and Heathcliff gradually lost his frown, and began to look quite pleasant. We were interrupted by the sound of the two Lintons arriving in the family carriage. From the window, we saw Catherine take a hand of each and bring them into the house. I urged my companion to hasten now and show his amiable humour; but ill luck would have it that, as he opened the door leading from the kitchen on one side, Hindley opened it on the other. They met, and the master, irritated at seeing him clean and cheerful, or perhaps eager to keep his promise to Mrs. Linton, shoved him back with a sudden thrust, crying, " Begone, you vagabond ! What ! you are attempting the coxcomb, are you ? Wait till I get hold of those elegant locks; see if I won't pull them a bit longer."

" They are long enough already," observed Master Linton, peeping from the doorway; " I wonder they don't make his head ache. It's like a colt's mane over his eyes."

He ventured this remark without any intention of insult; but Heathcliff was not prepared to endure the appearance of impertinence from one whom he seemed to hate, even then, as a rival. He seized a tureen of hot apple sauce, and dashed it full against the speaker's face and neck, who instantly commenced a lament that brought Isabella and Catherine hurrying to the place. Mr. Earnshaw snatched up the culprit directly, and conveyed him to his chamber, where doubtless he administered a rough remedy to cool the fit of passion. I got the dish-cloth, and rather spitefully scrubbed Edgar's nose and mouth, affirming that it served him right for meddling. His sister began weeping to go home, and Cathy stood by confounded, blushing for all.

" You should not have spoken to him ! " she expostulated with Master Linton. " He'll be flogged, and I hate him to be flogged. I can't eat my dinner. Why did you speak to him, Edgar ? "

" I didn't," sobbed the youth; " I promised mamma I wouldn't, and I didn't."

" Well, don't cry," replied Catherine contemptuously. " You're not killed. Don't make more mischief. My brother is coming. Be quiet, Isabella ! "

" There, there, children; to your seats ! " cried Hindley, bustling in. " That brute of a lad has warmed me nicely. I've locked him up, and he'll trouble us no more. Next time, Master Edgar, take the law into your own hands; it will give you an appetite."

The little party recovered its equanimity at sight of the fragrant feast. But though Catherine tried to assume an indifferent air, I perceived that she was in purgatory throughout the day, and wearying to find an opportunity to pay a visit to Heathcliff.

In the evening we had a dance, and the Gimmerton band (which goes the round of all the respectable houses at Christmas) arrived fifteen strong. And then she did manage to step upstairs to the door of the garret where Heathcliff was confined. He stubbornly declined answering her for a while; but she persevered, and finally persuaded him to hold converse through the boards. I left the poor things unmolested, till I thought the music and songs were going to cease, and the performers get some refreshment; then I clambered up the ladder to warn her. Instead of finding her outside, I heard her voice within. The little monkey had crept by the skylight of one garret, along the roof, and into the skylight of the other; it was only with the utmost difficulty I could coax her out again. When she did come, Heathcliff came with her, and she insisted I should take him into the kitchen, and give him food. I told them I intended by no means to encourage their tricks; but as the prisoner had never broken his fast since yesterday's dinner, I would wink at his cheating Mr. Hindley that once. I sat him on the stool by the fire, and offered him a quantity of good things; but he was sick and could eat little. He put his chin on his hands, and remained wrapped in dumb meditation. On my enquiring the subject of his thoughts, he answered gravely—

" I'm trying to settle how I shall pay Hindley back. I don't care how long I wait, if I can only do it at last. I hope he will not die before I do ! "

"For shame, Heathcliff!" said I. "It is for *God* to punish wicked people."

"No; God won't have the satisfaction I shall," he returned. "I only wish I knew the best way. Let me alone, and I'll plan it out; while I'm thinking of that I don't feel pain."

CHAPTER VII

THE clock in the room now struck eleven, and Mrs. Dean got up, apologising for having talked so long. "I forget," said she, "that these tales cannot divert you. You must be nodding for bed." But I protested that I was more than interested, and begged her to continue. She therefore sat down again, and went on as follows:—

Well, sir, I must now pass on to the next summer—the summer of 1778; nearly twenty-three years ago. One fine June morning my first bonny little nursling, and the last of the Earnshaw stock, was born. We were busy with the hay in a distant field when the girl that usually brought our breakfasts came running out an hour too soon, calling me as she ran.

"Oh, such a grand bairn!" she panted out. "The finest lad that ever breathed! But the doctor says the missis must go. He says she's been in consumption these many months, and will be dead before winter. You must come home directly. You're to nurse it, Nelly—to feed it with milk and sugar, and take care of it night and day."

"But is she very ill?" I asked, flinging down my rake and tying on my bonnet.

" I'll guess she is; yet she looks bravely, and talks as if she thought of living to see it grow a man. She's out of her head for joy, it's such a beauty."

I hurried home, eager to admire, though I was very sorry for Hindley's sake. He had room in his heart only for two idols—his wife and himself.

When we got to Wuthering Heights, there he stood at the front door. "How is the baby?" I asked as we passed in.

" Nearly ready to run about, Nell!" he replied, putting on a cheerful smile.

"And the mistress?" I ventured to inquire; "the doctor says—— "

"Damn the doctor!" he interrupted, reddening. "Frances is quite right; she'll be perfectly well by this time next week."

And till within a week of her death he persisted doggedly —nay, furiously—in affirming that her health improved every day. And Mrs. Earnshaw's gay heart never failed her. But one night, while leaning on his shoulder, in the act of saying she should be able to get up to-morrow, a fit of coughing seized her—a very slight one. He raised her in his arms; she put her two arms about his neck, her face changed—and she was dead.

As the girl had anticipated, the child Hareton fell wholly into my hands. Mr. Earnshaw, provided he saw him healthy and never heard him cry, was contented, as far as regarded him. For himself, he grew desperate; he cursed and defied—execrated God and man, and gave himself up to reckless dissipation. The servants could not bear his tyrannical and evil conduct long. Joseph and I were the only two that would stay.

The master's bad ways and bad companions formed a pretty example for Catherine and Heathcliff. His treatment of the latter was enough to make a fiend of a saint.

And, truly, it appeared as if the lad *were* possessed of something diabolical at that period. He delighted to see Hindley degrading himself past redemption, and became daily more notable for savage sullenness and ferocity. I could not half tell what an infernal house we had. Nobody decent came near us at last, unless Edgar Linton's visits to Miss Cathy might be an exception. At fifteen, haughty and headstrong as she was, she was the queen of the countryside. But Heathcliff kept his hold on her affections unalterably, and young Linton, with all his superiority, found it difficult to make an equally deep impression.

Catherine had kept up her acquaintance with the Lintons since her five weeks residence among them. In *their* company she had the sense to be ashamed of being rude, and from them she experienced an invariable courtesy. The old lady and gentleman loved her; she gained the admiration of Isabella, and the heart and soul of her brother. These acquaintances flattered her (for she was full of ambition), and led her to adopt a double character without exactly intending to deceive anyone. In the place where she heard Heathcliff termed " a vulgar young brute ", she took care not to act like him; but at home she had small inclination to practise politeness that would only be laughed at.

Mr. Edgar seldom mustered courage to visit Wuthering Heights openly. He had a terror of Earnshaw's reputation, and shrank from encountering him. And I rather think his appearance there was distasteful to Catherine. She had evidently an objection to her two friends meeting at all; for when Heathcliff expressed his contempt of Linton in his presence, she could not half coincide as she did in his absence; and when Linton evinced disgust and antipathy to Heathcliff, she dared not treat his sentiments with indifference, as if depreciation of her playmate was of scarcely any consequence to her. I might have pitied her distresses had not her pride prevented me from doing so.

Mr. Hindley had gone from home one afternoon, and Heathcliff had presumed to give himself a holiday on the strength of it. He had reached the age of sixteen, and, without having bad features or being deficient in intellect, he contrived to convey an impression of inward and outward repulsiveness that his present aspect retains no traces of. Continual hard work, and the complete cessation of his education, had contributed to this effect. His childhood's sense of superiority, instilled into him by the favours of old Mr. Earnshaw, had long since faded away. He made no attempt to improve himself. He had acquired a slouching gate and ignoble look; his naturally reserved disposition was exaggerated into an almost idiotic excess of unsociable moroseness, and he took a grim pleasure, apparently, in exciting the aversion of his few acquaintances.

Catherine was his constant companion still at his seasons of respite from labour, but he had ceased to express his fondness for her in words, and recoiled with angry suspicion from her girlish caresses, as if conscious that there could be no gratification in lavishing such marks of affection on him.

On this particular occasion he came into the house to announce his intention of doing nothing, while I was assisting Miss Cathy to arrange her dress. She had not reckoned on his being idle, and, imagining she would have the whole place to herself, she had managed by some means to inform Mr. Edgar of her brother's absence, and was then preparing to receive him.

" Cathy, are you busy this afternoon? " asked Heathcliff. " Are you going anywhere? "

" No, it is raining," she answered.

"Why have you that silk frock on, then? Nobody coming here, I hope?"

"Not that I know of," stammered miss; "but you should be in the field now."

"No. Hindley does not often free us from his accursed presence. I'll not work any more today; I'll stay with you."

So saying, he lounged to the fire and sat down. Catherine reflected an instant with knitted brows; she found it needful to smooth the way for an intrusion.

"Isabella and Edgar Linton talked of calling this afternoon," she said, at the conclusion of a minute's silence. "As it rains, I hardly expect them; but they may come, and if they do you run the risk of being scolded for no good."

"Order Ellen to say you are engaged. Don't turn me out for those silly friends of yours. I'm on the point, sometimes, of complaining that they—but I'll not."

"That they what?" cried Catherine, gazing at him with a troubled countenance.

"Nothing—only look at the almanac on the wall. The crosses are for the evenings you've spent with the Lintons, the dots for those you've spent with me. I've marked every day."

"Yes; very foolish—as if I took notice!" replied Catherine, in a peevish voice. "And where is the sense of that?"

"To show that I *do* take notice," said Heathcliff.

"And should I always be sitting with you?" she demanded, growing still more irritated. "You might as well be dumb for anything you say to amuse me."

"You never before told me I talked too little, or that you disliked my company," exclaimed Heathcliff in much agitation.

"It's no company at all, when people know nothing, and say nothing," she muttered.

Her companion rose up; but he hadn't time to express his feelings further, for a horse's feet were heard on the flags; and, having knocked gently, young Linton entered, his face brilliant with delight at the unexpected summons he had received. Doubtless Catherine marked the difference between her two friends as one came in and the other went out. The contrast resembled what you see in exchanging a bleak, hilly, coal country for a beautiful green valley.

"I am not come too soon, am I?" said Linton, in his sweet, low voice, casting a look at me. I had begun to wipe the plate and tidy some drawers at the far end of the dresser.

"No," answered Catherine. "What are you doing there, Nelly?"

"My work, miss" (Mr. Hindley had given me instructions to make a third party at any private visits Linton chose to pay).

She stepped behind me and whispered crossly, "Take yourself and your dusters elsewhere." I proceeded assiduously with my occupation; and this so angered her that, supposing Edgar could not see her, she snatched the cloth from my hand, and pinched me very hard and spitefully on the arm. I've said I did not love her, and rather relished mortifying her vanity now and then—besides, she hurt me extremely; so I started up from my knees and screamed out, "Oh, miss, that's a nasty trick! You've no right to nip me, and I'm not going to bear it."

"I didn't touch you, you lying creature!" cried she, her whole complexion in a blaze with passion.

"What's that, then?" I retorted, showing a decided purple witness to refute her.

She stamped her foot, wavered a moment, and then slapped me a stinging blow on the cheek.

"Catherine, love! Catherine!" interposed Linton,

greatly shocked by the double fault of falsehood and violence his idol had committed.

" Leave the room, Ellen ! " she repeated, trembling all over.

Little Hareton, who followed me everywhere, and was sitting near me on the floor, began to sob out complaints against " wicked Aunt Cathy " which drew her fury on his unlucky head. She seized his shoulders, and shook him till the poor child waxed livid, and Edgar thoughtlessly laid hold of her hands to deliver him. In an instant one was wrung free, and the astonished young man felt it applied over his own ear in a way that could not be mistaken for jest. He drew back in consternation. I walked off to the kitchen with Hareton in my arms, leaving the door of communication open, for I was curious to watch how they would settle their dispute. The insulted visitor moved to the spot where he had laid his hat, pale and with lips quivering.

" That's right ! " I said to myself. " Take warning and begone ! "

" Where are you going? " demanded Catherine, advancing to the door.

He swerved aside and attempted to pass.

" You shall not go ! " she exclaimed energetically.

" I must and shall ! " he replied in a subdued voice.

" No," she persisted, grasping the handle, " not yet, Edgar Linton. You shall not leave me in that temper. I should be miserable all night, and I won't be miserable for you ! "

" I cannot stay after you have struck me. You have made me ashamed and afraid of you. I shall not come here again."

" Very well, go, if you please—get away. And now I'll cry myself sick."

She dropped on her knees by a chair, and set to weeping

in serious earnest. Edgar persevered in his resolution as far as the court-yard. But there he wavered, turned abruptly, and hastened back into the house, shutting the door behind him. " Ah," I thought ; " there will be no saving him ; he's doomed and flies to his fall." And when I went in after a while to inform them that Earnshaw had come home rabid drunk, I saw that the quarrel had only effected a closer intimacy between them—had broken the outworks of youthful timidity, and enabled them to confess themselves lovers.

Intelligence of Mr. Hindley's arrival drove Linton speedily to his horse, and Catherine to her chamber.

Hindley entered, vociferating oaths fearful to hear, and caught me in the act of hiding his little son out of his way in the kitchen cupboard. Hareton was impressed with a wholesome terror of his father, never knowing whether he would encounter his wild beast's fondness or his madman's raging, and the poor thing remained quiet where I had put him.

" There, I've found it out at last," cried Hindley, pulling me back by the skin of my neck like a dog. " By heaven and hell, you've sworn between you to murder that child ! I know how it is, now that he is always out of my way. But, with the help of Satan, I shall make you swallow that carving-knife, Nelly ! I want to kill some of you. I shall have no rest till I do." And seizing the knife, he pushed the point between my teeth. But, for my part, I was never much afraid of his vagaries. I spat out, and declared it tasted detestably.

" Oh ! " said he, releasing me, " I see that hideous little villain is not Hareton. I beg your pardon, Nell. If it be, he deserves flaying alive for not coming to welcome me, and for screaming as if I were a goblin. Unnatural cub, come hither ! Hush, child, hush ! Whist, dry thy eyes— there's a joy ; kiss me. What ! it won't ? Damn thee, kiss me ! By God, as if I would rear such a monster ! As sure as I'm living, I'll break the brat's neck."

Poor Hareton was squalling and kicking in his father's arms with all his might, and redoubled his efforts when he carried him upstairs and held him over the banister. I ran to rescue him, and as I reached them, Hindley leant forward on the rails to listen to someone approaching below, almost forgetting what he had in his hands. "Who is that?" he asked, leaning right forward. I leant forward also, for the purpose of signing to Heathcliff, whose step I recognised, not to come farther, but at the instant my eye quitted Hareton, he gave a sudden spring, delivered himself of the careless grasp that held him—and fell.

There was scarcely time to experience a thrill of horror before we saw that the little wretch was safe. Heathcliff arrived underneath just at the critical moment; by a natural impulse he arrested the child's descent, and setting him on his feet, looked up to discover the author of the accident. A miser who has parted with a lucky lottery ticket for five shillings, and finds next day he has lost in the bargain five thousand pounds, could not show a blanker countenance than he did on beholding Mr. Earnshaw above. It expressed, plainer than words could do, the intense anguish he felt at having made himself the instrument of thwarting his own revenge. Had it been dark, I dare say he would have tried to remedy the mistake by smashing Hareton's skull on the steps. I ran down and caught my precious charge to my heart. Hindley descended more leisurely, sobered and abashed.

"It is your fault, Ellen," he said; "you should have taken him out of my sight. Is he injured anywhere?"

"Injured !" I cried angrily; "if he's not killed, he'll be an idiot. I wonder his mother does not rise from the grave to see how you use him—your own flesh and blood!"

He attempted to touch the child. At the first finger his father laid on him, however, little Hareton shrieked and struggled as though he would go into convulsions.

" You shall not meddle with him," I continued. " He hates you ; they all hate you—and no wonder. A happy family you have, and a pretty state you've come to."

" I shall come to a prettier yet, Nelly," laughed the misguided man. " Take yourself and the brat away—and you, Heathcliff, clear out of my sight and hearing." And saying this, he took a pint bottle of brandy from the dresser and poured some into a tumbler.

" Nay, don't ! " I entreated. " Have mercy on this unfortunate boy, if you care nothing for yourself. Have mercy on your own soul ! "

" Not I ! On the contrary, I shall have great pleasure in sending it to perdition to punish its maker. Here's to its hearty damnation ! "

He drank the spirits and, with oaths too bad to repeat, commanded us to go.

" It's a pity he cannot kill himself with drink," observed Heathcliff, when the door was shut. " He's doing his utmost, but his constitution defies him. Mr. Kenneth says he would wager his mare that he'll outlive any man this side of Gimmerton."

I went into the kitchen, and sat down to lull my little one to sleep. Heathcliff, as I thought, walked through to the barn. It turned out afterwards that he had only flung himself down, out of sight, on the other side of the settle. I was rocking Hareton when Miss Cathy put her head in at the door.

" Are you alone, Nelly ? " The expression on her face seemed troubled and anxious.

" Yes, miss," I replied.

" Where's Heathcliff ? "

" About his work in the stable," was my answer.

He did not contradict me; perhaps he had fallen into a doze. I saw that Catherine was crying. "Is she sorry for her shameful conduct?" I asked myself. "That will be a novelty." But no; she was sorry only for herself.

"Oh, dear! I'm very unhappy, Nelly."

"A pity," observed I. "You're hard to please. So few cares, and you can't make yourself content."

"Nelly, can you keep a secret for me?" she pursued, lifting her winsome eyes to my face.

"Is it worth keeping?" I enquired less sulkily.

"Yes, and it worries me, and I must let it out. Today Edgar Linton asked me to marry him, and I've given him an answer. Now, before I tell you whether it was a consent or denial, you tell me what it ought to have been."

"Really, Miss Catherine, how can I tell?" I replied. "If he asked you after the exhibition you performed in his presence this afternoon, he must be either hopelessly stupid or a venturesome fool."

"If you talk so, I won't tell you any more," she returned peevishly, rising to her feet. "I accepted him, Nelly. Be quick, and say whether I was wrong."

"You accepted him! Then what is the good of discussing the matter? You have pledged your word, and cannot retract."

"But say whether I should have done so—do!" she exclaimed, chafing her hands together and frowning.

"There are many things to be considered before that question can be answered properly," I said sententiously. "First and foremost, do you love Mr. Edgar?"

"Who can help it? Of course I do," she answered.

Then I put her through the following catechism. For a girl of twenty-two it was not injudicious.

"Why do you love him, Miss Cathy?"

"Nonsense; I do—that's sufficient."

"By no means; you must say why."

"Well, because he is handsome and pleasant to be with."

"Bad!" was my comment.

"And because he is young and cheerful."

"Bad, still."

"And because he loves me."

"Indifferent, coming there."

"And he will be rich, and I shall be the greatest woman in the neighbourhood."

"Worst of all. And now, say how you love him."

"As everybody loves. You're silly, Nelly."

"Not at all—answer."

"I love the ground under his feet, and the air over his head. I love his looks, and all his actions, and him entirely and altogether. There now!"

"And why?"

"Nay, you are making a jest of it. It is exceedingly ill-natured. It is no jest to me!" said the young lady, scowling and turning her face to the fire.

"I am very far from jesting, Miss Catherine," I replied. "You say you love Mr. Edgar because he is young, handsome and rich. He won't be young and handsome always, and may not always be rich. Would you love him then?"

"He is now; and I have only to do with the present. Do speak rationally."

"Well, that settles it. If you have only to do with the present, marry Mr. Linton."

"I don't want your permission for that—I *shall* marry him; and yet you have not told me whether I am right."

"Perfectly right, if people be right to marry only for the present. And now let us hear what you are unhappy about. You will escape from a disorderly, comfortless home into a wealthy, comfortable one; and you love Edgar, and Edgar loves you. All seems smooth and easy. Where is the objection?"

"*Here* and *here*," replied Catherine, striking one hand on her forehead and the other on her breast; "in whichever place the soul and heart lives. In my soul and in my heart I'm convinced I'm wrong."

"That's very strange. I cannot make it out!"

"It's my secret. But if you will not mock at me, I'll explain it. I can't do it distinctly, but I'll give you a feeling of how I feel."

She seated herself by me again; her countenance grew sadder and graver, and her clasped hands trembled.

"Nelly, do you never dream queer dreams?" she said suddenly, after some minutes' reflection.

"Yes; now and then," I answered.

"And so do I. I've dreamt in my life dreams that have stayed with me ever after, and changed my ideas; they've gone through and through me, like wine through water, and altered the colour of my mind. And this is one. I'm going to tell it; but take care not to smile at any part of it."

"Oh, don't, Miss Catherine!" I cried. "We're dismal enough without conjuring up ghosts and visions to perplex us. Come, come, be merry and like yourself! Look at little Hareton! *He's* dreaming nothing dreary. How sweetly he smiles in his sleep!"

"Yes; and how sweetly his father curses in his solitude! You remember him, I dare say, when he was just such another as that chubby thing—nearly as young and innocent. However, Nelly, I shall oblige you to listen; it's not long, and I've no power to be merry tonight."

"I won't hear it, I won't hear it!" I repeated hastily.

I was superstitious about dreams then, and am still; and Catherine had an unusual gloom in her aspect that made me dread something from which I might shape a prophecy and foresee a fearful catastrophe. She was

C

vexed, but she did not proceed. Apparently taking up another subject, she recommenced in a short time.

"If I were in heaven, Nelly, I should be extremely miserable."

"Because you are not fit to go there," I answered. "All sinners would be miserable in heaven."

"But it is not for that. I dreamt once that I was there."

"I tell you I won't hearken to your dreams, Miss Catherine! I'll go to bed," I interrupted again.

She laughed and held me down, for I made a motion to leave my chair.

"This is nothing," cried she. "I was only going to say that heaven did not seem to be my home, and I broke my heart with weeping to come back to earth; and the angels were so angry that they flung me out into the middle of the heath on the top of Wuthering Heights, where I woke sobbing for joy. That will do to explain my secret as well as the other. I've no more business to marry Edgar Linton than I have to be in heaven; and if the wicked man in there had not brought Heathcliff so low, I shouldn't have thought of it. It would degrade me to marry Heathcliff now, so he shall never know how I love him; and that not because he's handsome, Nelly, but because he's more myself than I am. Whatever our souls are made of, his and mine are the same; and Linton's is as different as a moonbeam from lightning, or frost from fire."

Ere this speech ended I became sensible of Heathcliff's presence. Having noticed a slight movement, I turned my head and saw him rise from the bench and steal out noiselessly. He had listened till he heard Catherine say it would degrade her to marry him, and then he stayed to hear no further. My companion, sitting on the ground, was prevented by the back of the settle from remarking his presence or departure; but I started and bade her hush.

" Why ? " she asked, gazing nervously round.

" Joseph is here," I answered, catching opportunely the roll of his cart-wheels up the road, " and Heathcliff will come in with him. I'm not sure whether he were not at the door this moment."

" Oh, he couldn't overhear me at the door," said she. " Give me Hareton while you get the supper, and when it is ready ask me to sup with you. I want to cheat my uncomfortable conscience, and be convinced that Heathcliff has no notion of these things. He has not, has he ? He does not know what being in love is ? "

" I see no reason that he should not know, as well as you," I returned ; " and if *you* are his choice, he'll be the most unfortunate creature that ever was born. As soon as you become Mrs. Linton, he loses friend, love, and all. Have you considered how you'll bear the separation, and how he'll bear to be quite deserted in the world ? Because, Miss Catherine—— "

" He quite deserted ! we separated ! " she exclaimed with an accent of indignation. " Who is to separate us, pray ? They'll meet the fate of Milo. Not as long as I live, Ellen—for no mortal creature ! Every Linton on the face of the earth might melt into nothing before I could consent to forsake Heathcliff. Oh, that's not what I intend—that's not what I mean ! I shouldn't be Mrs. Linton were such a price demanded ! He'll be as much to me as he has been all his lifetime. Edgar must shake off his antipathy, and tolerate him, at least. He will, when he learns my true feelings towards him. Nelly, I see now—you think me a selfish wretch ; but did it never strike you that if Heathcliff and I married, we should be beggars ? Whereas, if I marry Linton, I can aid Heathcliff to rise, and place him out of my brother's power."

" With your husband's money, Miss Catherine ? " I asked. " You'll find him not so pliable as you calculate upon; and, though I'm hardly a judge, I think that's the worst motive you've given yet for being the wife of young Linton."

"It is not!" retorted she; "it is the best! The others were the satisfaction of my whims; and for Edgar's sake, too—to satisfy him. This is for the sake of one who comprehends in his person my feelings to Edgar and myself. I cannot express it, but surely you and everybody have a notion that there is or should be an existence of yours beyond you. What were the use of my creation if I were entirely contained here? My great miseries in this world have been Heathcliff's miseries, and I watched and felt each from the beginning. My great thought in living is himself. If all else perished, and *he* remained, *I* should still continue to be. And if all else remained, and he were annihilated, the universe would turn to a mighty stranger—I should not seem a part of it. My love for Linton is like the foliage in the woods; time will change it, I'm well aware, as winter changes the trees. My love for Heathcliff resembles the eternal rocks beneath—a source of little visible delight, but necessary. Nelly, I *am* Heathcliff. He's always, always in my mind —not as a pleasure, any more than I am always a pleasure to myself, but as my own being. So don't talk of our separation again. It is impracticable, and—— "

She paused, and hid her face in the folds of my gown, but I jerked it forcibly away. I was out of patience with her folly.

"If I can make any sense of your nonsense, miss," I said, " it only goes to convince me that you are ignorant of the duties you undertake in marrying, or else that you are a wicked, unprincipled girl. But trouble me with no more secrets; I'll not promise to keep them."

" You'll keep that ? " she asked eagerly.

" No, I'll not promise," I repeated.

She was about to insist when the entrance of Joseph finished our conversation; and Catherine retired to a seat in the corner and nursed Hareton, while I made the supper. After it was cooked, Joseph and I began to quarrel who should carry some to Mr. Hindley, and it was nearly cold before we came to an agreement that we would let him ask if he wanted any.

"And how isn't that nowt comed in from the field be this time?" demanded the old man, looking round for Heathcliff.

"I'll call him," I replied. "He's in the barn, I've no doubt."

I went and called, but got no answer. On returning, I whispered to Catherine that he had heard a good part of our conversation, and told how I saw him quit the kitchen just as she complained of her brother's conduct regarding them. She jumped up in a fine fright, and ran out to seek for him herself. After a protracted absence she came hurrying back, breathless and agitated, and issued a hurried command to Joseph to run down the road, and wherever Heathcliff had rambled, find him, and make him re-enter directly. The old man objected at first, but seeing how much she was in earnest, he placed his hat on his head and walked grumbling forth. Meanwhile Catherine paced up and down the floor, exclaiming—

"I wonder where he is—I wonder where he *can* be? What did I say, Nelly? I've forgotten. Tell me what I said to grieve him. I do wish he would come."

"What a noise to make for nothing!" I cried, though rather uneasy myself. "Heathcliff cannot be far away. I'll engage he's sulking in the hay-loft. See if I don't ferret him out."

And with this, I departed. But neither my search nor Joseph's produced any results.

It was a very dark night, and appeared inclined to

thunder. I declared that the approaching rain would be certain to bring him home. But Catherine would not be persuaded into tranquillity. She kept wandering to and fro, in a state of agitation which permitted no repose, and finally took up a permanent situation on one side of the wall, near the road, regardless of the heavy rain that was now beginning to fall.

About midnight, while we still sat up, the storm came rattling over the Heights in full fury. There was a violent wind, as well as thunder, and either one or the other split a tree off at the corner of the building; a huge bough fell across the roof, and knocked off a portion of the east chimney-stack, sending a clatter of stones and soot into the kitchen fire. We thought a bolt had fallen into the midst of us, and Joseph swung on to his knees, beseeching the Lord to spare the righteous. But the uproar passed away in twenty minutes, without having awakened Mr. Earnshaw from his drunken slumbers. All of us were unharmed, except Cathy, who got thoroughly drenched for her obstinacy in refusing to take shelter. She came in and lay down on the settle, all soaked as she was, turning her face to the back, and putting her hands before it.

No expostulations would prevail on her to stir and take off her wet clothes, and when I came down in the morning, later than usual, she was still seated near the fireplace, unchanged. Hindley was there with her, and stood on the kitchen hearth, haggard and drowsy.

"What ails you, Cathy?" he was saying, when I entered; "you look as dismal as a drowned whelp. Why are you so damp and pale, my child?"

"I've been wet!" she answered reluctantly, "and I'm cold; that's all."

"Oh, she's naughty!" I cried, perceiving the master to be tolerably sober. "She got steeped in the shower of yesterday evening, and there she has sat the night through."

Mr. Earnshaw stared at us in surprise. "The night through!" he repeated. "What kept her up?"

Neither of us wished to mention Heathcliff's absence, so I replied that I did not know, and she said nothing. I threw back the lattice, and presently the room was filled with sweet scents from the garden; but Catherine called out peevishly, "Ellen, shut the window. I'm starving!" And her teeth chattered as she shrank closer to the embers.

"She's ill," said Hindley, taking her wrist. "Damn it! I don't want to be troubled with more sickness here. What took you into the rain?"

"Running after t' lads as usual," croaked Joseph, who had now joined us, and was quick to catch this opportunity, from our hesitation, of thrusting out his evil tongue. "If I war yah, maister, I'd slam t' boards i' their faces, all on 'em, gentle and simple. Never a day ut yah're off, but yon cat o' Linton comes sneaking hither; and Miss Nelly—shoo's a fine lass—shoo sits watching for ye i' t' kitchen; and as yah're in at one door, he's out at t'other, and then wer grand lady goes a-coorting of her side! It's bonny behaviour, lurking amang t' fields after twelve o' t' night wi' that fahl, flaysome divil of a gipsy, Heathcliff! They think *I'm* blind, but I'm noan—nowt ut t' soart! I seed it all yesterday."

"Silence, eavesdropper!" cried Catherine; "none of your insolence before me! Edgar Linton came yesterday by chance, Hindley, and it was *I* who told him to be off, because I knew you would not like to meet him as you were."

"You lie, Cathy, no doubt," answered her brother. "But never mind Linton at present; tell me—were you not with Heathcliff last night? Speak the truth, now.

You need not be afraid of harming him. Though I hate him as much as ever, he did me a good turn a short time since that will make my conscience very tender of breaking his neck. To prevent it, I shall send him about his business this very morning; and after he's gone, I'd advise you to look sharp."

" I never saw Heathcliff last night," answered Catherine, beginning to sob bitterly, " and if you turn him out of doors, I'll go with him. But perhaps you'll never have the opportunity; perhaps he's gone." Here she burst into uncontrollable grief, and the remainder of her words were inarticulate.

Hindley lavished on her a torrent of scornful abuse, and bade her get to her room immediately. I obliged her to obey, and I shall never forget the scene she acted when we reached her chamber. I thought she was going mad, and I begged Joseph to run for the doctor. It proved the commencement of delirium. Mr. Kenneth, as soon as he saw her, pronounced her dangerously ill with a fever.

Though I cannot say I made a gentle nurse, and Joseph and the master were no better, and though our patient was as wearisome and impatient as could be, somehow she weathered it through. Old Mrs. Linton paid us several visits, and when Catherine was better she insisted on conveying her to Thrushcross Grange, for which we were very grateful. But the poor dame had reason to repent her kindness. She and her husband both took the fever, and died within a few days of each other.

Our young lady returned to us, saucier and more passionate and haughtier than ever. Heathcliff had never been heard of since the evening of the thunderstorm. She would allow no one to cross or contradict her; and her brother at this time allowed her to demand whatever she pleased—not from affection, but from pride. He wished earnestly to see her bring honour to the family by an alliance with the Lintons. But he need not have feared. Edgar Linton was utterly infatuated, and believed himself to be the happiest man alive on the day he led her to Gimmerton Chapel, three years subsequent to his father's death.

Much against my inclination, I was persuaded to leave Wuthering Heights and accompany them here to the Grange. I could not bear to leave Hareton. But Catherine's tears were more powerful than mine or the child's. When I refused to go, she went lamenting to her husband and brother. The former offered me magnificent wages; the latter ordered me to pack up. He wanted no woman in the house, he said, now that there was no mistress. So I had no choice but to do as I was ordered. I kissed little Hareton good-bye, and since then he has been a stranger. I've no doubt that by this time he has completely forgotten all about Nelly Dean.

. . . . .

At this point of the housekeeper's story she chanced to glance towards the clock, and was in amazement at seeing the minute hand measure half-past one. She would not hear of staying a second longer—in truth, I felt rather disposed to defer the sequel of her narrative myself. And now that she is vanished to her rest, and I have meditated for another hour or two, I shall summon courage to go also, despite an aching laziness of head and limbs—the effect no doubt of my own ill-starred visit to Wuthering Heights.

CHAPTER VIII

A CHARMING introduction to a hermit's life. Four weeks' torture, tossing and sickness ! Oh, these bleak northern winds and skies, the impassable roads, and dilatory country surgeons ! And, oh, this dearth of the human physiognomy ! And worse than all, the terrible intimation of Doctor Kenneth that I shall not be out of doors till spring.

I am too weak to read, yet I feel I could enjoy something interesting. Why not have Mrs. Dean up to finish her tale ? I'll ring. She'll be delighted to find me capable of talking cheerfully.—I rang. Mrs. Dean came, and after an argument over some medicine which I had no disposition to swallow, I persuaded her to draw her knitting out of her pocket and settle herself.

" And now, if you please, continue the history of Mr. Heathcliff from where you left off to the present day. Did he finish his education on the Continent, and come back a gentleman ? Or did he get a sizar's place at college ? Or did he escape to America and make a fortune there ? "

" He may have done a little in all these vocations, Mr. Lockwood," said she, smiling, " but I couldn't give my word for any. I stated before that I didn't know how he gained his money, nor do I know what means he took to raise his mind from the savage ignorance to which it had sunk. But, with your leave, I'll proceed in my own fashion, if you think it will not weary you. Are you feeling better this morning ? "

" Much."

" That is good news."

I got Miss Catherine and myself to Thrushcross Grange, (said Mrs. Dean, now continuing her story), and, to my agreeable disappointment, she behaved infinitely better than I dared to expect. She seemed almost over-fond of Mr. Linton, and even to his sister she showed plenty of affection. But they were both very attentive to her comfort, and who can be ill-natured and disagreeable when they encounter neither ill-temper nor opposition? I observed that Mr. Edgar had a deep-rooted fear of ruffling her humour. He concealed it from her; but if ever he heard me answer her sharply, or saw any other servant grow cloudy at some imperious order of hers, he would show his trouble by a frown of displeasure that never darkened on his own account. Not to grieve a kind master, I learned to be less touchy; and for half a year the gunpowder lay as harmless as sand, because no fire came near to explode it; and though Catherine had seasons of gloom and silence now and then (which her husband ascribed to an alteration in her constitution produced by her illness), I believe I may assert that both husband and wife were possessed of a deep and growing happiness.

It ended.—One fragrant evening in September, I was coming from the garden with a heavy basket of apples I had been gathering. It had got dark; the moon looked over the high wall of the court. I stopped to rest near the house steps and was standing with my back to the door, when I heard a voice behind me say—

" Nelly, is that you? "

It was a deep voice, and foreign in tone, and yet somehow familiar. I turned to discover who spoke, fearfully; for the doors were shut, and I had seen nobody on approaching the steps. Something stirred in the porch—a tall man, in dark clothes, with dark face and hair. A ray fell on his features; the cheeks were sallow and half covered with black whiskers, the brows lowering, the eyes deep-set and singular. I recognised those eyes, and I drew back, starting.

" What! Heathcliff! Are you come back? "

"Yes, Nelly, it is me. I have waited here an hour, and the whole of that time all round me has been as still as death. I dared not enter!"

"Can it really be you!"

"Yes, it's me right enough. Are you not glad, Nelly? You need not be so disturbed.—Are they at home? Where is she? I want to have one word with her—your mistress. Go, and say that some person from Gimmerton desires to see her."

"How will she take it?" I exclaimed. "What will she do? The surprise bewilders me. It will put her out of her head. And you *are* Heathcliff, but altered! Nay, there's no comprehending it. Have you been for a soldier?"

"Go and carry my message," he interrupted impatiently. "I'm in hell till you do."

He lifted the latch, and I entered. Mr. and Mrs. Linton were in the parlour; they looked wonderfully peaceful, and I shrank from performing my errand. But at length I managed to stutter out, "A person from Gimmerton wishes to see you, ma'am."

"What does he want, Nelly?"

"I did not question him," I answered.

"Well, close the curtains, Nelly, and bring up tea. I'll be back again directly."

She quitted the apartment. Mr. Edgar inquired carelessly who it was.

"Someone the mistress does not expect," I replied. "That Heathcliff—you recollect him, sir—who used to live at Mr. Earnshaw's."

"What! the gipsy—the ploughboy?" he cried. "Why did you not say so to Catherine?"

"Hush! you must not call him by those names, sir. She'd be sorely grieved to hear you. She was nearly heart-broken when he ran off. I guess his return will make quite a jubilee to her."

Mr. Linton walked to a window that overlooked the court. He unfastened it and leant out. I suppose they were below, for he exclaimed quickly, " Don't stand there, love ! Bring the person in if it be anyone in particular." Ere long I heard the click of the latch, and Catherine flew upstairs, breathless and wild, too excited to show gladness; indeed, by her face, you would rather have surmised an awful calamity.

" Oh, Edgar, Edgar darling ! " she panted, flinging her arms round his neck. " Heathcliff's come back—he is ! " And she tightened her embrace to a squeeze.

" Well, well," said her husband crossly, " don't strangle me for that. He never struck me as such a marvellous treasure. There's no need to be frantic."

" I know you didn't like him," she answered, repressing a little the intensity of her delight. " Yet, for my sake, you must be friends now. Shall I tell him to come up ? "

He looked vexed, and suggested the kitchen as a more suitable place for him. Mrs. Linton eyed him with a droll expression—half angry, half laughing at his fastidiousness.

" No," she added, after a while; " I cannot sit in the kitchen.—Set two tables here, Ellen—one for your master and Miss Isabella, being gentry; the other for Heathcliff and myself, being of the lower orders. Will that please you, dear? Or must I have a fire lighted elsewhere? If so, give directions. I'll run down and secure my guest. I'm afraid the joy is too great to be real."

She was about to dart off again, but Edgar arrested her.

" *You* bid him step up, Ellen," he said; " and, Catherine, try to be glad without being absurd. The whole household need not witness the sight of your welcoming a runaway servant as a brother."

I descended and found Heathcliff waiting under the porch, evidently anticipating an invitation to enter. I ushered him upstairs into the presence of the master and mistress, whose flushed cheeks betrayed signs of warm talking. Catherine sprang forward, took both his hands, and led him to Linton; and then she seized Linton's reluctant fingers and crushed them into his. Now, fully revealed by the candlelight, I was more amazed than ever to behold the transformation in Heathcliff. He had grown a tall, athletic, well-formed man, beside whom my master seemed quite slender and youth-like. His upright carriage suggested the idea of his having been in the army. His countenance was much older in expression and decision than Mr. Linton's; it looked intelligent, and retained no marks of former degradation—though a half-civilised ferocity still lurked in his dark eyes. My master's surprise quite equalled mine. He remained for a minute at a loss how to address " the ploughboy ".

" Sit down, sir," he said at length. " Mrs. Linton, recalling old times, would have me give you a cordial reception; and, of course, I am gratified when anything occurs that pleases her."

" And I also," answered Heathcliff, " especially if it be anything in which I have a part. I shall stay an hour or two willingly."

He took a seat opposite Catherine, who kept her gaze fixed upon him, as though she feared he would vanish were she to remove it. He did not raise his to her often— a quick glance now and then sufficed; but it flashed back, each time more confidently, the undisguised delight he drank from hers. They were too much absorbed in their mutual joy to suffer embarrassment. Not so Mr. Edgar. He grew pale with pure annoyance—a feeling that reached its climax when his lady rose, and stepping across the rug, seized Heathcliff's hands again, and laughed like one beside herself.

" I shall think it a dream tomorrow ! " she cried. " I shall not be able to believe that I have seen, and touched, and spoken to you once more. And yet, cruel Heath-cliff, you do not deserve this welcome. To be absent and silent for three years, and never to think of me ! "

" A little more than you have thought of me," he murmured. " I heard of your marriage not long since, Cathy, and I determined that I would catch one last glimpse of your face, before settling my score with Hind-ley, and then prevent the law by doing execution on my-self. Your welcome has put these ideas out of my mind; but beware of meeting me with another aspect next time. You'll not drive me off again. I've fought through a bitter life since I last heard your voice; and you must forgive me, for I struggled only for you."

" Catherine, unless we are to have cold tea, please come to the table," interrupted Linton, striving to preserve his ordinary voice.

She took her post at the urn; and Miss Isabella came, summoned by the bell. I left the room. Their guest stayed only an hour that evening. I asked him, as he departed, if he were lodging at Gimmerton.

" No; at Wuthering Heights," he answered. " Mr. Earnshaw invited me when I called this morning."

Mr. Earnshaw invited *him* ! and *he* called on Mr. Earn-shaw ! I pondered this sentence painfully after he was gone. " Is he coming into the country to work mischief under a cloak ? " I mused. I had a presentiment that his coming would bring much evil.

In the middle of the night, I was wakened by Mrs. Linton coming into my room. She could not sleep, she said. Edgar was sulking because she had said a few sentences in commendation of Mr. Heathcliff; and she wanted some creature to keep her company in her happiness.

" What use is it praising Heathcliff to him ? " I answered. " They always had an aversion to each other.

It's human nature that he should dislike to hear you praise him."

"But does it not show great weakness?" pursued she. "I'm not envious of Isabella's yellow hair and white skin, and the fondness Edgar exhibits for her. I call her a darling and humour them both."

"You're mistaken, Mrs. Linton," said I; "they humour you. I know what there would be to do if they did not. You can well afford to indulge their passing whims. You may, however, fall out at last over something of equal consequence to you both; and then you will find that those you term weak are capable of being as obstinate as you."

"No!" returned Cathy, laughing. "I have such faith in Linton's love I believe I might kill him, and he would not wish to retaliate."

I advised her to value him the more for his affection.

"I do," she answered; "but he needn't resort to whining for trifles. He must get accustomed to my Heathcliff, and he may as well like him. Considering how Heathcliff has reason to object to Edgar, I'm sure he behaved excellently."

"What do you think of his going to Wuthering Heights?" I enquired. "Apparently he is offering the right hand of friendship to all his enemies around."

"He explained it," she replied. "He called to gather information concerning me from you, supposing you still resided there. Joseph told Hindley—who came out, fell to questioning him of what he had been doing, and finally desired him to walk in. There were some persons sitting at cards. Heathcliff joined them. My brother lost some money to him; and finding him plentifully supplied, asked him to come again in the evening, to which he consented. He means to fix himself at the Heights by offering liberal payment to my brother, whose covetousness will doubtless prompt him to accept the terms. In this way I shall have more opportunities of seeing him than if he settled at Gimmerton. And I mean to see him often."

"Have you no fears of the consequences?"

"None for *him*," she replied. "His strong head will keep him out of danger. A little for Hindley. But he can't be made morally worse than he is; and I stand between him and bodily harm. The event of this evening has reconciled me to God and humanity. If that creature knew what I have endured, he'd be ashamed to cloud its removal with idle petulance. It was kindness which induced me to bear it alone. However, it's over, and I'll take no revenge for his folly. I can afford to suffer anything hereafter. Should the meanest thing alive slap me on the cheek, I'd not only turn the other, but I'd ask pardon for provoking it; and as a proof I'll go and make my peace with Edgar instantly. Good-night! I'm an angel."

The success of her fulfilled resolution was obvious on the morrow. Mr. Linton not only abjured his peevishness (though his spirits were still subdued by Catherine's exuberance), but he ventured no objection to her taking Isabella with her to Wuthering Heights in the afternoon; and she rewarded him with such a summer of sweetness as made the house a paradise for several days.

Mr. Heathcliff used the liberty of visiting Thrushcross Grange cautiously at first, but he gradually established his right to be expected. The natural reserve which had always been characteristic of him prevented any startling demonstrations of feeling, and lulled my master's uneasiness—till further circumstances diverted it into a new channel.

Isabella Linton evinced a sudden and irresistible attraction towards the tolerated guest. She was at the time a charming young lady of eighteen, infantile in manners, though possessed of a keen wit, and a keen temper too, if irritated. Her brother, who loved her tenderly, was appalled at this fantastic preference. Leaving aside the degradation of an alliance with a nameless man, and the possible fact that his property, in default of male heirs, might pass into such a one's power, he had the sense to comprehend that, though Heathcliff's exterior was altered, his mind and disposition were unchanged and unchangeable. He would have recoiled still more had he been aware that her attachment rose unsolicited, and was bestowed where it awakened no answering sentiment, for the moment he discovered its existence he laid the blame on Heathcliff's deliberate designing.

We had all remarked, during some time, that Miss Linton fretted and pined over something—snapping at and teasing Catherine continually, at the imminent risk of exhausting her limited patience. We excused her, to a certain extent, on the plea of ill-health. She was fading and dwindling before our eyes. But one day, when she had been particularly wayward and complaining, Mrs. Linton peremptorily insisted that she should go to bed. Isabella exclaimed that her health was perfect, and it was only Catherine's harshness which made her unhappy.

" And when have I been harsh, you naughty fondling ? "

" Yesterday," sobbed Isabella, " and now."

" Yesterday ! " said her sister-in-law. " On what occasion ? "

" In our walk on the moor. You told me to ramble where I pleased, while you sauntered on with Mr. Heathcliff."

" Good heavens ! We didn't care whether you kept company with us or not. I merely thought Heathcliff's talk would have nothing entertaining for your ears."

" Oh, no," wept the young lady; " you wished me away because you knew I like to be there—with—— "

" Well? " said Catherine, perceiving her hesitation to complete the sentence.

" With him; and I won't always be sent off ! You are a dog in the manger, Cathy, and desire no one to be loved but yourself."

" You are an impertinent little monkey ! " exclaimed Mrs. Linton in surprise. " But I'll not believe this idiocy. It is impossible that you should covet the admiration of Heathcliff—that you consider him an agreeable person ! I hope I have misunderstood you."

" No, you have not," said the infatuated girl. " I love him more than you ever loved Edgar; and he might love me, if you would let him."

" Is she sane ! " exclaimed Catherine, in genuine consternation. " Nelly, help me to convince her of her madness. Tell her what Heathcliff is—an unreclaimed creature, without refinement; a fierce, pitiless, wolfish man. I'd as soon put that little canary into the park on a winter's day, Isabella, as recommend you to bestow your heart on him. He'd crush you like a sparrow's egg, if he found you a troublesome charge. I know he couldn't love a Linton, and yet he'd be quite capable of marrying your fortune and expectations. There's my picture; and I'm his friend—so much so, that had he thought seriously to catch you, I should perhaps have held my tongue, and let you fall into his trap."

Miss Linton regarded her sister-in-law with indignation.

" For shame ! for shame ! " she repeated angrily; " you are worse than twenty foes, you poisonous friend."

" Ah ! you won't believe me, then? " cried Catherine. " You think I speak from wicked selfishness. Try for yourself then, if that be your spirit. I have done, and yield the argument to your saucy insolence."

" And I must suffer for her egotism ! " sobbed Isabella, as Mrs. Linton left the room. " But she uttered false-hoods, didn't she, Nelly ? Mr. Heathcliff is not a fiend."

" Banish him from your thoughts, miss," I said. " He is a bird of bad omen—no mate for you. Mrs. Linton is better acquainted with his heart than anyone, and she would never represent him as worse than he is. Honest people do not hide their deeds. How has he been living ? How has he got rich ? Why is he staying at Wuthering Heights, at the house of a man he abhors ? Mr. Earnshaw is worse and worse since he came. I heard it from Joseph only a week ago. They sit up all night together continually, and Hindley has been borrowing money on his land, and does nothing but play and drink. Little by little Heathcliff is getting hold of all his money, and bringing him to ruin."

" You are leagued with the rest, Ellen ! " replied Isabella. " I'll not listen to your evil slanders."

Whether she would have got over this fancy if left to herself, I cannot say. But the day after, there was a justice meeting in the town, which my master, as a magistrate, was obliged to attend; and Heathcliff, aware of his absence, called rather earlier than usual. Catherine and Isabella were sitting in the library on hostile terms, but silent—the latter alarmed at the disclosures she had made of her secret feelings in a transient fit of passion; the former, on mature consideration, really offended with her companion. I was sweeping the hearth, and I observed a mischievous smile on Mrs. Linton's face as Heathcliff entered.

" Come in, that's right ! " she exclaimed gaily. " Here are two people sadly in need of a third to thaw the ice between them; and you are the very one we should choose.—Heathcliff, I'm proud to show you, at last, some body who dotes on you more than myself. I expect you to feel flattered. Nay it's not Nelly. My poor little sister-in-law is breaking her heart for you. It lies in your power to be Edgar's brother.—No, no, Isabella; you shan't run off," she continued, arresting, with feigned playfulness, the confounded girl, who had risen indignantly. "I will stand aside for you, as you told me I should do."

"Catherine!" said Isabella, calling up her dignity, and disdaining to struggle from the tight grasp that held her. "I'd thank you to adhere to the truth, and not to slander me, even in joke.—Mr. Heathcliff, be kind enough to bid this friend of yours to release me. She forgets that you and I are not intimate acquaintances; and what amuses her is painful to me beyond expression."

As the guest answered nothing, but took his seat, and looked thoroughly indifferent what sentiments she cherished concerning him, she turned and whispered an earnest appeal for liberty to her tormentor.

"By no means!" cried Mrs. Linton in anger. "I won't be named a dog in the manger again. Ever since the day before yesterday's walk, Heathcliff, she has fasted from sorrow and rage, because I dispatched her out of your society under the idea of its being unacceptable."

"I think you belie her," said Heathcliff, twisting his chair to face them. "She wishes to be out of my society now, at any rate."

And he stared hard at Isabella, as he might do at a strange, repulsive animal. The poor thing could not bear that. She grew red and white in rapid succession, and, while tears beaded her lashes, bent unavailingly the strength of her small fingers to loosen the firm hold of Catherine. At last, in desperation, she began to make use of her nails; and their sharpness presently ornamented the detainer's with crescents of red.

"There's a tigress!" exclaimed Mrs. Linton, setting

her free, and shaking her hand with pain. "Begone, for God's sake!—Look, Heathcliff! they are instruments that will do execution; you must beware of your eyes."

"I'd wrench them off her fingers if they ever menaced me," he answered brutally, when the door had closed after her. "But what did you mean by teasing the creature in that manner, Cathy? You were not speaking the truth, were you?"

"I assure you I was. She has been dying for you several weeks. But don't notice it further. I wished to punish her for her sauciness, that's all. I like her too well, my dear Heathcliff, to let you absolutely seize and devour her up."

"And I like her too ill to attempt it," said he, "except in a very ghoulish fashion. You'd hear of odd things if I lived alone with that mawkish, waxen face. Her eyes detestably resemble Linton's."

"Delectably," observed Catherine. "They are dove's eyes—angels."

"She's her brother's heir, is she not?" he asked, after a brief silence.

"I should be sorry to think so," returned his companion. "Half a dozen nephews shall erase her title, please heaven! You are too prone to covet your neighbour's goods. Remember *this* neighbour's goods are mine."

"If they were *mine*, they would be none the less that," said Heathcliff; "but though Isabella Linton may be silly, she is scarcely mad. In short, we'll dismiss the subject as you advise."

From their tongues they did dismiss it; but I felt certain, from his grim, ominous musings whenever Catherine happened to be absent from the apartment that evening, that Heathcliff had not dismissed it from his thoughts. I determined to watch his movements closely. His presence among us was an oppression past explaining.

CHAPTER IX

My uneasiness with regard to Mr. Earnshaw was growing daily; and had I not been aware that any interference would be hopeless, I would have visited the Heights and begged him to send Heathcliff away. But at last, going out of my way, I did pass the old gate on a journey to Gimmerton. Looking through the bars was an elf-locked, brown-eyed boy. It was my Hareton, not greatly altered since I had left him ten months since.

"God bless thee, darling!" I cried, hurrying forward. "Hareton, it's Nelly—Nelly, thy nurse."

He retreated an arm's length, and picked up a large flint.

"I am come to see thy father, Hareton," I added, guessing from the action that Nelly, if she lived in his memory at all, was not recognised as one with me.

He raised his missile and hurled it. The stone struck my bonnet; and then ensued, from the stammering lips of the little fellow, a string of curses, delivered with a practised emphasis, and an expression of shocking malignity. You may be certain this grieved more than it angered me. Fit to cry, I took an orange from my pocket, and offered it to propitiate him. He hesitated, and then snatched it from my hand, as if he fancied I only intended to tempt and disappoint him. I showed him another, keeping it out of his reach.

"Who taught you those fine words, my bairn?" I enquired—"the curate?"

"Damn the curate, and thee! Gie me that," he replied.

"Tell us who taught you, then, and you shall have it," said I.

"Heathcliff," was his answer.

I asked if he liked Mr. Heathcliff.

" Ay," he answered. " Daddy cannot bide me, and Heathcliff pays him back what he gies to me; he curses daddy for cursing me. He says I mun do as I will."

" And does not the curate still come to teach you to read and write? "

" No. Heathcliff has promised that the curate shall have his teeth dashed down his —— throat if he steps over the threshold."

I put the orange into his hand, and bade him tell his father that a woman called Nelly Dean was waiting to speak with him by the garden gate. He went into the house; but instead of Hindley Earnshaw, Heathcliff appeared on the door-stones; and I turned directly and ran down the road as hard as ever I could race, feeling as scared as if I'd raised a goblin.

The next time Heathcliff came to the Grange, Miss Linton chanced to be feeding some pigeons in the court. He had not been in the habit of bestowing a single unnecessary civility on *her*, I knew. Now, as soon as he beheld her, his first precaution was to take a sweeping survey of the house-front. I was standing by the kitchen window, but I drew back out of sight. He then stepped up to her, and said something. She seemed embarrassed and desirous of getting away. But he laid his hand upon her arm; and then, supposing himself to be unseen, the scoundrel had the impudence to embrace her.

" Judas! traitor! " I ejaculated. " You are a hypo-crite too, are you—a deliberate deceiver! "

" Who is, Nelly? " said Catherine's voice at my elbow. I had not seen her enter.

" Your worthless friend! " I answered warmly. " Ah, he has caught a glimpse of us; he is coming in! I wonder if he will have the heart to find a plausible excuse for making love to Miss when he told you he hated her? "

Mrs. Linton saw Isabella tear herself free, and run into the garden; and a minute later Heathcliff entered. I couldn't withhold giving some loose to my indignation; but Catherine threatened to order me out of the kitchen, if I dared to put in " my insolent tongue ". Then, turning to Heathcliff—

" What are you about, raising this stir ? I said you must let Isabella alone ! I beg you will, unless you wish Linton to draw the bolts against you."

" God forbid that he should try ! " answered the black villain. " God keep him meek and patient ! Every day I grow madder after sending him to heaven."

" Hush ! " said Catherine, shutting the inner door. " Why have you disregarded my request ? Did she come across you on purpose ? "

" What is it to you ? " he growled. " I have a right to kiss her, if she chooses; and you have no right to object. I am not *your* husband; *you* needn't be jealous of me."

" I'm not jealous of you," replied the mistress—" I'm jealous *for* you. Clear your face; you shan't scowl at me. If you like Isabella, you shall marry her. But do you like her ? There, you don't answer. I'm certain you don't."

" And would Mr. Linton approve of his sister marrying that man ? " I enquired.

" Mr. Linton should approve," returned my lady decisively.

" He might spare himself the trouble," said Heathcliff. " I could do as well without his approbation. As for you, Catherine, you have treated me infernally—infernally ! Do you hear ? If you think I can be consoled by flattery and sweet words, you are an idiot; and if you fancy I'll suffer unrevenged, I'll soon show you you're mistaken. Meanwhile I thank you for telling me your sister-in-law's secret. I swear I'll make the most of it."

"What new phase of his character is this?" exclaimed Mrs. Linton in amazement. "How have I treated you infernally? How will you take your revenge, ungrateful brute?"

"I seek no revenge on you," replied Heathcliff. "That's not the plan. You are welcome to torture me to death for your amusement; only you must allow me to amuse myself in the same style with those who are in *my* power. If I imagined you really wished me to marry Isabella, I'd cut my throat."

"Oh, the evil is that I'm not jealous, is it?" cried Catherine. "Well, I won't repeat my offer of a wife. It is as bad as offering Satan a lost soul. Your bliss is like his, in inflicting misery. You prove it. Edgar is restored from the ill-temper he gave way to at your coming. I begin to be secure and tranquil; and you appear resolved on upsetting everything. Quarrel with Edgar, if you please, and deceive his sister. You'll hit on exactly the most efficient method of revenging yourself on me."

The conversation ceased. Mrs. Linton sat down, flushed and gloomy. He stood on the hearth with folded arms, brooding on his evil thoughts. I left them, to seek the master, who was wondering what kept Catherine below so long.

"Ellen," said he, when I entered; "have you seen your mistress?"

"She's in the kitchen, sir," I answered. "She's sadly put out by Mr. Heathcliff's behaviour. And I do think it's time to arrange his visits on another footing. There's harm in being too soft, and now it's come to this——" And I related, as near as I dared, the scene in the court and the subsequent dispute.

"This is insufferable!" exclaimed Mr. Linton. "It is disgraceful that Catherine should own him as a friend, and force his company on me! Call me two men out of the hall, Ellen. I have humoured Catherine enough.''

He descended, and bidding the servants wait in the passage, entered the kitchen, followed by me. Mrs. Linton was scolding with renewed vigour; but Heathcliff, seeing the master first, motioned her to be silent.

" How is this ? " said Linton, addressing her. " What notion of propriety have you to remain here after the language that has been held to you by that blackguard ? "

" Have you been listening at the door, Edgar ? " asked the mistress, in a tone particularly calculated to provoke her husband. Heathcliff gave a sneering laugh—on purpose, it seemed, to draw Mr. Linton's attention to him. He succeeded; but Edgar did not mean to entertain him with any high flights of passion.

" I have been so far forbearing with you, sir," he said quietly; " but forbearance is exhausted. Your presence is a moral poison that would contaminate the most virtuous. Hereafter I shall deny you admission into this house, and must demand your instant departure. Three minutes' delay will render it involuntary and ignominious.''

Heathcliff measured the height and breadth of the speaker with an eye full of derision.

"Cathy, this lamb of yours threatens like a bull ! " he said. " By God, Mr. Linton, I'm mortally sorry you're not worth knocking down.''

My master signed me to fetch the men. I obeyed the hint; but Mrs. Linton, suspecting something, followed; and when I attempted to call them, she pulled me back, slammed the door to, and locked it.

" Fair means ! " she said, in answer to her husband's look of angry surprise. " If you have not the courage to attack him, make an apology, or allow yourself to be beaten. No, I'll swallow the key before you shall get it !

Edgar, I was defending you and yours; and I wish Heathcliff may flog you sick for daring to think an evil thought of me."

He tried to wrest the key from her, but for answer she flung it into the hottest part of the fire; whereupon his countenance turned deadly pale, and he was taken with a nervous trembling, which, try as he might, he could not control. Mingled anguish and humiliation overcame him completely.

"Oh, heavens! In the old days this would win you a knighthood!" cried Mrs. Linton. "Cheer up; you shan't be hurt. Your type is not a lamb, it is a sucking leveret."

"I wish you joy of the milk-blooded coward," exclaimed her friend. "And that is the slavering, shivering thing you preferred to me! I would not strike him with my fist, but I'd kick him with my foot, and experience considerable satisfaction. Is he weeping, or is he going to faint from fear?"

The fellow approached and gave the chair on which Linton rested a push. My master sprang erect and gave him a blow that would have levelled a slighter man. It took his breath a minute; and while he choked, Mr. Linton walked out by the back door into the yard, and thence to the front entrance.

"There! you're done with coming here," cried Catherine. "Get away, now. He'll return with a brace of pistols and half a dozen assistants. You've played me an ill turn, Heathcliff. But go—make haste. I'd rather see Edgar at bay than you."

Heathcliff swore that he would not go with the blow burning in his gullet He swore that he would crush my master's rib in like a rotten hazel-nut before he crossed the threshold. But upon my exclaiming that two gardeners and coachmen were in the court, each with a bludgeon, he resolved, on second thoughts, to avoid a struggle against these underlings. He seized the poker, smashed the lock from the inner door, and made his escape as they trampled in.

Mrs. Linton, much excited, bade me accompany her upstairs.

" I'm nearly distracted, Nelly ! " she exclaimed, throwing herself on the sofa. " A thousand smiths' hammers are beating in my head. Tell Isabella to shun me ; this uproar is owing to her. And tell Edgar I'm in danger of being seriously ill. What possessed him to turn listener ? Heathcliff's talk was outrageous after you left us ; but I could soon have diverted him from Isabella, and the rest meant nothing. Had Edgar never gathered our conversation, he would have been none the worse for it. Well, if I cannot keep Heathcliff for my friend, I'll try to break their hearts by breaking my own. That will be a prompt way of finishing all, when I am pressed to extremity. But it's a deed to be reserved for a forlorn hope ; I'd not take Linton by surprise with it. To this point he has been discreet in dreading to provoke me. You must represent to him the peril of quitting that policy, and remind him of my passionate temper, verging, when kindled, on frenzy. I wish you could dismiss that apathy from your countenance, and look rather more anxious about me."

The stolidity with which I received these instructions was, no doubt, rather exasperating, for they were delivered in perfect sincerity. But I did not wish to frighten her husband, and multiply his annoyances to serve her selfishness. I therefore said nothing when I met the master coming towards the parlour ; but I took the liberty of turning back to listen when he joined her there.

" Remain where you are, Catherine," I heard him say, in a voice of sorrowful despondency. " I shall not stay.

I wish only to know whether, after this evening's events, you intend to continue your intimacy with—— "

" Oh, for mercy's sake, let us hear no more of it now ! " interrupted the mistress, stamping her foot. " Your cold blood cannot be worked into a fever, but mine is boiling."

" You *must* answer my question," persevered Mr. Linton, ignoring her violence. " Will you give up Heathcliff hereafter, or will you give up me ? It is impossible for you to be *my* friend and *his* at the same time."

" I require to be let alone ! " exclaimed Catherine furiously. " I demand it ! Don't you see I can scarcely stand ? Edgar, you—you leave me."

She rang the bell till it broke with a twang. I entered leisurely, to find her dashing her head against the arm of the sofa, and grinding her teeth. Mr. Linton, stricken now with compunction and fear, told me to fetch some water. She had no breath for speaking. I brought a glass full ; and as she would not drink it, I sprinkled it over her face. In a few seconds she stretched herself out stiff, and turned up her eyes, while her cheeks, at once blanched and livid, assumed the aspect of death. Linton looked terrified.

" There is nothing in the world the matter," I whispered, not wanting him to yield.

" She has blood on her lips ! " he said, shuddering.

" Never mind ! " I returned tartly. And I told him how she had resolved, previous to his coming, on exhibiting a fit of frenzy ! I incautiously gave the account aloud, and she heard me. She started up, her eyes flashing. I made up my mind for broken bones at least ; but she only glared about her for an instant, and then rushed from the room. The master directed me to follow. I did ; but she hindered me from entering her chamber by locking the door against me.

The following day she remained in bed, refusing all

nourishment. Mr. Linton, on his part, spent his time in the library, and did not inquire concerning his wife's occupation. He had an hour's interview with Isabella, during which he tried to elicit from her some sentiment of proper horror for Heathcliff's advances; but he could make nothing of her evasive replies, and was obliged to close the examination, unsatisfactorily, adding, however, a solemn warning that if she were so insane as to encourage that worthless suitor, it would dissolve all bonds of relationship between himself and her.

§

While Miss Linton moped about the grounds, and her brother shut himself up miserably among his books that he never opened, and Catherine fasted pertinaciously, I went about my duties, determined to take no part in bringing about a reconciliation—much though I desired it.

On the third day Mrs. Linton unbarred her door, she had finished the water in her pitcher and decanter, and desired a fresh supply, and a basin of gruel, for she believed she was dying. That I set down to a speech meant for Edgar's ears. I believed no such thing, so I kept it to myself, and brought her some tea and toast. She ate and drank eagerly, and sank back on her pillow again, clenching her hands and exclaiming, " Oh, I will die, since no one cares anything for me. I wish I had not taken that." Then a good while after I heard her murmur, " No, I'll not die—he'd be glad—he does not love me—he would never miss me."

" Did you want anything, madam ? " I inquired, still preserving my external composure, in spite of her ghastly countenance and strange, exaggerated manner.

" What is that apathetic being doing ? " she demanded, pushing her entangled locks from her wasted face. " Has he fallen into a lethargy, or is he dead ? "

"Neither," replied I. "He's tolerably well, I think, though his studies occupy him rather more than they ought. He is continually among his books, since he has no other society."

"Among his books!" she cried, confounded. "And I dying! My God! does he know how I'm altered?" continued she, staring at her reflection in a mirror hanging against the opposite wall. "Is that Catherine Linton? He imagines me to be in a pet. Cannot you inform him it is frightful earnest? Nelly, if it be not too late, as soon as I learn how he feels I'll choose between these two—either to starve at once (that would be no punishment unless he had a heart), or to recover, and leave the country. Are you speaking the truth? Is he actually so indifferent for my life?"

"Why, ma'am," I answered, "the master has no idea of your being deranged; and of course he does not fear that you will let yourself die of hunger."

"Cannot you persuade him? Speak your own mind; say you are certain I will."

"You forget, Mrs. Linton, you have eaten with a good relish this evening."

"If I were only sure it would kill him," she interrupted, "I'd kill myself directly! These three awful nights I've never closed my lids, Nelly; I've been tormented— haunted! I thought, though everybody hated and despised each other, they could not avoid loving me. But now I begin to fancy you all dislike me. Oh, how dreary to meet death, surrounded by cold faces! Isabella afraid to enter the room; and Edgar standing solemnly by to see it over, and then thanking God for restoring peace to his house, and going back to his books. What in the name of all that feels has he to do with books when I am dying?"

She could not bear the notion which I had put into her head of Mr. Linton's philosophical resignation. She increased her feverish bewilderment to madness, and tore the pillow with her teeth; then, raising herself up, all burning, desired that I would open the window. We were in the middle of winter, and the wind blew strong from the north-east, and I objected. Both the expressions of her face and the changes of her mood began to alarm me terribly, and brought to my recollection her former illness, and the doctor's injunction that she should not be crossed. A minute previously she was violent; now, not noticing my refusal to open the window, she began to find childish diversion in pulling the feathers from the pillow, and ranging them on the sheet according to their different species. Her mind strayed to other associations.

"That's a turkey's," she murmured to herself; "and this is a wild duck's, and this is a pigeon's, and this is a lapwing's. Bonny bird, wheeling over our heads in the middle of the moor. It wanted to get to its nest, but Heathcliff set a trap for it, and it did not dare come. We saw its nest in the winter full of little skeletons. I made him promise he'd never shoot a lapwing after that, and he didn't. Yes, here are more. Did he shoot my lapwings, Nelly? Are they red, any of them? Let me look."

"Give over that baby-work," I interrupted, dragging the pillow away. "Lie down and shut your eyes.— You're wandering." I began to collect the feathers.

"I see in you, Nelly," she went on dreamily, "a withered hag, with grey hair and bent shoulders. That's what you'll come to in fifty years. But I know you're not so now; so you're mistaken. I'm not wandering. I'm conscious it's night, and there are two candles on the table making the press shine like jet."

"There is no press in the room, and never was," said I, resuming my seat, and looping up the curtain that I might watch her.

D

"Don't you see that face?" she inquired, gazing earnestly at the mirror.

Say what I would I could not make her comprehend that the face was her own; so I rose and covered the mirror with a shawl.

"It's behind there still!" she pursued anxiously. "And it stirred. Oh, Nelly, the room is haunted. I'm afraid of being alone."

I took her hand in mine and bade her be composed; for a succession of shudders convulsed her frame, and she would keep looking at the glass.

"There's nobody there," I insisted. "It was yourself, Mrs. Linton."

"Myself!" she gasped; "and the clock is striking twelve. It's true, then; that's dreadful!"

Her fingers clutched the clothes, and gathered them over her eyes. I attempted to steal to the door, with an intention of calling her husband; but I was summoned back by a frightful shriek. The shawl had fallen from the frame.

"Why, what is the matter?" cried I; "who is the coward now? Wake up! That is the mirror, Mrs. Linton; and you see yourself in it; and there am I, too, by your side."

Trembling and bewildered, she held me fast, but gradually the horror passed from her countenance.

"Oh, dear! I thought I was at home," she sighed, "in my own bedroom at Wuthering Heights. Because I am weak, my brain got confused. Don't say anything, but stay with me. I dread sleeping. My dreams appal me. Oh, if I were but in my own bed in the old house! And that wind sounding in the firs by the lattice. Do let me feel it—it comes straight from the moors—do let me have one breath!"

To pacify her, I held the casement ajar a few seconds.

A cold blast rushed through. I closed it, and returned to my post. She lay still now, her face bathed in tears.

"How long is it since I shut myself in here?" she asked, suddenly reviving.

"It was Monday," I replied, "and this is Thursday night—or rather Friday morning now."

"What! of the same week? It seems a weary number of hours. Surely it must be more. Before I recovered sufficiently to see and hear, it began to be dawn; and, Nelly, I'll tell you what thought has kept recurring till I feared for my reason. I thought I was enclosed in the oak-panelled bed at home; and my heart ached with some great grief, which, just waking, I could not recollect. And then, most strangely, the whole of the last seven years of my life grew a blank. I was a child again; my father was just buried, and my misery rose from the separation that Hindley had ordered between me and Heathcliff. Then memory burst in. My late anguish was swallowed up in paroxysm of despair. In a moment, from being a child twelve years old, I was Mrs. Linton, the wife of a stranger—an exile, an outcast from what had been my world.—Nelly, you should have spoken to Edgar—indeed you should—and compelled him to leave me quiet! I couldn't explain to him how certain I felt of going raving mad if he persisted in teasing me. Oh, I'm burning! I wish I were a girl again, half savage and hardy and free. Why am I so changed? Why does my blood rush into a hell of tumult at a few words? I'm sure I should be myself again were I once among the heather on those hills. Open the window wide—fasten it open! Quick! Why don't you move?"

"Because I won't give you your death of cold," I answered.

"You won't give me a chance of life, you mean," she

said sullenly. And sliding from the bed before I could hinder her, she crossed the room, threw it back, and bent out, careless of the frosty air that cut about her shoulders sharp as a knife. I entreated, and finally attempted to force her to retire. But I found her delirious strength (that she *was* delirious, I became convinced by her subsequent actions and ravings) beyond my control. There was no moon, and everything beneath lay in misty darkness. Not a light gleamed from any house, far or near; and those at Wuthering Heights were never visible—still she asserted she saw their shining.

"Look!" she cried eagerly; "that's my room with the candle in it, and the tree swaying before it; and the other candle is in Joseph's garret. He's waiting till I come home, that he may lock the gate. Well, he'll wait a while yet. It's a rough journey! We've braved its ghosts often together; and dared each other to stand by the graves and ask them to come. But, Heathcliff, if I dare you now, will you venture? If you do, I'll keep you. I'll not lie there by myself. They may bury me twelve feet deep, and throw the church down over me, but I won't rest till you are with me. I never will!"

Perceiving it vain to argue against her insanity, I was planning how I could reach something to wrap round her, without quitting my hold of herself by that gaping lattice, when, to my consternation, I heard the rattle of the door handle, and Mr. Linton entered. He had only then come from the library, and hearing our talking, had come to find out what it signified at that late hour.

"Oh, sir!" I cried, checking the exclamation that rose to his lips at the sight that met him, "my poor mistress is ill. I cannot manage her at all. Pray, forget your anger and come and help me."

"Catherine ill?" he said, hastening to us. "Shut the window, Ellen!—Catherine! Why——"

The haggardness of Mrs. Linton's appearance smote him speechless with horrified astonishment.

"She's been fretting here," I continued, "and eating scarcely anything. She would not admit any of us till this evening, so we couldn't inform you of her state. But it's nothing."

I felt I uttered my explanation awkwardly. The master frowned. "It is nothing, is it, Nelly Dean?" he said sternly. "You shall account more clearly for keeping me in ignorance of this." And he took his wife in his arms, and looked at her in anguish.

At first she gave him no sign of recognition, but by degrees she discovered who it was that held her.

"Ah, you are come, are you, Edgar Linton? You are one of those who are ever found when least wanted, and when you are wanted, never. I suppose we shall have plenty of lamentations now—I see we shall; but they can't keep me from my narrow home out yonder—my resting-place, where I'm bound before spring is over! There it is—not among the Lintons, mind, under the chapel roof—but in the open air, with a head-stone, and you may please yourself whether you go to them or come to me."

"Catherine, what have you done?" commenced the master. "Am I nothing to you any more? Do you love that wretch Heath——"

"Hush!" cried Mrs. Linton. "Mention his name, and I will end the matter instantly by a spring from the window! I don't want you, Edgar. I'm past wanting you."

"Her mind wanders, sir," I interposed. "She has been talking nonsense the whole evening. Hereafter we must be cautious how we vex her."

"I desire no further advice from you," answered Mr. Linton. "You knew your mistress's nature, and you encouraged me to harass her. And not to give me one hint of how she has been these three days! It was heartless! Months of sickness could not cause such a change!"

I began to defend myself, declaring that I had not supposed he would wish me to wink at Mr. Heathcliff's behaviour to humour her. I had performed only a faithful servant's duty in telling him.

"The next time you bring a tale to me, you shall quit my service," he replied.

"You'd rather hear nothing about it, I suppose, Mr. Linton?" said I. "Heathcliff has your permission to come a-courting miss, and drop in at every opportunity your absence offers? Very well; in future you may gather intelligence for yourself."

Confused as Catherine was, her wits were alert at applying our conversation.

"Ah! Nelly has played traitor," she exclaimed passionately. "Nelly is my hidden enemy. You witch! Let me go, and I'll make her rue! I'll make her howl a recantation."

A maniac's fury kindled under her brows; and leaving her struggling in her husband's arms, I quitted the chamber, resolving to seek medical aid on my own responsibility.

In passing the garden to reach the road, my eye was caught by something white, moving irregularly. I found to my horror that it was Miss Isabella's springer, Fanny, suspended by a handkerchief, and nearly at its last gasp. I quickly released the animal, wondering what mischievous person had treated it so. And while I did so, I caught the beat of horse's feet galloping at some distance. But there were so many things to occupy my reflections, that I hardly gave the circumstance another thought; though it was a strange sound in that place at two o'clock in the morning.

Mr. Kenneth was fortunately just coming from his house in the village to see a patient as I came up the street, and my account of Mrs. Linton's malady induced him to accompany me back immediately. He was a plain, rough man; and he made no scruples to speak his doubts of her surviving this second attack unless she were more submissive under his directions than she had shown herself before.

"Nelly Dean," said he, "I can't help fancying there's another cause for this. How did it begin?"

"The master will inform you," I answered guardedly. "But I may say this; it commenced in a quarrel. And in the height of it she flew off, and locked herself up, and refused to eat. Mr. Linton will break his heart if anything should happen to her. Don't alarm him more than necessary."

"Well, I told him to beware.—Hasn't he been intimate with Mr. Heathcliff lately?"

"Heathcliff visits frequently at the Grange," answered I, "though more on the strength of the mistress having known him as a boy than because the master likes him. At present he's forbidden the house, owing to some presumptuous aspirations after Miss Linton which he manifested. I hardly think he'll be admitted again."

"And does Miss Linton turn a cold shoulder on him?"

"I'm not in her confidence," returned I, reluctant to continue the subject.

"No; she's a sly one," he remarked, shaking his head. "But she's a real little fool. I have it on good authority that last night she and Heathcliff were walking above two hours in the plantation at the back of your house; and he pressed her not to go in again, but just to mount his horse and ride away with him. My informant said she could only put him off by pledging her word to be prepared on their next meeting."

This news filled me with fear. I outstripped Mr. Kenneth, and ran most of the way back. On ascending to Isabella's room my fears were confirmed. It was empty. Had I been a few hours sooner, Mrs. Linton's illness might have arrested her rash step. But what could I do now? *I* could not pursue them. And I dare not tell my master, absorbed as he was in his present calamity. There was nothing for it but to hold my tongue and suffer matters to take their course; and Kenneth being arrived, I went with a badly composed countenance to announce him. Catherine lay in a troubled sleep. Her husband hung over her pillow, watching every change of her painfully expressive features.

The doctor, on examining the case for himself, spoke hopefully to Mr. Linton of its having a favourable termination, if only we could preserve around her perfect and constant tranquillity. To me he signified that the threatening danger was not so much death, as permanent alienation of the intellect.

I did not close my eyes that night; nor did Mr. Linton—indeed, we never went to bed. Everyone was active but Miss Isabella; and the servants, up long before their usual hour, began to remark how sound she slept. Her brother became impatient for her presence, and I trembled lest he should send me to call her. But I was spared the pain of being the first proclaimant of her flight. One of the maids, a thoughtless girl, who had been on an early errand to Gimmerton, came panting upstairs, open-mouthed, and dashed into the chamber, crying that our young lady was gone—that she had run off with Mr. Heathcliff.

"What!" exclaimed Linton, rising in agitation. "It's not true. It's incredible. It cannot be. Ellen Dean, go to her room and seek her."

As he spoke he took the servant to the door, and

demanded her reasons for making such an assertion. The girl stammered that she had met the lad that brought the milk, and he had told her that, soon after midnight, a lady and gentleman had stopped at a blacksmith's shop two miles out of Gimmerton, to have a horse's shoe fastened. The blacksmith's lass had got up to spy on them, and had recognised both immediately. The lass had said nothing to her father of her discovery, but this morning she had told it all over Gimmerton.

I ran and peeped, for form's sake, into Isabella's room, confirming when I returned the servant's statement. Mr. Linton had resumed his seat by the bed. He sat silent, looking straight before him.

" What should we do? " I inquired. " Are we to try any measures for overtaking and bringing her back? "

" She went of her own accord," answered the master. " She had a right to go if she pleased. Trouble me no more about her. Hereafter she is my sister only in name —not because I disown her, but because she disowns me."

And that was all he said on the subject—except to direct me to send what property she had to her fresh home, when I knew it.

CHAPTER X

For two months the fugitives remained absent. In those two months Mrs. Linton conquered the worst shock of what was denominated as brain fever. Day and night Edgar nursed her, watching and patiently enduring all the annoyances that irritable nerves and a shaken reason could inflict. And he knew no limits in gratitude when her life was declared to be out of danger. Hour after hour he would sit beside her, tracing the gradual return to bodily health, and flattering his too sanguine hopes that her mind would settle back to its right balance also.

The first time she left her couch was at the commencement of the following March. Mr. Linton had put on her pillow, in the morning, a handful of garden crocuses. Her eye shone delighted as she gathered them eagerly together.

" These are the earliest flowers at the Heights," she exclaimed. " They remind me of soft thaw winds, and nearly melted snow. Edgar, is not the snow almost gone ? "

" The snow is quite gone down here, darling," replied her husband; " and I only see two white spots on the whole range of moors. The sky is blue, and the larks are singing. Catherine, last spring I was longing to have you under this roof; now I wish you were a mile or two up those hills; the air blows so sweetly, I feel sure it would cure you."

" I shall never go up there but once more," said the invalid; " and then you'll leave me, and I shall remain there for ever."

Linton lavished on her the fondest caresses, and tried to cheer her by the fondest words; but she let the tears collect on her lashes and stream down her cheeks unheeding. Thinking that a change of surroundings would help to cheer her, my master directed me to light a fire in the long-disused parlour. There he carried her, and she sat a long while enjoying the genial heat. By evening she was exhausted, but no arguments would induce her to return to her hated sick-chamber; and I had to arrange the parlour sofa for her bed, till another room could be prepared. To obviate the fatigue of mounting and descending the stairs, we fitted up a room on the same floor—this very room, sir, where you lie at present. She was soon strong enough to move from one to the other, leaning on Edgar's arm. I watched her recovery anxiously, for on her life depended that of another; we cherished the hope that in a little while Mr. Linton's heart would be gladdened, and his lands secured from a stranger's gripe, by the birth of an heir.

I should mention that Isabella sent her brother, some six weeks after her departure, a short note announcing her marriage to Heathcliff. It appeared dry and cold, but at the bottom was dotted in with a pencil an obscure apology, and an entreaty for kind remembrance and reconciliation. Linton did not reply to this, I believe; but in a fortnight more I got a long letter which I considered odd, coming from a bride just out of her honeymoon. I'll read it, for I keep it yet.

Dear Ellen (it begins) : I came to Wuthering Heights last night, and heard for the first time that Catherine has been very ill. I must not write to her, I suppose, and my brother is either too angry or too distressed to answer what I sent him. Still, I must write to somebody, and the only choice left me is you.

Inform Edgar that I'd give the world to see him again— that my heart returned to Thrushcross Grange in twenty-four hours after I left it. *I can't follow it, though;* they need not expect me.

And now I want to ask you two questions ; the first is— How did you contrive to preserve the sympathies of human nature when you resided here ? I cannot recognise any sentiment which those around share with me.

The second question I have great interest in ; it is this— Is Mr. Heathcliff a man ? If so, is he mad ? And if not, is he a devil ? I shan't tell you my reasons for making this inquiry, but I beseech you to explain, if you can, what I have married—that is, when you call to see me; and you must call, Ellen, very soon.

Now you shall hear how I have been received in my new home, as I am led to imagine the Heights will be.—It was dark when we dismounted in the paved yard of the farm-house, and your old fellow-servant Joseph issued out to receive us by the light of a dip candle. His first act was to raise it level with my face, squint malignantly, and turn away. Then he took the two horses and led them into the stables, reappearing to lock the outer gate, as if we lived in an ancient castle.

Heathcliff stayed to speak to him, while I entered the kitchen—a dingy, untidy hole now. I am sure you would hardly recognise it. By the fire stood a ruffianly child, strong in limb and dirty in garb, with a look of Catherine about his eyes and mouth.

"This is Hareton—Edgar's legal nephew," I reflected; "I must shake hands, and—yes—I must kiss him." But as I approached, he drew back with an oath and a threat to set Throttler on me if I did not "frame off".

"Hey, Throttler, lad!" whispered the little wretch, rousing a half-bred dog from its lair in the corner. "Now, wilt thou be ganging?" he asked authoritatively.

The instinct for self-preservation urged a compliance. I stepped back over the threshold into the yard, and, seeing Joseph, I begged him to accompany me into the house.

"None o' me," he answered. "I gotten something else to do." And, surveying my dress and countenance with sovereign contempt, he went back into the stables.

I walked through a wicket to another door, at which I took the liberty of knocking. After a short suspense it was opened by a tall, gaunt man, without neckerchief, and otherwise extremely slovenly; his features were lost in masses of shaggy hair that hung on his shoulders, and *his* eyes, too, were like a ghostly Catherine's with all their beauty annihilated.

"What's your business here?" he demanded grimly. "Who are you?"

"My name *was* Isabella Linton," I replied. "You've seen me before. I'm lately married to Mr. Heathcliff, and he has brought me here—I suppose by your permission."

"Is he come back, then?" asked the hermit, glaring like an angry wolf.

"Yes, we came just now," I said; "but he left me by the kitchen door, and your little boy frightened me off with the help of a bull-dog!"

"It's well the hellish villain has kept his word!" growled my future host, searching the darkness beyond me in the expectation of discovering Heathcliff; and then he indulged in a soliloquy of execrations, and threats of what he would have done had the "fiend" deceived him.

I repented having tried this second entrance, but before I could slip away, he ordered me in and refastened the door. There was a great fire, and that was all the light there was in the huge apartment, whose floor had grown a uniform grey, and the once brilliant pewter dishes were dusty and tarnished. I asked whether I might call the maid, and be conducted to a bedroom. Mr. Earnshaw vouchsafed no answer. He walked up and down, apparently forgetting that I was there. His abstraction was so deep, and his whole aspect so misanthropical, that I shrank from disturbing him again.—You can imagine, Ellen, how sad and despairing I felt to be thus imprisoned, only four miles from my old home, and finding that there was no one in the house who would be my ally against Heathcliff. I had sought refuge at the Heights almost gladly, knowing that I should thus be secured against living alone with him; but he knew the people we were coming amongst, and he did not fear for their intermeddling.

I sat and thought a doleful time. The clock struck eight and nine, and still my companion paced to and fro, his head bent on his breast. At last my wild regrets and dismal anticipations spoke audibly in irrepressible sighing and weeping. Earnshaw halted opposite, and gave me a stare of newly-awakened surprise, as if he had only just recollected my presence.

" I'm tired with my journey, and I want to go to bed ! " I exclaimed. " Where is the maidservant ? "

" We have none," he answered. " You must wait on yourself."

" Where must I sleep, then ? " I sobbed. I was beyond regarding self-respect.

" Joseph will show you Heathcliff's chamber," said he. " Open that door; he's in there."

I was going to obey, but he suddenly arrested me, and added in the strangest tone—

" Be so good as to lock your door and draw your bolt; don't omit it."

" Well ! " I said; " but why, Mr. Earnshaw ? " I did not relish the notion of deliberately fastening myself in with Heathcliff.

" Look here ! " he replied, pulling from his waistcoat a curiously constructed pistol, having a double-edged spring knife attached to the barrel. " That's a great tempter to a desperate man, is it not ? I cannot resist going up with this every night, and trying his door. If once I find it open, he's done for. There is some devil that urges me to thwart my own schemes by killing him."

I surveyed the weapon inquisitively. A hideous notion struck me. How powerful I should be, possessing such an instrument ! I took it from his hand and touched the blade. He looked astonished at the expression my face assumed during a brief second; it was not horror—it was covetousness. He snatched the pistol back, shut the knife, and returned it to its concealment.

" I don't care if you tell him," said he. " Put him on his guard, and watch for him. You know the terms we are on, I see. His danger does not shock you."

" What wrong has Heathcliff done you to warrant this appalling hatred? " I asked. " Wouldn't it be wiser to bid him quit the house? "

" No ! " thundered Earnshaw. " Should he offer to leave me, he's a dead man. Am I to lose *all* without a chance of retrieval? Is Hareton to be a beggar? Oh, damnation! I *will* have it back; and I'll have his gold too, and then his blood, and hell shall have his soul ! "

He now recommenced his moody walk, and, shuddering to be near him, I escaped into the kitchen. Joseph was bending over the fire, peering into a large pan that hung over it, and a wooden bowl of oatmeal stood on the settle close by. I conjectured that the contents of the pan was probably for our supper, and, being hungry, I resolved that it should be eatable; so, crying out sharply, " I'll make the porridge ! " I removed the vessel out of his reach, and proceeded to take off my hat and riding-habit. " Mr. Earnshaw," I continued, " directs me wait on myself. I will. I'm not going to act lady among you, for fear I should starve."

Ignoring his protestations that he would not submit himself to a mistress as well as two masters, I went briskly to work, sighing to remember a period when it would all have been merry fun. It racked me to recall past happiness, and the greater the peril there was of conjuring up its apparition, the quicker the thible ran round, and the faster the handfuls of meal fell into the water. Joseph beheld my style of cooking with growing indignation, exclaiming to Hareton that he wouldn't be able to sup his porridge tonight; it would be naught but lumps.

It was rather a rough mess, I own, when I poured it into the basins. Four had been provided, and a gallon pitcher of new milk was brought from the dairy, which Hareton seized and commenced drinking from the expansive lip. I expostulated, but, encouraged by Joseph, the infant continued sucking, and glowered up at me defyingly as he slavered into the jug.

"I shall have my supper in another room," I said. "Have you no place you call a parlour?"

"Parlour!" sneered Joseph—"*parlour*. Nay, we've noa *parlours*."

"Then I shall go upstairs," I answered. "Show me a chamber."

I put my basin on a tray, and fetched myself some more milk. With great grumblings, the fellow preceded me. We mounted to the garrets. He opened a door now and then to look into apartments we passed.

"Here's a rahm," he said at last, flinging back a cranky board on hinges. "It's weel eneugh to ate a few porridge in. There's a pack o' corn i' t' corner. If ye're feared o' muckying yer grand silk cloes, spread yer handkerchir o' t' top on 't."

The "rahm" was a kind of lumber-hole. Sacks of malt and grain were piled around, leaving a wide, bare space in the middle.

"Why, man!" I exclaimed, facing him angrily; "this is not a place to sleep in. I wish to see my bedroom."

"Bedrume!" he repeated, in a tone of mockery. "Yah's seen all t' *bedrumes* theer is. Yon's mine."

He pointed into a second garret, only differing from the first in being more naked about the walls, and having a large, low, curtainless bed at one end.

"What do I want with yours?" I retorted. "I suppose Mr. Heathcliff does not lodge at the top of the house, does he?"

"Oh, it's Maister *Hathecliff's* ye're wanting? That's just one ye cannut see. He allas keeps it locked, an' nob'dy iver mills on 't but hisseln."

"You've a nice house, Joseph," I could not refrain from observing, "and pleasant inmates. However, that's not the present purpose. There are other rooms. For heaven's sake be quick, and let me settle somewhere."

He made no reply, but plodded down the wooden steps, and halted before an apartment which from the superior quality of the furniture revealed when he opened the door, I conjectured to be the best one—though everything was covered in dust, and was damaged from deliberate rough handling. I was endeavouring to gather resolution to enter, when my fool of a guide announced, " This here is t' maister's." My supper by now was cold, my appetite gone, and my patience exhausted. I insisted on being provided instantly with a place of refuge and means of repose.

"Whear the divil?" began the religious elder. " The Lord forgie us! Whear the *hell* wold ye gang, ye marred, wearisome nowt? Ye've seen all but Hareton's bit of a cham'er. There's not another hoile to lay down in i' th' hoise."

I was so vexed, I flung my tray on the ground; then, seating myself at the stairs-head, I hid my face in my hands, and wept. Joseph continued scolding me for " flinging t' precious gifts o' God under fooit," and declared " that Maister Heathcliff would soon tame my wayward spirit." Then, still scolding, he went to his den beneath, leaving me in the darkness. I was beginning to meditate how I might clear the mess I had made outside Mr. Earnshaw's room before he discovered it, when an unexpected aid appeared in the shape of Throttler. The animal hastened to devour the porridge, while I groped from step to step, collecting the shattered bowl, and drying the spatters of milk from the banister with my pocket-handkerchief. Our labours were scarcely over before I heard Earnshaw approaching. I concealed myself in the nearest doorway. He passed on, entered his chamber, and shut the door. Soon after, Joseph came up with Hareton, to put him to bed. I had found shelter in Hareton's doorway, and the old man, seeing me, growled that the house below was empty now, and I might have it all to myself. I gladly availed myself of this intimation, and the minute I flung myself into a chair by the fire, I nodded and slept. But, too soon, Mr. Heathcliff awoke me. He had just come in, and demanded, in his loving manner, what I was doing there. I told him that he had the key of our room in his pocket. The adjective *our* gave mortal offence. He swore it was not, nor ever should be mine, and he'd—— But I'll not repeat his language, nor describe his habitual conduct. He is ingenious and un-resting to gain my abhorrence. I assure you that a tiger or a venomous serpent could not rouse terror in me equal to that which he awakens. I hate him—I am wretched—I have been a fool! Beware of uttering one word of this to anyone at the Grange. I shall expect you every day. Don't disappoint me.—Isabella.

§

As soon as I had read this epistle I went to the master and informed him that his sister had arrived at the Heights and sent me a letter expressing her ardent sorrow for Mrs. Linton's situation, and a wish that he would transmit to her, as early as possible, some token of his forgiveness.

"Forgiveness!" said Linton. "I have nothing to forgive her, Ellen. You may call at the Heights this afternoon, if you like, and say that I am not *angry*, but I'm *sorry* to have lost her—especially as I can never think she will be happy. But it is out of the question that I should go to see her; we are eternally divided, and should she really wish to oblige me, let her persuade the villain she has married to leave the country."

"And won't you write her a little note, sir?" I implored.

"No," he answered; "my communication with Heathcliff's family shall be as sparing as his with mine. It shall not exist."

Mr. Edgar's coldness depressed me exceedingly, and all the way from the Grange I puzzled my brains how to put more heart into what he said when I repeated it to Isabella. I dare say she had been on the watch for me since morning. I saw her looking through the lattice as I came up the causeway; but she drew back, as if afraid of being observed. I entered without knocking. There never was such a dismal scene as the formerly cheerful house now presented. Isabella already partook of the pervading spirit of neglect. Her pretty face was wan and listless— some locks hanging down, and some carelessly twisted round her head. Hindley was not there. Isabella came forward eagerly to greet me, and held out one hand for the expected letter. I shook my head; she would not take the hint, however; but followed me to a sideboard where I went to lay my bonnet, and importuned me in a whisper to give her directly what I had brought. Heathcliff guessed the meaning of her manœuvres and said—

"If you have anything for Isabella, Nelly—as no doubt you have—give it to her. You needn't make a secret of it. We have no secrets between us."

"Oh, I have nothing," I replied, thinking it best to speak the truth at once. "My master bade me tell his sister that she must not expect either a letter or a visit from him at present. He sends his love, ma'am, and his pardon for the grief that you have occasioned; but thinks that from this time there should be no communication between the households."

Mrs. Heathcliff's lip quivered, and she returned to her seat in the window. Her husband took his stand near me, and began to put questions concerning Catherine. I told him as much as I thought proper of her illness and its causes, and ended by hoping that he would follow Mr. Linton's example, and avoid future interference with his family.

"Mrs. Linton is now just recovering," I said. "She'll never be what she was, but her life is spared; and if you really have a regard for her, you'll shun crossing her way again—nay, you'll move out of the country entirely. Catherine Linton is so greatly changed, both in appearance and character. Only common humanity, and the remembrance of what she once was, can sustain her husband's affection for her."

"*That* is quite possible," replied Heathcliff. "But do you imagine I shall leave Catherine to his *humanity*? Can you compare my feelings respecting Catherine to his? Before you leave this house, I must exact a promise from you that you'll get me an interview with her. Consent or refuse, I *will* see her! What do you say?"

"You shall never see her through my means, Mr. Heathcliff. Another encounter between you and the master would kill her altogether."

"With your aid that may be avoided," he continued; "and should there be danger of such an event—should he be the cause of adding a single trouble more to her existence—why, I think I shall be justified in going to extremes. I wish you had sincerity enough to tell me whether Catherine would suffer greatly from his loss; the fear that she would restrains me. And there you see the difference between our feelings : had he been in my place, and I in his, though I hated him with a hatred that turned my life to gall, I never would have raised a hand against him. So long as Catherine desired his society, I would have died by inches before I touched a hair of his head ! ''

" And yet," I interrupted, " you have no scruples in completely ruining all her hopes of perfect restoration, by involving her in a new tumult of disorder and distress when she has nearly forgotten you."

" Catherine forgotten me ! " he exclaimed. " Oh, Nelly, you know she has not. You know as well as I do that for every thought she spends on that puny being she spends a thousand on me. He is scarcely nearer to her than her dog or her horse. It is not in him to be loved like me."

" Catherine and Edgar are as fond of each other as any two people can be," cried Isabella, with sudden vivacity ; " I will not sit in silence and hear him abused."

" Your brother is wondrous fond of you, too, isn't he ? " observed Heathcliff scornfully. " He turns you adrift on the world with surprising alacrity."

" He is not aware of what I suffer," she replied. " I didn't tell him that."

" You have been telling him something, then ? You have written, have you ? "

" To say that I was married, I did write. You saw the note."

" And nothing since ? "

" No."

" My lady is looking sadly worse for her change in condition," I remarked. " Somebody's love comes short in her case obviously."

" I should guess it was her own," said Heathcliff. " She degenerates into a mere slut. You'd hardly credit it, but on the very morrow of our wedding she was weeping to go home.   However, I'll take care she does not disgrace me by rambling abroad."

" Well, sir," returned I ; " I hope you'll consider that Mrs. Heathcliff is accustomed to be looked after and waited on.   You must let her have a maid to keep things tidy about her, and you must treat her kindly.   You must not forget how much she has sacrificed to live in this wilderness with you."

" She abandoned them under a delusion," he answered, " picturing in me a hero of romance, and expecting un-limited indulgences from my chivalrous devotion.   God knows why, for I never pretended devotion.   But at last I think she begins to know me.   You may tell your master, Nelly, that I never in all my life met such an abject thing as she is.   I've sometimes relented, from pure lack of invention, in my experiments on what she could endure, and still creep cringing back.   If she desired to go, she might ; but she'd thank no one for dividing us."

" Mr. Heathcliff," said I, " this is the talk of a madman. Your wife most likely is convinced that you are mad, and for that reason has borne with you hitherto.   But now that you say she may go, she'll doubtless avail herself of the permission.—You are not so bewitched, ma'am, are you ? as to remain with him of your own accord ? "

" He's a lying fiend ! " cried Isabella.   " Don't put faith in a single word he says.   I've been told I might leave before, and I've made the attempt, but I dare not repeat it.   Promise, Ellen, that you will not repeat a single word of his infamous conversation to my brother. He wishes to provoke Edgar to desperation.   He says he married me only to obtain power over *him*.   But he shan't obtain it.   I'll die first !   I pray he may forget his diabolical prudence and kill me. The single pleasure I can imagine is to die or to see him dead!"

"There—that will do for the present!" said Heathcliff.—"If you are called upon in a court of law you'll remember her language, Nelly. Take a good look at her countenance; she's near the point that would suit me.—No; you're not fit to be your own guardian, Isabella, now; and I must retain you in my custody, however distasteful the obligation may be. Go upstairs; I have something to say to Nelly Dean in private. That's not the way. Upstairs, I tell you. Why, this is the road upstairs, child."

He seized and thrust her from the room, and returned muttering—

"I have no pity! I have no pity! The more the worms writhe, the more I yearn to crush out their entrails!"

"No, you do not understand what the word pity means!" I cried, rising and hastening to resume my bonnet.

"Put that down!" he interrupted. "You are not going yet—not till you have undertaken to aid me in my determination to see Catherine. I swear I meditate no harm. I only wish to hear from herself how she is, and ask if anything I could do would be of use to her. Last night I was in the Grange garden six hours, and I'll return there tonight. I'll haunt the place every night, and every day, till I find an opportunity of entering. If Edgar Linton meets me I shall not hesitate to knock him down; and if his servants oppose me I shall frighten them off with these pistols. But wouldn't it be better to prevent my coming in contact with them or their master? You could arrange it so that my visit was unknown. You'll be hindering mischief."

I protested against playing that treacherous part in my

employer's house, and urged the cruelty of his destroying
Mrs. Linton's tranquillity for his satisfaction. "She's all
nerves," I said. "Don't persist, sir, or I shall be obliged
to inform my master of your designs, and he'll take
measures to secure his house from such unwarrantable
intrusion."

"In that case, I'll take measures to secure you, woman.
You shall not leave Wuthering Heights till tomorrow
morning. It is a foolish story to say that Catherine could
not bear to see me. You say that she is often restless and
anxious-looking. Is that a proof of tranquillity? Let us
settle the matter at once. Will you stay here, and am I
to fight my way to Catherine over Linton and his footman?
or will you be my friend, and do as I request?"

Well, Mr. Lockwood, I argued and complained, and
flatly refused him, fifty times; but in the end he forced
me into an agreement. I engaged to carry a letter from
him to my mistress; and should she consent, I promised
to let him have intelligence of Linton's next absence from
home; and to get myself and the servants out of the way
when he came. I knew it was wrong; but it was expedient, and, for all I knew, might create a favourable
crisis in Catherine's mental illness. I remembered also
Mr. Edgar's stern rebuke at my carrying tales, and I tried
to quiet my conscience by declaring that this betrayal of
trust should be my last. Nevertheless, my journey home-
ward was sadder than my journey thither, and many
misgivings I had ere I could prevail upon myself to put the
missive into Mrs. Linton's hand.

But here is Kenneth, Mr. Lockwood. I'll go down and
tell him how much better you are. My history is *dree*,
as we say, and will serve to while away another morning.

.   .   .   .   .

Dree and dreary, I reflected, as the good woman
descended to receive the doctor. But I must beware of

the fascination that lurks in Catherine Heathcliff's fine eyes. I should be in a curious plight if I surrendered my heart to that young person, and she turned out a second edition of the mother.

CHAPTER XI

ANOTHER week over, and I am so many days nearer health and spring ! I have now heard all my neighbour's history, at different sittings, and I'll set it down in Nelly's own words.

In the evening (she continued)—the evening of my visit to the Heights—I knew, as well as if I could see him, that Mr. Heathcliff was lurking about the Grange. But I had made up my mind not to give Mrs. Linton his letter, till my master went somewhere, as I could not guess how its receipt might affect Catherine. Consequently it was not till Sunday, when it had been in my pocket four days (and the household had gone to church), that I brought it to her. Only one servant was left in the house, and him I sent to the village to get some oranges for my mistress, to be paid for on the morrow. Then I went upstairs.

Mrs. Linton sat in a loose white dress with a light shawl over her shoulders, in the recess of the open window. Her thick, long hair had been partially removed at the beginning of her illness, and was simply combed over her temples and neck. Her appearance was indeed altered; but when she was calm there seemed an unearthly beauty in the change. She was very pale. Her eyes, once bright and flashing, were soft, dreamy, and melancholy; they appeared to gaze beyond—out of this world, you would have said.

A book lay open, but unread, on the sill before her. Linton had placed it there; he spent many hours trying to entice her attention to some subject which had formerly been her amusement. In her better moods she endured his efforts placidly, only showing their uselessness by now and then suppressing a weary sigh, and checking him at last with the saddest of smiles and kisses. At other times she would push him petulantly away, and then he took good care to leave her alone.

" There's a letter for you, Mrs. Linton," I said, gently inserting it in one hand that rested on her knee. " You must read it immediately, because it wants an answer." But her mind was far away; and the letter fell unheeded from her fingers.

" It is from Mr. Heathcliff, ma'am," I said, breaking the seal and replacing it in her lap.

There was a start and a troubled glare of recognition, and a struggle to arrange her ideas. She lifted the letter, seemed to peruse it, and when she came to the signature she sighed; but it was clear she had not gathered its import.

" He's in the garden, ma'am, and wishes to see you."

As I spoke I observed a large dog lying outside on the sunny grass raise its ears and begin to bark. Mrs. Linton bent forward and listened breathlessly. The minute later Heathcliff's step traversed the hall. With straining eagerness Catherine gazed towards the door of her chamber. He did not hit the right room directly. She motioned me to admit him, but he found it out ere I could reach the door, and in a stride or two was at her side, and had grasped her in his arms.

He neither spoke nor loosed his hold for some five minutes, during which period he bestowed more kisses than he ever gave in his life before, I dare say; but then my mistress had kissed him first, and I plainly saw that he could hardly bear, for downright agony, to look in her face. A single glance had been sufficient to reveal to him that she was fated, sure to die. "Oh, Cathy! Oh, my life! how can I bear it?" was the first sentence he uttered, in a tone that did not seek to disguise his despair. And his eyes burned with anguish.

"What now?" said Catherine, leaning back and returning his look with a suddenly clouded brow. "You and Edgar have broken my heart between you! And you both come to bewail the deed to me, as if *you* were the people to be pitied! I shall not pity you, not I. You have killed me—and thriven on it, I think. How strong you are! How many years do you mean to live after I am gone?"

Heathcliff had knelt on one knee to embrace her. He attempted to rise, but she seized his hair and kept him down.

"I wish I could hold you," she continued bitterly, "till we were both dead! I shouldn't care what you suffered. I care nothing for your sufferings. Why shouldn't *you* suffer? I do! Will you forget me? Will you be happy when I am in the earth? Will you say twenty years hence, 'That's the grave of Catherine Earnshaw. I loved her long ago, and was wretched to lose her; but it is past. I've loved many others since. My children are dearer to me than she was, and at death I shall not rejoice that I am going to her; I shall be sorry that I must leave them. Will you say so, Heathcliff?'"

"Don't torture me till I'm as mad as yourself," cried he, wrenching his head free and grinding his teeth.

The two, to a cool spectator, made a strange and fearful picture. Well might Catherine deem that heaven would be a land of exile to her, unless with her mortal body she cast away her moral character also. Her present countenance had a wild vindictiveness in its white cheek,

and a bloodless lip and a scintillating eye; and she retained in her closed fingers a portion of the locks she had
been grasping. As to her companion, while raising himself with one hand, he had taken her arm with the other,
and so inadequate was his stock of gentleness to the
requirements of her condition that on his letting go I saw
four distinct impressions left blue in the colourless skin.

" Are you possessed with a devil," he pursued savagely,
" to talk in that manner to me when you are dying? Do
you reflect that all those words will be branded in my
memory, and eating deeper eternally after you have left
me? You know you lie to say I have killed you; and,
Catherine, you know that I could as soon forget you as my
existence! Is it not sufficient for your infernal selfishness
that, while you are at peace, I shall writhe in the torments
of hell?"

" I shall not be at peace," moaned Catherine, recalled
to a sense of physical weakness by the violent, unequal
throbbing of her heart, which beat visibly and audibly
under this excess of agitation. She said nothing further
till the paroxysm was over, then she continued more
kindly—

" I'm not wishing you greater torment than I have,
Heathcliff. I only wish us never to be parted; and should
a word of mine distress you hereafter, think I feel the
same distress underground, and for my own sake forgive
me! Come here and kneel down again. You never
harmed me in your life. Nay, if you nurse anger, that will
be worse to remember than my harsh words. Won't you
come here again? Do!"

Heathcliff went to the back of her chair and leant over,
but not so far as to let her see his face, which was livid
with emotion. She bent round to look at him. He
would not permit it. Turning abruptly, he walked to the
fireplace, where he stood, silent, with his back towards us.

Mrs. Linton's glance followed him suspiciously. Every movement woke a new sentiment in her. After a pause and a prolonged gaze she resumed, addressing me in accents of indignant disappointment—

"Oh, you see, Nelly, he would not relent a moment to keep me out of the grave! *That* is how I'm loved! Well, never mind. That is not *my* Heathcliff. I shall love mine yet, and take him with me; he's in my soul. And," added she musingly, "the thing that irks me most is this shattered prison, after all. I'm tired of being enclosed here. I'm wearying to escape into that glorious world, and to be always there—not seeing it dimly through tears, and yearning for it through the walls of an aching heart, but really with it and in it. Nelly, you think you are better and more fortunate than I, in full health and strength. You are sorry for me. Very soon that will be altered. I shall be sorry for *you*. I shall be incomparably beyond and above you all. I *wonder* he won't be near me!" she went on to herself. "I thought he wished it.—Heathcliff dear, you should not be sullen now. Do come to me, Heathcliff."

In her eagerness she rose and supported herself on the arm of the chair. At that earnest appeal he turned to her, looking absolutely desperate. His eyes, wide and wet, at last flashed fiercely on her; his breast heaved convulsively. An instant they held asunder, and then how they met I hardly saw, but Catherine made a spring, and he caught her, and they were locked in an embrace from which I thought my mistress would never be released alive—in fact, to my eyes, she seemed directly insensible. He flung himself into the nearest seat, and on my approaching hurriedly to ascertain if she had fainted, he gnashed at me and foamed like a mad dog, and gathered her to him, so I stood off and held my tongue in great perplexity.

A movement of Catherine's relieved me a little presently. She put up her hand to clasp his neck, and bring her cheek to his as he held her; while he, in return, covering her with frantic caresses, said wildly—

"You teach me now how cruel you have been—cruel and false. *Why* did you despise me? *Why* did you betray your own heart, Cathy? I have not one word of comfort. You deserve this. You have killed yourself. Yes, you may kiss me, and cry, and wring out my kisses and tears; they'll blight you—they'll damn you. You loved me; then what right had you to leave me? What right—answer me—for the poor fancy you felt for Linton? Because misery, and degradation, and death, and nothing that God and Satan could inflict would have parted us, *you*, of your own will, did it. I have not broken your heart—you have broken it; and in breaking it you have broken mine. So much the worse for me that I am strong. Do I want to live? What kind of living will it be when you—O God! would *you* like to live with your soul in the grave?"

"Let me alone! Let me alone!" sobbed Catherine. "If I've done wrong, I'm dying for it. It is enough! You left me too; but I won't upbraid you. I forgive you. Forgive me."

"It is hard to forgive, and to look at those eyes, and feel those wasted hands," he answered. "Kiss me again, and don't let me see your eyes. I forgive what you have done to me. I love *my* murderer—but *yours*! How can I?"

They were silent—their faces hid against each other, and washed by each other's tears. At least, I suppose the weeping was on both sides, as it seemed Heathcliff *could* weep on a great occasion like this.

I grew very uncomfortable, meanwhile, for the afternoon wore fast away, the man whom I had sent off returned from his errand, and I could distinguish by the shine of the western sun up the valley a concourse thickening outside Gimmerton chapel porch.

"Service is over," I announced. "My master will be here in half an hour."

Heathcliff groaned a curse, and strained Catherine closer. She never moved.

Ere long I perceived a group of the servants passing up the road towards the kitchen wing. Mr. Linton was not far behind. He opened the gate himself, and sauntered slowly up, probably enjoying the lovely afternoon, that breathed as soft as summer.

"Now he is here!" I exclaimed. "For heaven's sake hurry down! You'll not meet any one on the front stairs. Do be quick, and stay among the trees till he is fairly in."

"I must go, Cathy," said Heathcliff, seeking to extricate himself from his companion's arms. "But if I live I'll see you again before you are asleep. I won't stray five yards from your window."

"You must not go!" she answered, holding him as firmly as her strength allowed. "You *shall* not, I tell you."

"For one hour," he pleaded earnestly.

"Not for one minute," she replied.

"I *must*; Linton will be up immediately," persisted the alarmed intruder.

He would have risen and unfixed her fingers by the act; she clung fast, gasping. There was mad resolution in her face.

"No!" she shrieked. "Oh, don't, don't go! It is the last time! Edgar will not hurt us. Heathcliff, I shall die! I shall die!"

"Damn the fool! There he is!" cried Heathcliff, sinking back into his seat. "Hush, my darling! Hush,

hush, Catherine ! I'll stay. If he shot me so, I'd expire with a blessing on my lips."

And there they were fast again. I heard my master mounting the stairs. The cold sweat ran from my forehead; I was horrified.

"Are you going to listen to her ravings?" I said passionately. "She does not know what she says. Will you ruin her because she has not wit to help herself? Get up ! You could be free instantly. That is the most diabolical deed that ever you did. We are all done for—master, mistress and servant."

I wrung my hands and cried out, and Mr. Linton hastened his step at the noise. In the midst of my agitation I was sincerely glad to observe that Catherine's arms had fallen relaxed, and her head hung down.

"She's fainted or dead," I thought; "so much the better. Far better that she should be dead than lingering, a burden and a misery-maker to all about her."

Edgar sprang to his unbidden guest, blanched with astonishment and rage. What he meant to do I cannot tell. However, the other stopped all demonstrations at once by placing the lifeless-looking form in his arms.

"Look there ! " he said. "Unless you be a fiend, help her first; then you shall speak to me ! "

He walked into the parlour and sat down. Mr. Linton summoned me, and with great difficulty, and after resorting to many means, we managed to restore her to sensation; but she was all bewildered. She sighed and moaned, and knew nobody. Edgar, in his anxiety for her, forgot her hated friend. I did not. I went at the earliest opportunity and besought him to depart, affirming that Catherine was better, and he should hear from me how she passed the night.

"I shall not refuse to go out of doors," he answered, "but I shall stay in the garden; and, Nelly, mind you

keep your word tomorrow. I shall be under those larch
trees. Mind! or I pay another visit, whether Linton be
in or not.''

He sent a rapid glance through the half-open door of
the chamber; and ascertaining that what I stated was
apparently true, delivered the house of his luckless
presence.

CHAPTER XII

AT twelve o'clock that night was born the Catherine you
saw at Wuthering Heights—a puny seven-months child;
and two hours after the mother died, having never
recovered sufficient consciousness to miss Heathcliff or
know Edgar. The latter's distraction at his bereavement
is too painful a subject to dwell on. A great addition to
his sorrow, in my eyes, was his being left without an heir.
I bemoaned as I gazed on the feeble orphan, and I mentally
abused old Linton for—what was only natural partiality—
the securing of his estate to his own daughter instead of
his son's.

Morning came at last; and Edgar Linton laid his head
on the pillow beside his wife's, and sank into an exhausted
sleep. I felt certain that Mr. Heathcliff was still in the
garden—and there I found him, leaning against an old
ash tree, his hat off, his hair soaked with the dew. He
raised his eyes as I approached, and spoke.

'' She's dead! '' he said. '' I've not waited for you to
tell me that. Don't snivel before me, damn you! She
wants none of your tears.''

I perceived that he had somehow got intelligence of the

E

catastrophe. " Yes, she's dead ! " I answered, checking my sobs and drying my tears—" Gone to heaven, I hope, where we may all join her, if we take due warning, and leave our evil ways to follow good."

" Did *she* take due warning, then ? " said Heathcliff, attempting a sneer. " Did she die like a saint ? Come, tell me the truth ? How did—— "

He endeavoured to pronounce the name, but could not manage it ; and compressing his mouth, he held a silent combat with his inward agony, defying, meanwhile, my sympathy with an unflinching, ferocious stare. But after the struggle I saw that he was trembling, in spite of himself, to his very finger-ends.

" Poor wretch ! " I thought ; " you have a heart and nerves the same as your brother men ! Why should you be anxious to conceal them ?—She died quiet as a lamb," I answered aloud.

" And—did she ever mention me ? "

" Her senses never returned. She recognised no one from the time you left her. Her life closed in a gentle dream. May she wake as kindly in the other world ! "

" May she wake in torment ! " he cried with frightful vehemence. " Why, she's a liar to the end. Where is she ? Not *there*—not in heaven—not perished—where ?— Oh ! you said you cared nothing for my sufferings ! I pray one prayer—I repeat it till my tongue stiffens— Catherine Earnshaw, may you not rest so long as I am living. You say I killed you—haunt me, then ! The murdered do haunt their murderers, I believe. Be with me—take any form—drive me mad—only *do* not leave me in this abyss, where I cannot find you. Oh God ! it is unutterable ! I cannot live without my life ! I cannot live without my soul ! "

He dashed his head against the knotted trunk, and howled like a savage beast being goaded to death. His hand and forehead became stained with blood. The sight hardly moved my compassion—it appalled me; still I felt reluctant to quit him so. But the moment he recollected himself enough to notice me watching, he thundered a command for me to go, and I obeyed. He was beyond my skill to quiet or control.

Mrs. Linton's funeral was to take place the following Friday. Linton spent his hours in her chamber—a ceaseless guardian beside the corpse. Heathcliff spent his nights, at least, outside, equally a stranger to repose. I held no communication with him. Still I was conscious of his desire to enter; and on Tuesday, a little after dark, when my master, from sheer fatigue, had been compelled to retire for a couple of hours, I opened one of the windows, to give him a chance of taking a last view of his faded idol. He did not omit to avail himself of the opportunity, but so cautiously and briefly that I should not have known he had been there but for the disarrangement of the drapery about Catherine's face, and for observing on the floor a light curl of hair fastened with a silver thread, which I knew had been kept in a locket that hung round Catherine's neck. On examining the trinket, I found he had replaced it by a black lock of his own. I twisted the two and enclosed them together.

Mr. Earnshaw was, of course, invited to attend his sister's funeral. He sent no excuse, but he never came; so that, besides her husband, the mourners were wholly composed of tenants and servants. Isabella was not asked. The place of interment was on a green slope in a corner of the kirkyard, where the wall is so low that heath and bilberry plants have climbed over it from the moor, and peat-mould almost buries it. Her husband lies in the same spot now, and they have each a simple headstone above, and a plain grey block at their feet to mark the graves.

§

The sun shone on the morning we buried her; but in the evening the weather broke. The wind moved from south to north-east, and brought rain first, and then sleet and snow. My master kept his room; I took possession of the lonely parlour, converting it into a nursery, and the following afternoon I was sitting there with the moaning doll of a child laid on my knee, rocking it to and fro, when the door opened and Isabella stood before me !

" I have run the whole way from Wuthering Heights," she gasped. " Oh, I am aching all over ! Don't be alarmed ! There shall be an explanation as soon as I can give it, only just have the goodness to step out and order the carriage to take me to Gimmerton, and tell a servant to seek up a few clothes in my wardrobe."

She was dressed only in a silk frock and light slippers. Her hair streamed from her shoulders. Her face was pale and bruised; and under one ear was a deep cut which only the cold prevented from bleeding profusely.

" My dear young lady," I exclaimed, " I'll stir nowhere and do nothing till you have put on dry clothes; and certainly you shall not go to Gimmerton tonight, so it is needless to order the carriage."

" Certainly I shall," she said—" walking or riding." And not till I had carried out her instructions would she permit me to bathe her wound or change her attire.

" Now, Ellen," she said, when my task was finished, and she was seated in an easy-chair near the fire, with a cup of tea before her, " I dare not stay lest Heathcliff should take it into his head to come after me—and I have not come suing Edgar's assistance. I ought and I wish to remain, to cheer Edgar and take care of the baby. But I tell you the brute wouldn't let me. Do you think he could bear to see me grow fat and merry, and not resolve on poisoning our comfort? Now I have the satisfaction of knowing he detests me to the point of its annoying him seriously to have me within earshot or eyesight. Now, therefore, is my chance to get away. I feel certain that he would not chase me over England supposing I contrive a clear escape. He has extinguished my love effectually, and so I'm at my ease. He is a monster. Catherine had an awfully perverted taste to esteem him so dearly, knowing him so well. Would that he could be blotted out of creation, and out of my memory!"

"Hush, hush! He is a human being," said I. "There are worse men than he is yet."

"He is not a human being," she retorted, "and he has no claim on my charity. I gave him my heart, and he took it and pinched it to death, and flung it back at me. People feel with their hearts, Ellen, and since he has destroyed mine, I have not power to feel for him, though he groaned from this till his dying day, and wept tears of blood for Catherine! No, indeed, indeed, I wouldn't!"

And here Isabella began to cry; but immediately dashing the water from her lashes, she recommenced, "You are wondering, no doubt, what has driven me to flight at last? I was compelled to attempt it, because I had succeeded in rousing his anger to a pitch above malignity. He was worked up to forget the fiendish prudence he boasted of, and proceeded to murderous violence."

"Yesterday, you know, Mr. Earnshaw should have been at the funeral. He had kept himself tolerably sober for the purpose, and consequently rose in suicidal, low spirits, as fit for the church as for a dance; and instead of going there, he sat down by the fire and swallowed gin by tumblerfuls.

"Heathcliff has been a stranger to the house from last Sunday till today. He has just come home at dawn, and locked himself up in his chamber. It was impossible for me to avoid regarding this season of deliverance from degrading oppression as a holiday, and I even recovered sufficient spirits to hear Joseph's lectures without weeping, and to move up and down the house less like a frightened thief. Mr. Earnshaw does not interfere with me. He is quieter now than he used to be, if no one provokes him— more sullen and depressed, and less furious.

" Yester-evening I sat in my nook by the fire, reading some old books, till near twelve o'clock. It seemed so dismal to go upstairs, with the wild snow blowing outside, and my thoughts kept reverting to the new-made grave. Hindley sat opposite, his head on his hands, perhaps meditating on the same subject. Hareton and Joseph were fast asleep in bed. There was no sound through the house but the moaning of the wind.

" The doleful silence was broken at length by the sound of the kitchen latch. Heathcliff had returned from his watch earlier than usual, owing, I suppose, to the sudden storm. That entrance was fastened, and we heard him coming round to get in by the other. I rose with an irrepressible expression of what I felt on my lips, which induced Hindley to exclaim :—

" ' I'll keep him out for five minutes. You won't object ? '

" ' No; you may keep him out the whole night for me,' I answered. ' Do; put the key in the lock and draw the bolts.'

Hindley accomplished this ere his guest reached the front. He then came and brought his chair close to me, and finding in my eyes a sympathy with the burning hate that gleamed from his, he went on :—

" ' You and I have a great debt to settle with that man out yonder. If we were neither of us cowards, we might combine to discharge it. Are you as soft as your brother? Are you willing to endure to the last, and not once attempt a repayment?'

"'I'm weary of enduring now,' I replied, 'and I'd be glad of a retaliation that didn't recoil on myself. But treachery and violence recoil. They wound those who resort to them worse than their enemies.'

"'Treachery and violence are a just return for treachery and violence!' cried Hindley. 'Mrs. Heathcliff, I'll ask you to do nothing but sit still and be dumb. Can you? He'll be your death, and *my* ruin. Damn the hellish villain! He knocks at the door as if he were master here already. Promise to hold your tongue, and in three minutes you'll be a free woman.'

"'I'll not hold my tongue,' I said; 'you mustn't touch him. Let the door remain shut and be quiet.'

"'No! I've formed my resolution, and, by God, I'll execute it!' cried the desperate being. 'I'll do you a kindness in spite of yourself, and Hareton justice. And you needn't trouble to screen me. Nobody alive would regret me; it's time to make an end.'

"I might as well have struggled with a bear. The only resource left to me was to run to the lattice and warn his intended victim.

"'You'd better seek shelter somewhere else tonight,' I exclaimed, in rather a triumphant tone. 'Mr. Earnshaw has a mind to shoot you if you persist in endeavouring to enter.'

"'You'd better open the door, you—' he answered.

"'I shall not meddle in the matter,' I retorted again. 'Come in and get shot, if you please. I've done my duty.'

"And with that I shut the window and returned to my place by the fire. Earnshaw swore passionately at me, affirming that I loved the villain yet. But a moment later the casement behind me was banged to the floor by a blow, and Heathcliff's black countenance looked blightingly through. The stanchions stood too close to suffer his shoulders to follow, and I smiled, exulting in my fancied security.

" ' Isabella, let me in, or I'll make you repent ! ' he cried.

" ' I cannot commit murder,' I replied. ' Mr. Earnshaw stands sentinel with a knife and loaded pistol. But why do you come ? It's a poor love of yours that cannot bear a shower of snow ! If I were you, Heathcliff, I'd go and stretch myself over her grave, and die like a faithful dog.'

" ' He's there, is he ? ' exclaimed my companion, rushing to the gap. ' If I can get my arm out I can hit him ! ' But as he attempted to do so, Heathcliff flung himself on Earnshaw's weapon, and wrenched it from his grasp.

" The charge exploded, and the knife, in springing back, closed on the owner's wrist. Heathcliff pulled it away by main force, slitting up the flesh as it passed on, and thrust it deep into his pocket. He then took a stone, struck down the division between the two windows, and sprang in. Hindley had fallen senseless with excessive pain. Blood gushed from his wound. The ruffian kicked and trampled on him, and dashed his head repeatedly against the flags, holding me with one hand meantime to prevent me summoning Joseph. Finally he desisted and dragged the inert body to the settle. There he tore the sleeve off Earnshaw's coat, and bound the deep gash with brutal roughness, cursing and spitting as he did so. Being at liberty, I lost no time in seeking the old servant, who, having gathered by degrees the purport of my hasty tale, hastened below.

" ' And so ye've been murtherin' on him ! ' exclaimed Joseph, as he entered. ' If iver I seed a seeght loike this ! May the Lord——'

"Heathcliff gave him a push on to his knees in the middle of the blood, commanding him to hold his tongue and wipe up the mess. But, instead of doing so, he joined his hands and began a prayer, which, in my excited state, caused me to burst out into laughter.

"'Oh, I forgot you,' said the tyrant. 'You shall do that. Down with you! And you conspire with him against me, do you, viper? There, that is work fit for you!'

"He shook me till my teeth rattled, and pitched me beside Joseph, who steadily concluded his supplications, and then rose, vowing he would set off for the Grange directly. Mr. Linton was a magistrate, and though he had fifty wives dead, he should inquire into this. Only when he understood that Earnshaw had been the aggressor, did he change his intention, and turn to succour his master— who presently regained consciousness. Heathcliff, aware that his opponent was ignorant of the treatment he had received while insensible, called him deliriously intoxicated, and advised him to go to bed. To my joy, he left us, after giving this judicious counsel. Hindley stretched himself on the hearthstone, and I departed to my own room, marvelling that I had escaped so easily.

"This morning, when I came down, about half an hour before noon, Mr. Earnshaw was sitting by the fire, deadly sick. Heathcliff, almost as gaunt and ghastly, leant against the chimney. Neither appeared inclined to dine; and having waited till all was cold on the table, I commenced alone. I ate heartily; and after I had done, I ventured on the unusual liberty of drawing near the fire, kneeling on the floor in the corner where Earnshaw sat.

"Heathcliff did not glance my way. He stood, abstracted, his forehead shaded with a heavy cloud, and his basilisk eyes nearly quenched by sleeplessness and weeping. His lips were sealed in an expression of unspeakable sadness. Had it been another, I would have covered my face in the presence of such grief. In *his* case, I was gratified. I couldn't miss the chance of sticking a dart into my fallen enemy. His weakness was the only time I could taste the delight of paying wrong for wrong.

"Hindley wanted some water. I handed him a glass, and asked him how he was.

"'Not as ill as I would wish,' he replied. 'But, leaving out my arm, every inch of me is as sore as if I had been fighting with a legion of imps.'

"'Yes, no wonder,' said I. 'Catherine used to boast that she stood between you and bodily harm. She meant that certain persons would not hurt you for fear of offending her. It's as well people don't *really* rise from their graves, or last night she might have witnessed a repulsive scene! Are not you bruised and cut over your chest and shoulders?'

"'What do you mean? Did he dare to strike me when I was down?'

"'He trampled on and kicked you and dashed you on the ground,' I whispered. 'And his mouth watered to tear you with his teeth; because he's more fiend than man.'

"Mr. Earnshaw looked up, like me, to the countenance of our mutual foe, who, absorbed in his anguish, seemed insensible to anything around him.

"'Oh, if God would but give me strength to strangle him in my last agony, I'd go to hell with joy,' groaned Hindley, writhing to rise.

"'Nay, it's enough that he has murdered one of you,' I observed aloud. 'At the Grange every one knows your sister would have been living now, if he had not come there and disturbed her happiness.'

"Heathcliff's attention was roused. Most likely he

noticed more the truth of what was said than the spirit
of the person who said it, for his eyes rained down tears
upon the ashes, and he drew his breath in suffocating
sighs. I stared full at him, and laughed aloud.

" ' Get up, and begone out of my sight,' he exclaimed.

" ' I beg your pardon,' I replied, no longer afraid of
him; ' but I loved Catherine too; and her brother
requires attendance, which, for her sake, I shall supply.
Now that she is dead, I see her in Hindley. Hindley has
exactly her eyes, if you had not tried to gouge them out,
and made them black and red. And her—— '

" ' Get up, wretched idiot, before I stamp you to
death ! ' he cried.

" ' But then,' I continued, holding myself ready to flee,
' if poor Catherine had trusted you, and assumed the
degrading title of Mrs. Heathcliff, she would soon have
presented a similar picture. She wouldn't have borne
your abominable behaviour quietly. Her detestation
and disgust must have found voice.'

" The back of the settle interposed between him and
me ; so instead of endeavouring to reach me, he snatched
a dinner-knife from the table and flung it at my head. It
struck beneath my ear, and stopped the sentence I was
uttering ; but, pulling it out, I sprang to the door, and
delivered another taunt, which I hope went deeper than
his missile. The last glimpse I caught of him was a
furious rush on his part, checked by the embrace of his
host ; and both fell locked together on the hearth. And
then, in a moment, I was out of the house, flying hither
over the moor, like a soul escaped from purgatory. And
far rather would I be condemned to a perpetual dwelling
in the infernal regions than, even for one night, abide
beneath the roof of Wuthering Heights again."

Isabella ceased speaking, and took a drink of tea.
Then she rose, and turning a deaf ear to my entreaties for

her to remain another hour, she bid me put on her bonnet and a great shawl I had brought, kissed Edgar's and Catherine's portraits, bestowed a similar salute on me, and descended to the carriage. She was driven away, never to revisit the neighbourhood; but a regular correspondence was later established between her and my master. I believe her new abode was in the south, near London; and there she had a son born, a few months subsequent to her escape. He was christened Linton, and, from the first, she reported him an ailing, peevish creature.

Mr. Heathcliff, meeting me one day in the village, inquired where she lived. I refused to tell. He remarked that it was not of any moment, only she must beware of coming to her brother. She should not be with him, if he had to keep her himself. Afterwards he discovered both her place of residence and the existence of the child. Still he did not molest her, for which forbearance she might thank his aversion, I suppose. He declared, however, that he would take the child when it suited his convenience to do so.

Fortunately the mother died before that time arrived— when little Linton was twelve years old.

Catherine's death transformed my master into a complete hermit. He threw up his office of magistrate, and ceased even to attend church. But he was too good to be thoroughly unhappy long. Time brought resignation and a melancholy sweeter than common joy. He recalled his wife's memory with an ardent, tender love.

And he had earthly consolation also.—At first he had seemed regardless of the puny successor to the departed, but it was not long before the tiny thing came to wield a despot's sceptre over his heart. It was named Catherine —*Cathy* he always called her; the shortened name formed a distinction from its mother, and yet a connection; and his attachment sprang from its relation to her far more than from its being his own.

How different was his conduct from Earnshaw's in similar circumstances. Both had been fond husbands. But while Earnshaw had abandoned himself to evil ways after *his* loss, my master trusted God, and God comforted him. One despaired, the other hoped.—The end of Earnshaw was what might have been expected; it followed fast on his sister's. He died within six months of her, drunk as a lord, and only twenty-seven years old. His unwelcome guest had cheated him out of all his property; Earnshaw had mortgaged every yard of land he owned to supply his mania for gambling; so Wuthering Heights passed into Heathcliff's hands, and there he continued to reside—a hateful presence to all of us at the Grange.

I insisted on Mr. Earnshaw's funeral being respectable. Heathcliff said I might have my own way there, only desiring me to remember that the money came out of his pocket. He had the hypocrisy to represent a mourner; and previous to following the coffin from the house with Hareton, he lifted the unfortunate child on to the table, and muttered, with particular gusto, "Now, my bonny lad, you are *mine*! And we'll see if one tree won't grow as crooked as the other, with the same wind to twist it!" The unsuspecting thing was pleased at the speech, and stroked Heathcliff's cheek; but I divined it's meaning, and observed tartly, "That boy must go back with me to Thrushcross Grange, sir. There is nothing in the world less yours than he is."

"Does Linton say so?" he demanded.

"Of course; he is his nephew, and he has ordered me to take him," I replied.

"Well," said the scoundrel, "we'll not argue the subject now; but I have a fancy to try my hand at rearing a young one, so near to your master. And you may tell him this : if he takes Hareton away I'll be pretty sure to supply his place with my own bairn."

The hint was enough to tie our hands; and thus Hareton remained at the Heights, reduced to a state of complete dependence on his father's enemy. To this day he remains a servant in the house that should have been his own, deprived of the advantage of wages, and quite unable to right himself, because of his friendlessness and his ignorance that he has been wronged.

CHAPTER XIII

THE twelve years that followed this dismal period (continued Mrs. Dean) were the happiest of my life. My greatest troubles rose from our little lady's trifling illnesses, which she had to experience in common with all children, rich and poor. For the rest, after the first six months, she grew like a larch. She was soon the most winning thing that ever brought sunshine into a desolate house—a real beauty in face, with the Earnshaw's handsome dark eyes, but the Linton's fair skin and small features and yellow curling hair. To Mr. Linton she was everything in the world. I never heard him speak a harsh word to her. He took her education on himself, and, being a child of lively curiosity and quick intellect, she learned rapidly and eagerly.

Till she reached the age of thirteen, she had not been beyond the range of the park by herself. Linton would take her with him a mile or two outside on rare occasions; but he trusted her to no one else. Wuthering Heights and Mr. Heathcliff did not exist for her. She was a perfect recluse, and, apparently, perfectly contented. Sometimes, indeed, while surveying the country from her nursery window, she would observe—

"Ellen, how long will it be before I can walk to the top of those hills? I wonder what lies on the other side. Is it the sea?"

"No, Miss Cathy," I would answer. "Beyond Peniston Crags it is the hills again, just like these—only wilder and steeper."

"How do you know, Ellen? Have you seen them? Have you walked on those other hills beyond?"

"Yes, miss, I have."

"Oh! Then I can go, too, when I am a woman. Has papa been there?"

"Papa would tell you, miss," I answered hastily, "that they are not worth the trouble of visiting. The moors where you ramble with him are much nicer; and Thrushcross Park is the finest place in the world."

"But I know the park, and I don't know those. I should delight to look around me from the brow of that tallest point. My little pony Minny shall take me there some time."

She teased Mr. Linton on the subject, and he promised she should make the journey when she got older. But Miss Catherine measured her age by months, and, "Now am I old enough to go to Peniston Crags?" was the constant question in her mouth. The road thither wound close by Wuthering Heights. Edgar had not the heart to pass it, so she received as constantly the answer; "Not yet, love; not yet."

I have said Mrs. Heathcliff lived only a dozen years after quitting her husband. Her family were of a delicate constitution. She and Edgar both lacked the ruddy health you generally meet in these parts. When she knew that her life was drawing to an end, she wrote to ask her brother to come and see her, for she had much to settle. Her hope was that little Linton might be left with him. His father, she would fain convince herself, had no desire to assume the burden of his maintenance or education.—My master lost no time in complying with her request. Reluctant as he was to leave home at ordinary calls, he flew to answer this, commending Catherine to my particular vigilance, in his absence, with reiterated orders that she must not wander out of the park, even under my vigilance. He did not calculate on her going unaccompanied.

He was away three weeks. The first day or two my charge sat in a corner of the library, too sad for either reading or playing. But after that she became fretful and impatient; and, being too busy and too old then to run up and down amusing her, I used to send her on her travels round the grounds, now on foot and now on her pony, indulging her with a patient audience of all her adventures, real and imaginary, when she returned.

The summer shone in full prime, and she took such a taste for this solitary rambling that she often contrived to remain out from breakfast till tea. I did not fear her breaking bounds, because the gates were generally locked, and I thought she would scarcely venture forth alone, even if they had been open.

Unfortunately my confidence proved misplaced. One day she set off as usual, and when tea-time came she did not return. I became anxious, and at last went out in search of her. There was a labourer working at a fence on the borders of the grounds. I inquired of him whether he had seen our young lady.

"I saw her at morn," he replied. "She leapt her Galloway over the hazel hedge yonder, where it is lowest, and galloped out of sight."

You may guess how I felt at hearing this news. It

struck me directly she must have started for Peniston Crags. I pushed my way through the gap the man was repairing, and making straight for the highroad, I walked as if for a wager, mile after mile, till a turn brought me in view of the Heights; but no Catherine could I detect far or near. The Crags lie about a mile and a half beyond Mr. Heathcliff's place, and that is four from the Grange, so I began to fear that night would fall ere I could reach them. "And what if she should have slipped in clambering among them," I reflected, "and been killed or broken some of her bones?" My suspense was truly painful; and at first it gave me delightful relief to observe, in hurrying by the Heights, my young lady's pony, tethered to a tree. I opened a wicket and ran to the door, knocking vehemently for admittance. A woman whom I knew, and who had formerly lived at Gimmerton, answered. She had been a servant there since the death of Mr. Earnshaw.

"Ah," said she, "you are coming a-seeking your little mistress! Don't be frightened. She's here safe; but I'm glad it isn't the master."

"Mr. Heathcliff is not at home, then, is he?" I panted.

"No, no. Both he and Joseph are off, and I think they won't return this hour or more. Step in and rest you a bit."

I entered, and beheld my stray lamb seated on the hearth, rocking herself in a little chair that had been her mother's when a child. She seemed perfectly at home, laughing and chattering in the best spirits imaginable, to Hareton—now a great strong lad of eighteen, who stared at her with considerable curiosity and astonishment, comprehending little of the fluent succession of remarks and questions which her tongue poured forth.

"Very well, miss!" I exclaimed, concealing my joy under an angry countenance. "This is your last ride

till papa comes back.   Put on that hat and come home at
once.   I'll not trust you out of my sight again."

Miss Cathy, who had welcomed my coming with a happy
smile and run gaily to my side, now began to pout and
cry.

"Don't be too hard on the bonny lass, Mrs. Dean," said
the servant.   "We made her stop.   She'd fain have
ridden forward, afeard you should be uneasy.   Hareton
offered to go with her, and I thought he should.   It's a
wild road over the hills."

Hareton stood with his hands in his pockets, too awkward to speak, though he looked as if he did not relish my
intrusion.

"How long am I to wait?" I continued, disregarding
the woman's interference.   "Come along at once, Miss
Cathy."

I picked up her hat and approached to reinstate it;
but she, seeing that the people of the house took her part,
began dodging behind the furniture, rendering it ridiculous
for me to pursue.   Hareton and the woman began to
laugh, and she joined them, till I cried out in great
irritation—

"Do you hear me, Miss Cathy?   If you were aware
whose house this is, you'd be glad enough to get out."

"It's *your* father's, isn't it?" said she, turning to
Hareton.

"Nay," he replied, looking down, and blushing bash-
fully.

"Whose, then—your master's?" she asked.

He coloured deeper; muttered an oath, and turned
away.

"Who is his master?" continued the tiresome girl.
"He talked about 'our house', and 'our folk'.   I
thought he was the owner's son.   And he never said miss.
He should have done, shouldn't he, if he's a servant?"

Hareton grew black as a thunder-cloud at the childish speech. I silently shook my questioner, and at last succeeded in getting her ready for departure.

" Now get my horse," said she, addressing her unknown kinsman as she would one of the stable-boys at the Grange. " Make haste ! Get my horse, I say."

" I'll see thee damned before I be thy servant," growled the lad.

" You'll see me *what* ? " asked Catherine in surprise.

" Damned, thou saucy witch ! " he replied.

" Ellen," cried she, staring, fixed in astonishment, " how dare he speak to me so ?—You wicked creature, I shall tell papa what you said."

Hareton did not appear to feel this threat, so the tears sprang to her eyes with indignation. " *You* bring the pony," she exclaimed, turning to the woman. " Bring it this instant."

" Softly, miss," answered she addressed ; " you'll lose nothing by being civil. Though Mr. Hareton be not the master's son, he's your cousin ; and I was never hired to serve you."

" He my cousin ! " cried Cathy with a scornful laugh.— " Papa is gone to fetch my cousin from London. My cousin is a gentleman's son."

" Hush, hush ! " I whispered ; " people can have many cousins, and of all sorts, Miss Cathy, without being the worse for it ; only they needn't keep their company, if they be disagreeable and bad."

" But—he—*he's* not my cousin, Ellen ! " cried Cathy, bursting into tears, and flinging herself into my arms as a refuge from the idea.

I was much vexed at her and the servant for their mutual revelations. It was certain that little Linton's approaching arrival would be communicated to Heath-cliff ; and Catherine's first thought on her father's return would be to seek an explanation of her relationship to Hareton. Pausing in her lamentations, she surveyed him with a glance of horror, and then burst forth anew.

But at last we were away, sadly out of sorts. I could not wring from my little lady how she had spent the day. But I gathered that, as she had passed the farmhouse on her way to the Crags, Hareton had issued forth. She had asked him the way, and finally beguiled him to accompany her. He had opened to her the mysteries of the Fairy Cave and twenty other queer places. And evidently her guide had been quite a favourite till she had hurt his feelings by calling him a servant, and Heathcliff's house-keeper had hurt hers by calling him her cousin. Then the language he had held to her rankled in her heart. She was always "love" and "darling" and "angel" to everyone at the Grange, and to be insulted so shockingly by a stranger! She did not comprehend it. I had hard work to obtain a promise that she would not lay her grievance before her father. I explained how he objected to the whole household at the Heights, and how sorry he would be to find she had been there; but I insisted most on the fact that if she revealed my negligence of his orders to her father, he would probably be so angry that I should have to leave; and Cathy could not bear that prospect. She pledged her word, and kept it, for my sake. After all, she was a sweet little girl.

§

A letter edged with black, announced the day of my master's return. Isabella was dead; and he wrote to bid me get mourning for his daughter, and arrange a room for his youthful nephew. Catherine ran wild with joy at the idea of welcoming her father back, and indulged in the most sanguine anticipations of the innumerable excellencies of her "real" cousin.

At length the day came. The travelling carriage rolled in sight. Cathy was out of the house in a moment, shrieked and stretched out her arms as soon as she caught her father's face looking from the window. He descended, nearly as eager as herself; and a considerable interval elapsed ere they had a thought for any but themselves. While they exchanged caresses, I took a peep in to see after Linton. He was almost asleep in one corner—a pale, delicate, effeminate boy, who might have been taken for my master's younger brother, so strong was the resemblance; but there was a sickly peevishness in his countenance that Edgar Linton never had.

Cathy was now all anxiety to see her cousin. Mr. Linton warned her that the boy was not as strong and merry as she was. "And remember, darling," he added, "he has lost his mother a short time since, so don't expect him to run about and play with you directly. Let him be quiet this evening, at least, will you?"

"Yes, yes, papa," answered Catherine; "but I do want to see him, and he hasn't once looked out."

My master roused the sleeper, and lifted him to the ground.

"This is your cousin Cathy, Linton," he said, putting their hands together. "She's fond of you already. Try to be cheerful now; the travelling is at an end, so you can now rest and amuse yourself as you please."

"Let me go to bed, then," wailed the boy, shrinking from Catherine's salute.

"Come, come, there's a good child," I whispered, leading him in. "You'll make her weep too. See how sorry she is for you!"

I did not know whether it was sorrow for him, but his cousin put on a countenance as sad as himself. Tea was ready in the library. I proceeded to remove Linton's cap and mantle, and placed him in a chair by the table;

but he was no sooner seated than he began to cry afresh, declaring that he was too exhausted to sit in a chair.

"Go to the sofa, then," said his uncle, patiently; "and Ellen shall bring you some tea there."

Linton slowly trailed off, and lay down. Cathy carried a footstool and a cup of tea to his side. At first she sat silent; but that could not last. She had resolved to make a pet of her little cousin, and she commenced stroking his curls, and kissing him, and offering him tea in her saucer, like a baby. This pleased him. He dried his eyes, and lightened into a faint smile.

"Oh, he'll do very well," said the master to me, after watching them a minute—"very well, if we can keep him, Ellen. The company of a child of his age will instil new spirit into him soon."

"Ay, if we can keep him!" I mused to myself, and sore misgivings came over me that there was slight hope of that. And then I thought, however will that weakling live at Wuthering Heights? Between his father and Hareton, what playmates and instructors he'll have! Our doubts were decided even earlier than I had expected. I had only just taken the children upstairs, and seen Linton asleep, when a maid informed me that Mr. Heathcliff's servant Joseph was at the door, and wished to speak with the master.

"I shall ask him what he wants first," I said, in considerable trepidation. "A very unlikely hour to be troubling people; and only this instant returned from a long journey! I don't think the master will see him."

Joseph was in the hall. He had donned his Sunday garments, and his most sanctimonious and sourest face.

"Good evening, Joseph," I said coldly. "What business brings you here tonight?"

"It's Maister Linton I mun speak to," he answered, waving me disdainfully aside.

"Mr. Linton is going to bed. Unless you have something very particular to say, you had better entrust your message to me."

"Which is his rahm?" pursued the fellow, surveying the range of closed doors.

I perceived that he was bent on refusing my mediation, so very reluctantly I went up to the library and announced the unseasonable visitor. Mr. Linton had no chance of sending him away, for he had followed me into the room.

"Heathcliff has sent me for his lad, and I munn't goa back 'bout him," he announced in an elevated tone, as if anticipating opposition.

Edgar Linton was silent a minute; an expression of extreme sorrow overcast his features. He was mindful no doubt of Isabella's hopes and fears, and was searching in his heart how he might avoid yielding the child up. No plan offered itself. The very exhibition of any desire to keep him would have rendered the claimant more peremptory. However, he was not going to rouse him from his sleep.

"Tell Mr. Heathcliff," he answered calmly, "that his son shall come to Wuthering Heights tomorrow. He is in bed, and too tired to go the distance now. You may also tell him that his health is very precarious, and that his mother desired him to remain under my guardianship."

"Noa!" cried Joseph. "I mun tak him t'neight."

"Most certainly you shall not," answered Linton decisively. "Walk downstairs at once, and repeat to your master what I have said.—Ellen—show him down.—Go!"

And aiding the indignant elder with a lift by the arm, he rid the room of him, and closed the door.

"Varrah well!" shouted Joseph, as he slowly drew off. "To-morn, he's come hisseln; and thrust *him* out, if ye darr!"

§

To obviate the danger of this threat being fulfilled, Mr.
Linton commissioned me to take the boy home early,
on Catherine's pony; and said he—

" As we can now have no influence over his destiny, you
must say nothing of where he is gone to my daughter,
lest she should be restless to visit the Heights.   Merely
tell her his own father sent for him suddenly."

Little Linton was very reluctant to be roused from his
bed at five o'clock, and astonished to be informed that he
must prepare for further travelling; but I softened off the
matter by stating that he was going to spend some time
with his father, Mr. Heathcliff, who was very anxious to
see him.

" My father !   Mamma never told me I had a father.
Where does he live ?   I'd rather stay with uncle."

" Just beyond those hills—not so far.   You may walk
over and see us when you get hearty."

" But why have I not heard of my father before ?   Why
didn't he and mamma live together, as other people do ? "

" He had business to keep him in the north," I answered,
" and your mother's health required her to remain in the
south."

" And why didn't mamma speak to me about him ? "
persevered the child.   " She often talked of *uncle*, and I
learned to love him long ago.   How am I to love papa ?
I don't know him."

" Oh, all children love their parents," I answered.
" Your mother, perhaps, thought you would want to be
with him if she mentioned him.   Let us make haste.
It is a beautiful morning for an early ride."

" Is *she* to go with us—the little girl I saw yesterday."

" Not now," I replied.

" Is uncle ?"

" No. I shall be your companion there."

" I won't go without uncle," he cried. He lay down again in his bed, and resisted all my coaxing to rise from it. I was obliged to call for my master's assistance, and the poor thing was finally got off, with several delusive assurances that the absence would be short. The pure heather-scented air, the bright sunshine, and the gentle canter of the pony relieved his despondency after a while. He began to ask questions about his new home and its inhabitants, which I answered as cheerfully as I was able. As we approached the Heights, I could see that his private feelings entirely disapproved of the exterior of his new abode. But he had the sense to postpone complaining. There might be compensations within.

Before he dismounted, I went and opened the door; the servant was clearing the breakfast-table. Joseph stood by his master's chair, telling some tale about a lame horse. Hareton was preparing for the hayfield.

" Hello, Nelly ! " said Mr. Heathcliff when he saw me. " I feared I should have to come down and fetch my property myself. You've brought it, have you? Let us see what we can make of it."

He got up and strode to the door, Hareton and Joseph following. Poor Linton ran a frightened eye over the faces of the three. Heathcliff, having stared his son into an ague of confusion, uttered a scornful laugh.

" God ! What a beauty ! what a lovely, charming thing ! " he exclaimed. " Haven't they reared it on snails and sour milk, Nelly? Oh, damn my soul ! but that's worse than I expected, and the devil knows I was not sanguine."

I bade the trembling and bewildered child get down and enter. He did not thoroughly comprehend his father's speech; indeed, he was not certain that the grim sneering stranger was his father. But he clung to me with growing trepidation; and on Mr. Heathcliff's taking a seat and bidding him " come hither ", he hid his face on my shoulder and wept.

" Tut, tut ! " said Heathcliff, dragging him roughly between his knees, and holding up his head by the chin. " None of that nonsense ! We're not going to hurt thee, Linton. Isn't that thy name? Thou art thy mother's child entirely. Where is *my* share in thee, puling chicken?—Yes, I am thy father. You've heard of me, I dare say."

" No," replied Linton, raising his great blue eyes to the other's face.

" No ! What a shame of your mother not to waken your filial regard for me ! Your mother was a wicked slut to leave you in ignorance of the sort of father you possessed. Now, don't wince and colour up. Be a good lad, and I'll do for you.—Nelly, if you're not tired, you'd better get home again. This thing won't be settled while you linger about it."

" Well," I replied, " I hope you'll be kind to the boy, Mr. Heathcliff, or you'll not keep him long. He's all the kin you have in the world, remember."

" I'll be kind to him, you needn't fear," he said, laughing. " Only nobody else must be kind to him. I'm jealous of monopolising his affection. Joseph, bring the lad some breakfast. Hareton, you infernal calf, begone to your work.—Yes, Nell," he added, when they had departed, " my son is the prospective owner of your place—Edgar Linton's place—and I should not wish him to die till I was certain of being his successor. I despise him for himself, and hate him for all the memories he revives. But he shall be tended as carefully as your master tends his own. I have a room upstairs furnished for him in handsome style I've engaged a tutor to come three times a week, from twenty miles distance. I've ordered Hareton to obey him; and, in fact, I've arranged everything to preserve the gentleman in the whey-faced whining wretch."

The poor child clung to me while I tried to make my departure. But, muttering as many consoling words as I was able, I managed at last to get away, his father's grip preventing him from following me. I mounted Minny, and urged her into a trot. And so my master's brief guardianship of his nephew ended.

CHAPTER XIV

WE had sad work with Cathy that day. She rose in high glee, eager to join her cousin, and such passionate tears and lamentations followed the news of his departure that Edgar himself was obliged to soothe her by affirming that he should come back soon. He added, however, " if I can get him," and there were no hopes of that. This promise poorly pacified her; but time was more potent; and though at intervals she still inquired when Linton would return, before she did see him again his features had waxed so dim in her memory that she did not recognise him.

When I chanced to encounter the housekeeper of Wuthering Heights, in paying business visits to Gimmerton, I used to ask how the young master got on. I gathered that he continued in weak health, and was a tiresome inmate. Mr. Heathcliff, she said, seemed to dislike him more than ever, though he took some trouble to conceal it. Mr. Edgar encouraged me to gain information about the boy. He thought a great deal about him, I fancy, and would have taken some risk to see him. He told me to ask the housekeeper if he ever came into the village. She said he had only been twice, on horseback, with his father, and both times pretended to be quite knocked up for days afterwards. That housekeeper left two years after he came, and another woman I did not know took her place. She lives there still.

Time wore on at the Grange in its former pleasant way till Miss Cathy reached her sixteenth birthday. On a beautiful spring day, and when her father had retired to his library, my lady came down, dressed for going out. Mr. Linton had given her leave to go with me, if we went only a short distance and were back within the hour.

" So make haste, Ellen ! " she cried. " I know where I wish to go—where a colony of moor game are settled. I want to see if they have made their nests yet. It's not very far. I've gone very near with papa."

I put on my bonnet and sallied out, thinking nothing more of the matter. She bounded before me, returned to my side, and was off again like a young greyhound ; and at first I found plenty of entertainment enjoying the warm, sweet sunshine, and watching her, my pet and my delight, with her golden ringlets flying loose behind, and her bright cheek, as soft and pure in its bloom as a wild rose, and her eyes radiant with cloudless pleasure. She was a happy creature in those days. It's a pity she could not be content.

" Well," said I, " where are your moor-game, Miss Cathy ? We should be at them. The Grange park fence is a great way off now."

" Oh, a little farther—only a little farther, Ellen," was her answer. " When we have climbed that hillock, and we shall be almost there." And she ran ahead, far outstripping me, and either not hearing my calls for her to come back, or determined not to hear them. Finally she dived into a hollow, and before I came in sight of her again she was two miles nearer Wuthering Heights than her own home; and I beheld a couple of persons arrest her, one of whom I felt convinced was Mr. Heathcliff himself. Cathy had been caught in the act of hunting out the nests of his grouse. She was on his land, and he was reproving the poacher.

" I've neither taken any eggs nor found any," she said, as I toiled up to them, expanding her hands in corroboration of this statement. " I didn't mean to take them; but papa told me there were quantities here, and I wished to see them."

Heathcliff glared at me with an all-meaning smile, expressing his malevolence, and demanded who " papa " was, though he must have known what the answer would be.

" Mr. Linton of Thrushcross Grange," she replied. " I thought you did not know me, or you wouldn't have spoken in that way."

" You suppose papa is highly esteemed and respected, then ? " he said sarcastically.

" And who are you ? " inquired Catherine, gazing curiously on the speaker. And then, pointing to Hareton, who stood by him, " That man I've seen before. Is he your son ? " (Hareton had gained nothing but increased bulk and strength. He seemed as awkward and rough as ever.)

" Miss Cathy," I interrupted, " it will be three hours instead of one that we are out presently. We really must go back."

" No, that man is not my son," answered Heathcliff, pushing me aside. " But I have one, and you have seen him before too. If you will turn this nab of heath and walk into my house, you shall see him again. I promise you shall receive a kind welcome."

I whispered to Catherine that she must on no account accede to the proposal.

"Why?" she asked aloud. "I want a rest, and the ground is too dewy to sit upon. He says I've seen his son. I'm sure he's mistaken. But I guess where he lives—at the farmhouse I visited in coming from Peniston Crags. Don't you?"

"I do," said Heathcliff, overhearing. "Come, Nelly, hold your tongue; it will be a treat for her to look in on us; Hareton, get forward with the lass. You shall walk with me, Nelly."

"No, she is not going to any such place," I cried. "I know you mean no good. And if she sees Linton, all will be told to her father as soon as ever we return; and I shall have all the blame."

"I want her to see Linton," he answered. "He's looking better these days. It's not often he's fit to be seen. And we'll soon persuade her to keep the visit secret. Where's the harm of it?"

"I have a duty to my master," said I; "and I am convinced you have a bad design in encouraging her."

"My desire is as honest as possible. I'll inform you of its whole scope—that the two cousins may fall in love and get married. I'm acting generously to your master. His young chit has no expectations, and should she second my wishes, she'll be provided for at once as the joint successor with Linton."

"If Linton dies," I answered, "Catherine would be the heir!"

"No, she would not. There is no clause in the will to secure it so. His property would go to me. But to prevent disputes I desire their union, and am resolved to bring it about."

"And I am resolved she shall never approach your home

again," I returned, as we reached the gate, where Miss
Cathy waited our coming.

Heathcliff bade me be quiet, and hastened forward to
open the door. My young lady gave him several looks, as
if she did not quite know what to make of him; but now
he smiled when he met her eye, and softened his voice in
addressing her; and I was foolish enough to imagine that
the memory of her mother might disarm him from desiring
her injury. Linton stood on the hearth. He had just
been out walking, for his cap was on, and he was calling to
Joseph to bring him dry clothes. He had grown tall for
his age—still some months short of sixteen. His features
were pretty yet, and his eye and complexion were
brightened by his exercise.

"Now, who is that?" asked Mr. Heathcliff, turning to
Cathy. "Can you tell?"

"Your son?" she said, having doubtfully surveyed
first one and then the other.

"Yes, yes," answered he. "But is this the only time
you have beheld him? Think! Ah! you have a short
memory.—Linton, don't you recall your cousin that you
used to tease us so with wishing to see?"

"What Linton!" cried Cathy, kindling into joyful
surprise at the name. "Is that little Linton? He's
taller than I am!—are you Linton?"

The youth stepped forward and acknowledged himself.
She kissed him fervently, and they gazed with wonder
at the change time had wrought in the appearance of each.
Catherine had reached her full height; her whole aspect
sparkled with health and spirits. Linton's looks and
movements were very languid, but there was a grace in
his manner which rendered him not unpleasing. After
exchanging numerous marks of fondness with him,
Catherine went up to Mr. Heathcliff, who stood by the
door.

" And you are my uncle, then ! " she cried, reaching up
to salute him. " I thought I liked you, though you were
so cross at first. Why don't you visit at the Grange with
Linton ? To live all these years such close neighbours, and
never see us, is very odd."

" I visited it once or twice too often before you were
born," he answered. " There—damn it ! If you have
any kisses to spare, give them to Linton—they are wasted
on me."

" Naughty Ellen ! " exclaimed Catherine, flying to
attack me next with her lavish caresses. " Wicked
Ellen, to try and hinder me from entering ! But I'll
take this walk every morning in future—may I, uncle ?—
and sometimes bring papa."

" Of course ! " replied the uncle, with a hardly suppressed grimace, resulting from his deep aversion to both
the proposed visitors. " But stay. I'd better tell you at
once. Mr. Linton has a prejudice against me. We
quarrelled at one time of our lives with unchristian
ferocity, and if you mention coming here to him, he'll put
a veto on your visits altogether. If you want to see your
cousin again, you must not mention it."

" Why did you quarrel ? " asked Catherine, considerably crestfallen.

" He thought me too poor to wed his sister," answered
Heathcliff, " and was grieved I got her. His pride was
hurt, and he'll never forgive it."

" That's wrong," said the young lady. " Sometime
I'll tell him so. But Linton and I have no share in your
quarrel. I'll not come here then ; he shall come to the
Grange."

" It will be too far for me," murmured her cousin ;
" the distance would kill me. No, come here, Miss
Catherine—not every morning, but once or twice a
week."

The father launched towards his son a glance of bitter contempt.

"I am afraid, Nelly, I shall lose my labour," he muttered to me. "Miss Catherine, as the ninny calls her, will discover his value, and send him to the devil. Now, if it had been Hareton! Do you know that twenty times a day I covet Hareton? I'd have loved the lad had he not been Hindley's child.—Oh, confound the vapid weakling! He's absorbed in drying his feet and never looks at her.—Linton!"

"Yes, father," answered the boy.

"Have you nothing to show your cousin anywhere about? Before you change your shoes, take her into the stable to see your horse."

But Linton kept his seat, and shrank closer to the fire. Heathcliff went out into the yard and called Hareton; and presently the two re-entered. The young man had been washing himself, as was visible by the glow on his cheeks and wetted hair.

"Oh, I'll ask you, uncle," said Miss Cathy, recollecting the housekeeper's assertion. "That is not my cousin, is he?"

"Yes," he replied—"your mother's nephew. Don't you like him? Is he not a handsome lad?"

Catherine smiled, and, rising on tiptoe, whispered a sentence in Heathcliff's ear. He laughed. Hareton darkened. I perceived he was very sensitive to suspected slights. But his master or guardian chased the frown by exclaiming—

"You'll be the favourite among us, Hareton! She says you're a—what was it? Well, something very flattering. Here, you go with her round the farm. And behave like a gentleman, mind. Speak slowly; don't use any bad words, and keep your hands out of your pockets. Be off, and entertain her as nicely as you can."

F

He watched the couple walking past the window. Earnshaw's countenance was completely averted from his companion. Catherine took a sly look at him, expressing small admiration, and then tripped merrily on, seeking out objects of amusement for herself.

"I've tied his tongue," observed Heathcliff. "He'll not venture a word all the time. Nay, you recollect me at his age. Did *I* ever look so stupid and oafish?"

"Worse," I replied, "because more sullen with it."

"I've a pleasure in him," he continued. "He has satisfied my expectations. If he were a born fool I should not enjoy his degradation half so much. But he's no fool; and I can sympathize with his feelings, having felt them myself. I know what he suffers now, for instance, exactly. But it's merely a beginning of what he's going to suffer. And he'll never be able to emerge from his bathos of coarseness and ignorance. I've got him faster than his scoundrel of a father secured me, and lower, for he takes a pride in his brutishness. I've taught him to scorn all refinements as silly and weak. And the best of it is, he's damnably fond of me. He thinks I'm the one friend he has in the world. You'll own I've outmatched Hindley there."

I made no reply, because I saw he expected none. Meanwhile our young companion, who sat too far from us to hear what was said, began to evince symptoms of uneasiness, probably repenting that he had denied himself the treat of Catherine's society for fear of a little fatigue. His father remarked his restless glance towards the window.

"Get up, you idle boy!" he exclaimed, with assumed heartiness. "Away after them! They are just at the corner, by the stand of the hives."

Linton gathered his energies and left the hearth. The lattice was open, and as he stepped out I heard Cathy inquiring of her unsociable attendant what was that inscription over the door. Hareton scratched his head like a true clown.

" It's some damnable writing," answered Hareton, " I cannot read it."

" Can't read it? " cried Catherine. " I can read it; it's English. But I want to know why it's there."

Linton giggled—the first appearance of mirth he had exhibited.

" He does not know his letters," he said to his cousin. " Could you believe in the existence of such a colossal dunce? "

" Is he all he should be? " asked Miss Cathy seriously; " or is he simple—not right. Each time I ask him a question he looks so stupid."

Linton repeated his laugh, and glanced at Hareton tauntingly—who certainly did not seem quite clear of comprehension at the moment.

" There's nothing the matter but laziness—is there, Earnshaw? " he said. " My cousin fancies you are an idiot. There you experience the consequence of scorning ' book-larning ', as you would call it.—Have you noticed, Catherine, his frightful Yorkshire pronunciation? "

" Why, where the devil is the use on't? " growled Hareton, more ready in answering his daily companion. He was about to enlarge further, but the two youngsters broke into a noisy fit of merriment.

" Come, Hareton! " tittered Linton. " Papa told you not to say any bad words. Do try to behave like a gentleman! "

" If thou weren't more a lass than a lad, I'd fell thee this minute, I would, pitiful lath of a crater! " retorted the angry boor, retreating, his face burning with indignation—for he was now conscious of being insulted.

We stayed till afternoon—I could not tear Miss Cathy

away sooner; but happily my master had not quitted his apartment, and remained ignorant of our prolonged absence. I would fain have enlightened her on the character of the people with whom she had become acquainted, but any explanation from me was impossible, and she remained convinced that I was prejudiced against them. She did not mention the visit that night, because she did not see Mr. Linton. Next day it all came out, sadly to my chagrin. And still I was not altogether sorry. I thought the burden of directions and warning would be more efficiently borne by him than by me.

" Papa ! " she exclaimed after the morning's salutations, " guess whom I saw in my walk on the moors. Ah, papa, you started ! You have not done right, have you, now ? I saw—— But listen, and you shall hear how I found you out."

She gave a faithful account of her excursion and its consequences; and my master, though he cast more than one reproachful glance at me, said nothing till she had concluded. Then he drew her to him, and asked if she knew why he had concealed Linton's near neighbourhood from her.

" It was because you disliked Mr. Heathcliff," she answered.

" No, darling; it was not because I dislike Mr. Heathcliff, but because Mr. Heathcliff dislikes me, and is a most diabolical man, delighting to wrong and ruin those he hates, if they give him the slightest opportunity. I knew that you could not keep up an acquaintance with your cousin without being brought into contact with him; so for your own good, and nothing else, I took precautions that you should not see him again. I meant to explain this sometime when you grew older, and I'm sorry I delayed it."

" But Mr. Heathcliff was quite cordial, papa," observed

Catherine, not at all convinced; " and he said I might come to his house whenever I pleased. *You* are the one to be blamed. He is willing to let Linton and I be friends —and you are not."

My master, perceiving that she would not take his word for her uncle-in-law's evil disposition, gave a hasty sketch of his conduct to Isabella, and of the manner in which Wuthering Heights became his property. And Miss Cathy appeared so deeply shocked and impressed (that any human being could be so evil had never before dawned on her) that Mr. Edgar deemed it unnecessary to pursue the subject. She kissed her father, and sat down quietly with him to her lessons. But in the evening, when she retired to her room, and I went to help her undress, I found her crying on her knees by the bedside

" Oh, fie, silly child ! " I exclaimed. " If you had any real griefs you'd be ashamed to waste a tear on this little contrariety. You must put Wuthering Heights and all its occupants out of your head."

" I'm not crying for myself, Ellen," she answered—" it's for him—Linton. He expected to see me again tomorrow; he'll be so disappointed when I don't come."

" Nonsense ! " said I. " Hasn't he Hareton for a companion ? Linton will conjecture how it is, and trouble himself no more about you."

" But may I not write him a note and tell him why I cannot come ? " she asked, rising to her feet; " and just send him those books I promised him ? "

" No, indeed ! no, indeed ! " replied I, with decision. " Then he would write you, and there'd never be an end of it. The acquaintance must be dropped entirely."

" But how can one little note—— " she recommenced, putting on an imploring countenance.

" Silence ! " I interrupted. " We'll not begin your little notes. Get into bed ! "

She threw at me a very naughty look—so naughty that I would not kiss her good-night at first. I covered her up and shut her door in great displeasure; but repenting half-way, I returned softly, and lo! there was miss standing at the table with a bit of blank paper before her, and a pencil in her hand, which she guiltily slipped out of sight on my entrance.

"You'll get nobody to take that, Catherine," I said, "if you write it; and at present I shall put out your candle."

I set the extinguisher on the flame, receiving as I did so a slap on my hand. I then quitted her again, and she drew the bolt in one of her worst, most peevish humours. But the letter was finished and forwarded to its destination by a milk-fetcher who came from the vlllage—though I did not learn that for some time afterwards. Weeks passed, and Cathy recovered her temper, though she grew wondrous fond of stealing off to corners by herself. She also got a trick of coming down early in the morning and lingering about the kitchen, as if she were expecting the arrival of something; and she had a small drawer in a cabinet in the library which she now took special care to keep locked.

These circumstances gradually aroused my suspicions. I determined to take a peep at her mysterious treasures; so one night, as soon as she and my master were safe upstairs, I searched and readily found among my house-keys one that would fit the lock. And in the drawer I discovered a mass of correspondence—daily, almost, it must have been—from Linton Heathcliff, answers to letters sent by her. The earliest ones were embarrassed and short; gradually, however, they expanded into copious love-letters, foolish, as the age of the writer rendered natural, yet with touches here and there which I thought were borrowed from a more experienced source.

After turning over as many as I thought proper, I tied them in a handkerchief and set them aside, relocking the vacant drawer.

Following her habit, my young lady descended early the next morning and visited the kitchen. I watched her go to the door on the arrival of a certain little boy and while the dairy-maid filled his can, she tucked something into his jacket pocket, and plucked something out. I went round by the garden and succeeded in waylaying the messenger, and extracting the epistle, though he fought valorously for his trust. Then, remaining under the wall, I perused Miss Cathy's affectionate epistle. It was more simple and eloquent than her cousin's—very pretty and very silly. I shook my head and went meditating into the house. The day being wet, she could not divert herself with rambling about the park; so, at the conclusion of her morning studies, she resorted to the solace of her drawer. Her father sat reading at a table, and I, on purpose, had sought a bit of work in some unripped fringes of the window-curtain, keeping my eye steadily fixed on her proceedings. The anguished "Oh!" which she uttered on discovering the disappearance of her treasures caused Mr. Linton to look up.

"What is the matter, love? Have you hurt yourself?" he said.

The tone and look assured her that *he* had not been the finder of her hoard.

"No, papa," she gasped.—"Ellen! Ellen! come upstairs! I'm sick!"

I obeyed her summons and accompanied her out.

"Oh, Ellen, you have got them!" she commenced immediately, dropping on her knees, when we were enclosed alone. "Oh, give them to me, and I'll never, never do it again. Don't tell papa! You have not told papa, Ellen?"

With grave severity I bade her stand up.

" So," I exclaimed, " Miss Catherine, you may well be ashamed of yourself. A fine bundle of trash you study in your leisure hours ! I haven't shown it yet, but you needn't imagine I shall keep your ridiculous secrets. For shame ! And you must have led the way in writing such absurdities. He would not have thought of it, I'm certain."

" I didn't ! I didn't ! " sobbed Catherine, fit to break her heart. " I didn't once think of loving him till—— "

" *Loving !* " cried I, scornfully. " *Loving !* Did anybody ever hear the like ! Why, you've only seen Linton twice in your life. I'm going with the babyish trash to your father, and we'll see what *he* says to such loving."

She sprang at her precious epistles, but I held them above my head ; and then she poured out further entreaties that I would burn them—do anything rather than show them.

And being really fully as much inclined to laugh as to scold—for I esteemed it all girlish vanity—I at length relented in a measure, and asked—

" If I consent to burn them, will you promise faithfully neither to send nor receive a letter from him again ? Unless you will, here I go."

" I promise, Ellen ! " she cried, catching my dress. " Oh, put them in the fire !—do, do ! "

I unknotted the handkerchief, and commenced dropping them in from an angle. The flame curled up the chimney, while Cathy stood weeping beside me. At last it was done. I stirred up the ashes, and interred them under a shovelful of coals ; and she mutely, and with a sense of intense injury, retired to her private apartment. I descended to tell my master that the young lady's qualm of sickness was almost gone, but I judge it best for her to lie down a while. She wouldn't dine ; but she reappeared at tea, pale and red about the eyes, and marvellously subdued in outward aspect. Next morning I answered the letter by a slip of paper inscribed, " Master Heathcliff is requested to send no more notes to Miss Linton, as she will not receive them." And thenceforth the little boy came with vacant pockets.

CHAPTER XV

SUMMER drew to an end, and early autumn. It was past Michaelmas; but the harvest was late that year, and a few of our fields were still uncleared. Mr. Linton and his daughter would frequently walk out among the reapers. At the carrying of the last sheaves they stayed till dusk, and the evening happening to be chill and damp, my master caught a bad cold, that settled obstinately on his lungs, and confined him indoors throughout the whole of the winter, nearly without intermission.

Poor Cathy, frightened from her little romance, had been considerably sadder and duller since its abandonment; and her father insisted on her reading less, and taking more exercise. She had his companionship no longer. I esteemed it a duty to supply its lack, as much as possible, with mine—an inefficient substitute, for I could only spare two or three hours from my numerous diurnal occupations to follow her footsteps, and then my society was obviously less desirable than his.

One grey afternoon, in October or the beginning of November, I requested my young lady to forgo her ramble, because I was certain of showers. She refused, and I unwillingly donned a cloak and took my umbrella to accompany her on a stroll to the bottom of the park—a formal walk which she generally affected if low-spirited (and that she invariably was when Mr. Edgar's health had been worse than ordinary). She went sadly on. There was no running or bounding now. And often, from the side of my eye, I could detect her raising a hand and brushing something off her cheek.

"Catherine, why are you crying, love?" I asked, approaching and putting my arm over her shoulder. "You mustn't cry because papa has a cold. Be thankful it is nothing worse."

She now put no further restraint on her tears; her breath was stifled by sobs.

"Oh, it *will* be something worse!" she said. "And what shall I do when papa and you leave me, and I am by myself? How life will be changed, how dreary the world will be, when papa and you are dead!"

"None can tell whether you won't die before us," I replied. "It's wrong to anticipate evil. We'll hope there are years and years to come before any of us go. All you have to do is to wait well on your father, and cheer him by letting him see you cheerful, and avoid giving him anxiety on any subject. Mind that, Cathy! I'll not disguise but you might kill him if you were wild and reckless, and cherished a foolish, fanciful affection for the son of a person who would be glad to have him in his grave, and allowed him to discover that you fretted over the separation he has judged it expedient to make."

"I fret about nothing on earth except papa's illness," answered my companion. "I care for nothing in comparison with papa. And I'll never—never—oh, never, while I have my senses, do an act or say a word to vex him. I love him better than myself, Ellen, and I know it by this: I pray every night that I may live after him, because I would rather be miserable than that he should be. That proves I love him better than myself."

"Good words," I replied. "But deeds must prove it also. And after he is well, remember you don't forget resolutions formed in the hour of fear."

As we talked, we neared a door that opened on the road; and my young lady, lightening into sunshine again, climbed up and seated herself on the top of the wall, reaching over to gather some hips that bloomed scarlet on the summit branches of the wild rose trees shadowing the highway side. The lower fruit had disappeared, but only birds could touch the upper, except from Cathy's present station. In stretching to pull them, her hat fell off, and as the door was locked she proposed scrambling down to recover it. I bade her be cautious lest she got a fall, and she nimbly disappeared. She was still trying to clamber back when I heard the sound of a horse approaching.

"Who is that?" I whispered.

"Ellen, I wish you could open the door," whispered back my companion anxiously.

"Ho, Miss Linton!" cried a deep voice (the rider's). "I'm glad to meet you. Don't be in haste to enter, for I have an explanation to ask and obtain."

"I shan't speak to you, Mr. Heathcliff," answered Catherine. "Papa says you are a wicked man, and you hate both him and me; and Ellen says the same."

"That is nothing to the purpose," said Heathcliff. (He it was.) "I don't hate my son, I suppose, and it is concerning him that I demand your attention. Yes, you have cause to blush. Two or three months since were you not in the habit of writing to Linton—making love in play, eh? You deserved, both of you, flogging for that— you especially, the elder, and less sensitive, as it turns out. I've got your letters, and if you give me any pertness I'll send them to your father. I presume you grew weary of the amusement and dropped it, didn't you? Well, you dropped Linton with it into a Slough of Despond. He was in earnest—in love, really. As true as I live, he's dying for you, breaking his heart at your fickleness—not figuratively, but actually. He'll be under the sod before summer unless you restore him."

"How can you lie so glaringly to the poor child?" I called from the inside. "Pray ride on!—Miss Cathy, I'll knock the lock off with a stone. You won't believe that vile nonsense. You can feel in yourself it is impossible that a person should die for love of a stranger."

"I was not aware there were eavesdroppers," muttered the detected villain. "Worthy Mrs. Dean, I like you, but I don't like your double-dealing," he added aloud. "How could *you* lie so glaringly as to affirm I hated the 'poor child', and invent bugbear stories to terrify her from my door-stones? Catherine Linton (the very name warms me), my bonny lass, I shall be from home all this week; go and see if I have not spoken the truth; do—there's a darling! I swear, on my salvation, that my son is going to his grave, and none but you can save him!"

The lock gave way, and I issued out.

"I swear Linton is dying," repeated Heathcliff, looking hard at me. "And grief and disappointment are hastening his death. Nelly, if you won't let her go, you can walk over yourself. But I shall not return till this time next week; and I think your master himself would scarcely object to her visiting her cousin."

"Come in," said I, taking Cathy by the arm and forcing her to re-enter; for she lingered, viewing with troubled eyes the features of the speaker, too stern to express his inward deceit.

He pushed his horse close, and bending down, observed:
"Miss Catherine, I'll own to you that I have little

patience with Linton; and Hareton and Joseph have less. I'll own that he's with a harsh set. He pines for kindness as well as love, and a kind word from you would be his best medicine. Don't mind Mrs. Dean's cruel cautions, but be generous and contrive to see him. He dreams of you day and night, and cannot be persuaded that you don't hate him, since you neither write nor call.''

I closed the door, and rolled a stone to assist the loosened lock in holding it; and spreading my umbrella, I drew my charge underneath, for the rain began to drive through the moaning branches of the trees, and warned us to avoid delay. Our hurry prevented any comment on the encounter with Heathcliff as we stretched towards home, but I divined instinctively that Catherine's heart was clouded now in double darkness. Her features were so sad they did not seem hers. She evidently regarded what she heard as every syllable true.

The master had retired to rest before we came in. Cathy stole to his room to inquire how he was; he had fallen asleep. She returned and asked me to sit with her in the library. We took our tea together, and afterwards she lay down on the rug, and told me not to talk for she was weary. I got a book, and pretended to read. As soon as she supposed me absorbed in my occupation she recommenced her silent weeping; it appeared, at present, her favourite diversion. I suffered her to enjoy it a while; then I expostulated, deriding and ridiculing all Mr. Heathcliff's assertions about his son, as if I were certain she would coincide. Alas! I had not skill to counteract the effect his account had produced; it was just what he intended.

"You may be right, Ellen," she answered, "but I shall never feel at ease till I know. And I must tell Linton it is not my fault that I don't write, and convince him that I shall not change."

What use were anger and protestations against her silly credulity? We parted that night hostile, but next day beheld me on the road to Wuthering Heights by the side of my wilful young mistress's pony. I couldn't bear to witness her sorrow, to see her pale dejected countenance and heavy eyes; and I yielded, in the faint hope that Linton himself might prove, by his reception of us, how little of the tale was founded on fact.

CHAPTER XVI

THE rainy night had ushered in a misty morning, half frost, half drizzle, and temporary brooks crossed our path, gurgling from uplands. My feet were thoroughly wetted. I was cross and low—exactly the humour suited for making the most of these disagreeable things. We entered the farmhouse by the kitchen way, to ascertain whether Mr. Heathcliff were really absent, because I put slight faith in his own affirmation.

Joseph seemed sitting in a sort of elysium alone, beside a roaring fire, a quart of ale on the table near him, bristling with large pieces of toasted oat-cake, and his black, short pipe in his mouth. Catherine ran to his hearth to warm herself. I asked if the master was in.

" Na-ay ! " he snarled, or rather screamed through his nose. "Na-ay! yah mun goa back whear yah coom frough."

" Joseph ! " cried a peevish voice, simultaneously with me, from the inner room. " How often am I to call you? There are only a few red ashes now. Joseph ! Come this moment."

Vigorous puffs and a resolute stare into the grate

declared he had no ear for this appeal. The house-keeper and Hareton were invisible—one gone on an errand, and the other at his work probably. We knew Linton's tones, and entered.

"Oh, I hope you'll die in a garret, starved to death," said the boy, mistaking our approach for that of his negligent attendant.

He stopped on observing his error. His cousin flew to him.

"Is that you, Miss Linton?" he said, raising his head from the arm of the great chair in which he reclined. "No, don't kiss me; it takes my breath. Dear me! Papa said you would call," continued he, after recovering a little from Catherine's embrace, while she stood by looking very contrite. "Will you shut the door, if you please? You left it open; and those—those *detestable* creatures won't bring coals to the fire. It's so cold."

I stirred up the cinders, and fetched a scuttleful myself. The invalid complained of being covered with ashes; but he had a tiresome cough, and looked feverish and ill, so I did not rebuke his temper.

"Well, Linton," murmured Catherine, when his corrugated brow relaxed, "are you glad to see me? Can I do you any good?"

"Why didn't you come before?" he asked. "You should have come, instead of writing. It tired me dreadfully writing those long letters. I'd far rather have talked to you. Now, I can neither bear to talk nor anything else. I wonder where Zillah is! Will you"—looking at me—"step into the kitchen and see?"

"Nobody is out there but Joseph," said I.

"I want to drink," he exclaimed fretfully, turning away. "Zillah is constantly gadding off to Gimmerton since papa went; it's miserable! And I'm obliged to come down here: they resolved never to hear me upstairs."

"Is your father attentive to you, Master Heathcliff?"
I asked, perceiving Catherine to be checked in her friendly
advances.

"Attentive? He makes *them* a little more attentive at
least," he cried. "The wretches! Do you know, Miss
Linton, that brute Hareton laughs at me! I hate him!
Indeed, I hate them all! They are odious beings."

Cathy began searching for some water; she lighted on a
pitcher in the dresser, filled a tumbler, and brought it.
He bade her add a spoonful of wine from a bottle on the
table; and having swallowed a small portion, appeared
more tranquil, and said she was very kind.

"And are you glad to see me?" asked she, reiterating
her former question, and pleased to detect a faint dawn of
a smile.

"Yes, I am. It's something new to hear a voice like
yours!" he replied. "But I have been vexed because
you wouldn't come. And papa swore it was owing to me.
He called me a pitiful, shuffling, worthless thing, and said
you despised me, and if he had been in my place he would
have been more the master of the Grange than your father
by this time. But you don't despise me, do you,
Miss——"

"I wish you would call me Catherine, or Cathy," interrupted my young lady. "Despise you? No! Next to
papa and Ellen, I love you better than anybody living.
I don't love Mr. Heathcliff, though; and I dare not come
when he returns. Will he stay away many days?"

"Not many," answered Linton; "but he goes on to the
moors frequently since the shooting season commenced,
and you might spend an hour or two with me in his
absence. Do say you will. I think I should not be peevish
with you. You'd not provoke me, and you'd always be
ready to help me, wouldn't you?"

"Yes," said Catherine, stroking his long, soft hair.

" If I could only get papa's consent I'd spend half my time with you. Pretty Linton! I wish you were my brother."

" And then you would like me as well as your father? " observed he, more cheerfully. " But papa says you would love me better than him and all the world if you were my wife; so I'd rather you were that."

" No, I should never love anybody better than papa," she returned gravely. " And people hate their wives sometimes, but not their sisters and brothers; and if you were the latter you would live with us, and papa would be as fond of you as he is of me."

Linton firmly denied that people ever hated their wives; but Cathy affirmed they did, and in her wisdom instanced his own father's aversion to her aunt. I endeavoured to stop her thoughtless tongue. I couldn't succeed till everything she knew was out. Master Heathcliff, much irritated, asserted her relation was false.

" Papa told me, and papa does not tell falsehoods," she answered pertly.

" *My* pap scorns yours! " cried Linton. " He calls him a sneaking fool."

" Yours is a wicked man," retorted Catherine, " and you are very naughty to dare to repeat what he says. He must be wicked to have made Aunt Isabella leave him as she did."

" She didn't leave him," said the boy. " You shan't contradict me."

" She did," cried my young lady.

" Well, I'll tell *you* something," said Linton. " Your mother hated your father. Now then."

" Oh! " exclaimed Catherine, too enraged to continue.

" And she loved mine," added he.

" You little liar! I hate you now! " she panted, and her face grew red with passion.

" She did! she did!" sang Linton, sinking into the recess of his chair, and leaning back his head to enjoy the agitation of the other disputant, who stood behind.

" Hush, Master Heathcliff!" I said. " That's your father's tale too, I suppose."

" It isn't. You hold your tongue!" he answered.— " She did! she did, Catherine! She did! She did!"

Cathy, beside herself, gave the chair a violent push, and caused him to fall against one arm. He was immediately seized by a suffocating cough that soon ended his triumph. It lasted so long that it frightened even me. As to his cousin, she wept with all her might, aghast at the mischief she had done, though she said nothing. I held him till the fit exhausted itself. Then he thrust me away, and leant his head down silently. Catherine quelled her lamentations also, took a seat opposite, and looked solemnly into the fire.

" How do you feel now, Master Heathcliff? " I inquired, after waiting ten minutes.

" I wish *she* felt as I do," he replied—" spiteful, cruel thing! Hareton never touches me; he never struck me in his life. And I was better today; and there—— " His voice died in a whimper.

" *I* didn't strike you!" muttered Cathy, chewing her lip to prevent another burst of emotion.

He sighed and moaned like one under great suffering, and kept it up for a quarter of an hour, on purpose to distress his cousin, apparently, for whenever he caught a stifled sob from her he put renewed pain and pathos into the inflections of his voice.

" I'm sorry I hurt you, Linton," said she at length, racked beyond endurance. " But *I* couldn't have been hurt by that little push, and I had no idea that you could either. You're not much hurt, are you, Linton? Don't

let me go home thinking I've done you harm.   Answer !
Speak to me ! "

" I can't speak to you," he murmured.   " You've hurt
me so that I shall lie awake all night choking with this
cough.   If you had it you'd know what it was; but *you'll*
be comfortably asleep while I'm in agony, and nobody
near me.   I wonder how you would like to pass those
fearful nights."   And he began to wail aloud, for very pity
of himself.

" Since you are in the habit of passing dreadful nights,"
I said, " it won't be miss who spoils your ease; you'd be
the same had she never come.   However, she shall not
disturb you again; and perhaps you'll get quieter when
we leave you."

" Must I go ? " asked Catherine dolefully, bending over
him.   " Do you want me to go, Linton ? "

" You can't alter what you've done," he replied pet-
tishly, shrinking from her, " unless you alter it for the
worse by teasing me into a fever."

She lingered, and resisted my persuasions to departure a
tiresome while; but as he neither looked up nor spoke, she
finally made a movement to the door, and I followed.
We were recalled by a scream.   Linton had slid from his
seat on to the hearth-stone, and lay writhing in the mere
perverseness of an indulged plague of a child, determined
to be as grievous and harassing as it can.   I saw at once
it would be folly to attempt humouring him.   Not so my
companion.   She ran back in terror, knelt down, and
cried, and soothed, and entreated, till he grew quiet from
lack of breath, by no means from compunction at dis-
tressing her.

" I shall lift him on to the settle," I said, " and he may
roll about as he pleases.   We can't stop to watch him.
I hope you are satisfied, Miss Cathy, that *you* are not the
person to benefit him, and that his condition of health is

not occasioned by attachment to you. Now, then, there he is! Come away. As soon as he knows there is nobody by to care for his nonsense, he'll be glad to lie still."

She placed a cushion under his head, and offered him some water. He rejected the latter, and tossed uneasily on the former, as if it were a stone or a block of wood. She tried to put it more comfortably.

"I can't do with that," he said; "it's not high enough."

Catherine brought another to lay above it.

"That's *too* high," murmured the provoking thing.

"How must I arrange it, then?" she asked despairingly.

He twined himself up to her, as she half knelt by the settle, and converted her shoulder into a support.

"Now, that won't do," I said. "You'll be content with the cushion, Master Heathcliff. Miss has wasted too much time on you already; we cannot remain five minutes longer."

"Yes, yes; we can!" replied Cathy. "He's good and patient now. He's beginning to think I shall have far greater misery than he will tonight if I believe he is the worse for my visit, and then I dare not come again.—Tell the truth about it, Linton; for I mustn't come if I have hurt you."

"You must come, to cure me," he answered. "You ought to come, because you have hurt me; you know you have extremely. I was not as ill when you entered as I am at present—was I?"

"But you've made yourself ill by crying and being in a passion."

"I didn't do it all," said his cousin. "However, we'll be friends now."

"And you want me—you would wish to see me sometimes, really?"

"I told you I did," he replied impatiently. "Sit on

the settle and let me lean on your knee. That's as mamma used to do, whole afternoons together. Sit quite still and don't talk; but you may sing a song, if you can sing, or you may say a nice long interesting ballad—one of those you promised to teach me—or a story. I'd rather have a ballad, though. Begin."

Catherine repeated the longest she could remember. The employment pleased both mightily. Linton would have another, and after that another, notwithstanding my strenuous objections; and so they went on until the clock struck twelve, and we heard Hareton in the court, returning for his dinner.

"And tomorrow, Catherine—will you be here tomorrow?" asked young Heathcliff, holding her frock as she rose reluctantly.

"No," I answered, "nor next day neither."

She however, gave a different response evidently, for his forehead cleared as she stooped and whispered in his ear.

"You won't go tomorrow, recollect, miss," I commenced, when we were out of the house. "You are not dreaming of it, are you?"

She smiled.

"Oh, I'll take good care," I continued. "I'll have that lock mended, and you can escape by no way else."

"I can get over the wall," she said, laughing. "The Grange is not a prison, Ellen, and you are not my gaoler. And besides, I'm almost seventeen; I'm a woman. And I'm certain Linton would recover quickly if he had me to look after him. I'm older than he is, you know, and wiser—less childish, am I not? And he'll soon do as I direct him, with some slight coaxing. He's a pretty little darling when he's good. I'd make such a pet of him if he were mine. We should never quarrel, should we, after we were used to each other? Don't you like him, Ellen?"

"Like him!" I exclaimed. "The worst-tempered bit

of a sickly slip that ever struggled into its teens.   Happily, as Mr. Heathcliff conjectured, he'll not win twenty. I doubt whether he'll see spring, indeed.   And small loss to his family whenever he drops off.   And lucky it is for us that his father took him : the kinder he was treated, the more tedious and selfish he'd be.   I'm glad you have no chance of having him for a husband, Miss Catherine."

My companion waxed serious at hearing this speech. To speak of his death so regardlessly wounded her feelings.

" He's younger than I," she answered, after a pro-tracted pause of meditation, " and he ought to live the longest.   It's only a cold that ails him—the same as papa has.   You say papa will get better, and why shouldn't he ? "

" Well, well," I cried, " after all, we needn't trouble ourselves ; for listen, miss—and mind I'll keep my word : if you attempt going to Wuthering Heights again, with or without me, I shall inform Mr. Linton ; and unless he allows it, the intimacy with your cousin must not be revived."

" It has been revived," muttered Cathy sulkily.

" Must not be continued, then," I said.

" We'll see," was her reply ; and she set off at a gallop, leaving me to toil in the rear.

We both reached home before our dinner-time ; my master supposed we had been wandering through the park, and therefore he demanded no explanation of our absence.

For the next three weeks I was laid up with a cold. The wetting I had received on the way to Wuthering Heights had done the mischief.   My little mistress be-haved like an angel, dividing her day between her father and me.   No amusement usurped a minute.   She neg-lected her meals, her studies, and her play, and she was the fondest nurse that ever watched.   But I generally needed nothing after six o'clock, and the master retired early, so the evenings were her own.   Poor thing ! I never considered what she did with herself after tea.   And though I sometimes remarked a fresh colour on her cheek, when she looked in to bid me good-night, I laid it to the charge of a hot fire in the library.

At last I was able to quit my chamber and move about the house.   On the first occasion of my sitting up in the evening, I observed that she began to grow restless.

" Ellen, are you not tired ? " she asked, after glancing several times towards the window.   " Hadn't you better lie down now ?   You'll be sick keeping up so long."   I protested that I was not at all tired, and asked her to read to me.   She did so for a while, but it was evident that she had no relish for her occupation.   At eight o'clock she laid down her book, began yawning and stretching, complained of weariness and a headache, and saying she intended to lie down, went upstairs and left me.   I remained a long while, and before retiring, went to ask how she was.   Her chamber was empty.   Nor could I discover her anywhere else in the house.

I returned to her apartment, extinguished my candle, and seated myself in the window.   The moon shone bright ; and presently I detected a figure creeping along the inner fence of the park.   It stepped into the light, and I saw that it was one of the grooms.   He stood a considerable period viewing the carriage-way through the grounds, then started off at a brisk pace, as if he had detected something.   Presently he reappeared, leading Miss Cathy's pony, and there she was, just dismounted, walking by its side.   The man took his charge stealthily across the grass by the stable.   Cathy entered by the casement window of the drawing-room, and glided noiselessly upstairs to where I awaited her.   The surprise petrified her an instant.

" My dear Miss Cathy," I began, too vividly impressed

by her recent kindness to break into a scold; "where have you been riding out at this late hour? You must have been doing wrong, or you wouldn't have deceived me."

She burst into tears and threw her arms round my neck.

"Well, Ellen, I was so afraid of your being angry. Promise not to be angry, and you shall know the truth. I hate to hide it."

We sat down in the window-seat. I assured her I would not scold whatever her secret might be, and I guessed it, of course : so she commenced—

"I've been to Wuthering Heights, Ellen, and I've never missed going a day since you were ill. I was generally there by half-past six, and stayed till half-past eight. The groom promised to keep silence about my excursions. I told him how my cousin wished me to visit him, because he was sick, and couldn't come to the Grange, and how papa would object to my going. You mustn't scold him either, mind.

"And truly, Ellen, it was not to please myself that I went. Now and then I was happy—once a week, perhaps. At first I expected there would be sad work persuading you to let me keep my word to Linton, for I had engaged to call again next day when we quitted him. But as you stayed upstairs on the morrow, I escaped that trouble.

"On my second visit Linton seemed in lively spirits. Zillah, the housekeeper, made us a clean room and a good fire, and told us that as Joseph was out at a prayer-meeting and Hareton away with his dogs—robbing our wood of pheasant, as I heard afterwards—we might do as we liked. She brought me some warm wine and some gingerbread; and Linton and I talked and laughed so merrily together, and found so much to say, and he looked so pretty. We planned where we would go, and what we would do in summer. I needn't repeat that, because you would call it silly. But later, when we played some games, he became peevish and sulky because I beat him every time. In the end, however, we made it up, and kissed, and were friends; and I promised to come again the next evening. ' I shall have another happy evening,' I told myself, ' and, what delights me more, my pretty Linton's well.'

" It was a beautiful moonlight after tea on the morrow. I rode fast over the moors, and I was trotting up their garden when that fellow Earnshaw met me, took my bridle, and bade me go in by the front entrance. He patted Minny's neck, and said she was a bonny beast, and appeared as if he wanted me to speak to him. I only told him to leave my horse alone, or it would kick him. However, he moved forward to open the door for me, and as he raised the latch, he looked at the inscription above, and said with a stupid mixture of awkwardness and elation—

" ' Miss Catherine, I can read yon now.'

" ' Wonderful ! ' I exclaimed. ' Pray let us hear you; you *are* grown clever.'

" He spelt and drawled over the syllables, the name, ' Hareton Earnshaw.'

" ' And the figures ? ' I cried encouragingly, perceiving he came to a dead halt.

" ' I cannot tell them yet,' he answered.

" ' Oh, you dunce ! ' I said, laughing at his failure.

" The fool stared, a grin hovering over his lips, and a scowl gathering over his eyes, as if uncertain whether he might not join in my mirth—whether it were not pleasant familiarity, or what it really was, contempt. I settled his doubt by ordering him to go away, for I came to see Linton not him, and he skulked off a picture of mortified vanity."

" Stop, Miss Catherine, dear ! " I interrupted. " I shall not scold, but I do not like your conduct here. If you had remembered that Hareton was your cousin as much as Master Heathcliff, you would have felt how improper it was to behave in that way. You had made him ashamed of his ignorance before, I have no doubt, and he wished to remedy it and please—which was very praiseworthy. To sneer at his imperfect attempt was very bad breeding. Had you been brought up as he has been, would you be less rude and ignorant?"

"Well, Ellen, you won't cry about it, will you?" she exclaimed, surprised at my earnestness. "But wait, and you shall hear if he conned his ABC to please me, and if it were worth being civil to the brute.—I entered and found Linton lying on the settle, looking very pale. He welcomed me by saying that he was feeling very ill, and that I must do all the talking tonight, while he listened. I had brought him some of my nicest books, and was about to read to him when Earnshaw burst in, seized Linton by the arm, and swung him off the seat.

"'Get to thine own room!' he cried, in a voice almost inarticulate with passion. 'Take her there if she comes to see thee; thou shalln't keep me out of this. Begone wi' ye both!' And he almost threw Linton into the kitchen. I followed. He kicked the door after me, and shut us out. Linton, white and trembling (he did not look pretty then, Ellen), grasped the handle and started shaking it, crying, 'If you don't let me in I'll kill you! Devil! devil! I'll kill you! I'll kill you!'

"I took hold of his hands, and tried to pull him away, but he only shrieked the louder. Blood gushed from his mouth, and he fell to the ground. I ran into the yard, sick with terror, calling for Zillah as loud as I could. She came out to me from the cowshed, where she was milking, and inquired what was to do. I hadn't the breath to explain. Dragging her in, I looked about for Linton. Hareton had come in to examine the mischief he had caused, and was carrying the thing upstairs. I ascended after, but Hareton stopped me at the top of the stairs, and said I shouldn't go in. I must go home. I exclaimed that he had killed Linton, and I would enter. Joseph, who had now appeared from somewhere, declared that I should do 'no sich stuff'. I stood crying, and defying them all; and then Zillah took hold of me and nearly carried me out of the house. At length they compelled me to depart. I mounted my pony and rode away. But I had not gone two hundred yards before Hareton issued suddenly from the shadow of the roadside, and checked Minnie and took hold of me.

" ' Miss Catherine, I'm ill grieved,' he began, ' but its rayther too bad—— '

" I gave him a cut with my whip, thinking perhaps he would murder me. He let go, thundering one of his horrid curses, and I galloped home more than half out of my senses.

" I didn't go to Wuthering Heights the next evening. But on the third day I took courage. I went at five o'clock and walked, fancying I might creep up to Linton's room unobserved. However, the dogs gave notice of my approach. Zillah received me, and said ' the lad was mending nicely '. She showed me into a small, tidy, carpeted apartment, where, to my inexpressible joy, I beheld Linton laid on a little sofa, reading one of my books. But he would neither speak nor look at me for a whole hour; and when he did open his mouth it was to utter the falsehood that I had occasioned the whole uproar, and Hareton was not to blame. I was so angry, I got up and walked out of the room (which he had not expected), and would not heed his cries calling me back.

" But the next day I was so miserable and so sorry for him, that I went back and made it up with him. He said I must make allowances for his moodiness, as it was more

the effect of his illness than his own fault.   He said it was
so much easier for me to be sweet and kind and good-
tempered, because I was so strong and healthy, and had
been surrounded by love all my life. I felt there was
much truth in this, and I felt I must forgive him again.
Poor Linton ! He'll never let his friends be at ease,
because he'll never be at ease himself.—I have always
gone to his parlour since that night, because his father
returned the day after.—Now, Ellen, you have heard all.
I can't be prevented from going to Wuthering Heights
except by inflicting misery on two people ; whereas, if
you'll only not tell papa, my going need disturb the
tranquillity of none.—You'll not tell, will you ?   It'll be
very heartless if you do."

" I'll make up my mind on that point tomorrow, Miss
Catherine," I said.   " It requires some study.   You go to
your rest."

I thought it over aloud in my master's presence, walking
straight from her room to his, and relating the whole
story, except her conversations with her cousin, and any
mention of Hareton. Mr. Linton was greatly alarmed
and distressed. In the morning Catherine learned of my
betrayal of her confidence, and she learned also that her
secret visits were to end. In vain she wept and writhed
against the verdict, but Mr. Linton would not give way.

CHAPTER XVII

" THESE things happened last winter, sir," said Mrs.
Dean—" hardly more than a year ago. Last winter I did
not think, at another twelve months end, I should be

amusing a stranger by relating them.—Yet who knows how long you'll be a stranger? You're too young to rest always contented, living by yourself, and I'm sure no one could see Catherine Linton and not love her. You smile; but why do you look so lively and interested when I talk about her? and why have you asked me to hang her picture over your fireplace? and why—— "

" Stop, my good friend ! " I cried. " It may be very possible that *I* should love her, but would she love me? I doubt too much to venture my tranquillity by running into temptation. And then my home is not here. I belong to the busy world, and to its arms I must return.— Go on. Was Catherine obedient to her father's commands? "

She was (continued the housekeeper). Her affection for him was still the chief sentiment of her heart; and he spoke without anger—he spoke in the deep tenderness of one about to leave his treasure amid perils and foes, where his remembered words would be the only aid he could bequeath to guide her.

Regarding Catherine's attachment to her cousin, he sometimes questioned me about him.

" Is he changed for the better, Ellen? Is there a prospect of his health improving as he grows older? "

" He is very delicate, sir," I replied, " and scarcely likely to reach manhood; but this I can say, he does not resemble his father. If Miss Catherine had the misfortune to marry him, he would not be beyond her control, unless she were very foolish and indulgent. However, master, you'll have plenty of time to get acquainted with him, and see whether he would suit her. It wants four years and more to his being of age."

Edgar sighed, and walking to the window, looked out towards Gimmerton Kirk.

" No," he said, his face still averted; " time for me is

running short. What am I to do for Cathy? How must I quit her?—I'd not care one moment for his being Heathcliff's son," he continued, coming back into the room, " if he would console her for my loss. I'd not care that Heathcliff gained his ends, and triumphed in robbing me of my last blessing. But should Linton prove unworthy—only a feeble tool to his father—I cannot abandon her to him."

Spring advanced, yet my master gained no real strength, though he resumed his walks in the grounds with his daughter. He wrote to Linton, expressing his great desire to see him; and had the invalid been presentable, I've no doubt his father would have permitted him to come. As it was, being instructed, he returned an answer, intimating that Mr. Heathcliff objected to his calling at the Grange; but his uncle's kind remembrances delighted him, and he hoped to meet him sometimes in his rambles, and personally petitioned that his cousin and he might not remain so utterly divided. ' We have done nothing to deserve this separation,' he wrote; ' you have no reason to dislike me, or be angry with me. Dear uncle, send me a kind note tomorrow, and leave to join you anywhere you please, except Thrushcross Grange.'

Edgar, though he felt for the boy, could not grant his request, because he could not accompany Catherine. He said in summer perhaps they might meet. Meanwhile he wished him to continue writing. Linton complied, and had he been unrestrained, would probably have spoiled all by filling his letters with complaints and lamentations; but his father kept a sharp eye on him, and of course insisted on every line my master sent being shown. So instead of penning his peculiar personal sufferings, he harped on the cruel obligation of being held asunder from his friend and love, and gently intimated that Mr. Linton must allow an interview with her soon, or he should fear he was purposely deceiving him with empty promises.

Cathy was a powerful ally at home, and between them they at length persuaded my master to allow them to walk or ride together once a week—under my guardianship, for June still found my master's strength declining. Though he had set aside yearly a portion of his income for my young lady's fortune, he had a natural desire that she might retain—or at least in a short time return to—the house of her ancestors; and he considered her only prospect of doing so was by a union with his heir. He had no idea that the latter was failing almost as fast as himself; and for my part I believed that the young man must be rallying, when he actually mentioned riding or walking on the moors. I could not picture a father treating his dying child so tyrannically and wickedly as I afterwards learned Heathcliff had treated him, to compel this apparent eagerness, his efforts redoubling the more imminently his avaricious plans were threatened with defeat by death.

§

Summer was already past its prime when, with Edgar's reluctant consent, Catherine and I set out on our first ride to join her cousin. It was a close, sultry day. Our place of meeting had been fixed at the guide-stone by the crossroads. On arriving there, however, a herd-boy, dispatched as a messenger, told us that ' Master Linton'd be much obliged if we'd gang a bit further to meet him?' But when we reached him, it was scarcely a mile from his own door. He had no horse. He lay on the heath awaiting our approach, and did not rise till we came within a few yards. Then he walked so feebly, and looked so wasted and pale, that the ejaculation of joy on Miss Cathy's lips changed to one of alarm. He clutched her hand as if needing its support, while his large blue eyes wandered timidly over her.

"Oh, Linton, you have been worse? You are thinner, and——"

"I'm tired," he interrupted hurriedly. "It's too hot for walking; let us rest here. In the morning I often feel sick. Papa says I grow too fast."

Badly satisfied, Cathy sat down, and made him recline against her, while she tried to cheer him with her conversation. But Linton hardly seemed to be listening to her. An indefinite change had come over his whole manner and person. The pettishness that might be caressed into fondness had yielded to a listless apathy. Cathy perceived, as well as I did, that he held it rather a punishment than a gratification to endure our company, and she made no scruple of proposing presently to depart. That proposal roused Linton from his lethargy. He glanced fearfully towards the Heights, begging her to remain another half-hour at least.

"But I think you'd be more comfortable at home than sitting here," said Cathy. "If I could amuse you, I'd willingly stay."

"Stay to rest yourself," he replied. "And, Catherine, don't think or say I'm very unwell. It's the heavy weather and heat that make me dull. Tell uncle I'm in tolerable health, will you?"

"I'll tell him *you* say so, Linton; I couldn't affirm that you are," observed my young lady, wondering at his pertinacious assertion of what was evidently an untruth.

"And be here again next Thursday," continued he. "And give him my best thanks for permitting you to come. And——and if you *did* meet my father, don't lead him to suppose I've been silent and stupid. He'll be angry."

"I care nothing for his anger," exclaimed Catherine.

"But I do," said her cousin, shuddering. "Don't provoke him against me, for he is very hard."

"Is he severe on you, Master Heathcliff?" I inquired. "Has he grown weary of indulgence, and passed from passive to active hatred?"

Linton looked at me, but did not answer; and after keeping her seat by his side another ten minutes (during which his head fell drowsily on his breast and he uttered nothing but suppressed moans of exhaustion or pain), Cathy began to seek solace by looking for bilberries.

"Is it half an hour now, Ellen?" she whispered at last. "I can't tell why we should stay. He's asleep, and papa will be wanting us back."

"We can't leave him asleep," I answered. "Till he wakes we must be patient. It seems to me you longing for poor Linton's company has soon evaporated."

"Why did *he* wish to see me?" returned Cath rine. "It's just as if it were a task he was compelled to perform for fear his father should scold him. But I'm hardly going to come and see him just to please Mr. Heathcliff, whatever reason he may have for ordering Linton to undergo this penance. And though I'm glad he's in better health, I'm sorry he's so much less pleasant, and so much less affectionate to me."

"You think he is in better health, then?" I asked.

"Yes," she answered, "because he always made a great deal of his sufferings, you know. He is not tolerably well, as he told me to tell papa; but he's better very likely."

"There I disagree with you, Miss Cathy. I should conjecture him to be far worse."

Here Linton awoke and sat up trembling, saying he thought he had heard his father's voice.

"There is no one here but us," Catherine assured him. "Only Ellen and I were disputing about your health. Are you truly better, Linton—*truly*?"

G

" Yes, yes, I am ! " replied Linton, tears gushing from his eyes.

Cathy rose. " For today we must part," she said. " And I won't conceal that I've been sadly disappointed in our meeting, though I'll mention it to no one but you— not that I stand in awe of Mr. Heathcliff."

" Hush ! " murmured Linton ; " for God's sake, hush ! He's coming ! " And he clung to her arm, striving to detain her ; but at that announcement she hastily disengaged herself, and with a promise to be there again in a week, she mounted her pony.

And so we left him, scarcely conscious of our departure, so absorbed was he in anticipating his father's approach.

Before we reached home, Catherine's displeasure softened into a perplexed sensation of pity and regret, blended with vague, uneasy doubts about Linton's circumstances. My master requested an account of our ongoings. His nephew's message of thanks was duly delivered, Miss Cathy gently touching on the rest. I also threw little light on his inquiries, for I hardly knew what to hide and what to reveal.

§

In the seven days that followed, Edgar Linton's health declined rapidly, and Miss Cathy's next excursion to her cousin was made very reluctantly ; for, realising now that his death was approaching, she grudged every moment that did not find her leaning over her father's pillow, or seated by his side.

We discovered Linton watching at the same spot he had selected before. He received us with greater animation on this occasion ; but it looked to me like the animation of fear.

" It is late," he said, speaking shortly and with difficulty.

" Is not your father very ill? I thought you would not come? "

" *Why* won't you be candid? " cried Catherine, swallowing her greeting. " Why cannot you say at once you don't want me? It is very strange, Linton, that for the second time you have brought me here for no reason, apparently, but to distress us both."

Linton glanced at her, half supplicating, half ashamed; but his cousin's patience was not sufficient to bear this enigmatical behaviour. " My father *is* very ill," she said; " and why am I called from his bedside? Why didn't you send to absolve me from my promise? Come! I desire an explanation. I cannot dance attendance on your affections now."

" My affections! " he murmured; " what are they? For heaven's sake, Catherine, don't look so angry! Despise me as much as you please. I am a worthless, cowardly wretch.—I can't be scorned enough; but I'm too mean for your anger. Hate my father, and spare me for contempt."

" Nonsense! " cried Catherine, in a passion. " Foolish, silly boy! Heavens! he trembles, as if I were really going to touch him. Get off! I shall return home. It is folly to be dragging you from your hearth-stone, and pretending—what we do pretend? Let go my frock.— Ellen, tell him how disgraceful this conduct is.—Rise, and don't degrade yourself into an abject reptile— *don't*."

With straining face and an expression of agony, Linton had thrown himself on the ground.

" Oh! " he sobbed. " I cannot bear it! Catherine! Catherine, I'm a traitor too, and I dare not tell you. But leave me and I shall be killed! Dear Catherine, my life is in your hands, and you have said you love me, and if you did, it wouldn't hurt you. You'll not go then, kind,

sweet, good Catherine? And perhaps you *will* consent—
and he'll let me die with you!"

My young lady, witnessing his intense anguish, was
moved to pity and alarm.

"Consent to what?" she asked. "To stay? Tell me
the meaning of this strange talk, and I will. Be calm and
frank, and confess all that weighs on your heart. You
wouldn't injure me, would you, Linton? I'll believe
you are a coward for yourself, but not a cowardly betrayer
of your best friend."

"But my father threatened me," gasped the boy,
"and I dread him—I dread him! I *dare* not tell!"

"Oh, well," said Catherine, with scornful compassion,
"keep your secret. *I'm* no coward. Save yourself.
I'm not afraid."

Her magnanimity provoked his tears. He wept wildly,
kissing her supporting hands, and yet could not summon
courage to speak out. I was cogitating what the mystery
might be, when, hearing a rustle among the ling, I looked
up and saw Mr. Heathcliff almost close upon us, descending the Heights. He didn't cast a glance towards my
companions, though they were sufficiently near for Linton's sobs to be audible, but hailing me in an almost
hearty tone, he said—

"It is something to see you so near to my house, Nelly.
How are you at the Grange? The rumour goes," he
added in a lower tone, "that Edgar Linton is on his
deathbed; perhaps they exaggerate his illness?"

"No. My master is dying," I replied; "it is true
enough."

"How long will he last, do you think?" he asked.

"I don't know," I said.

"Because," he continued, looking at the two young
people, who were fixed under his eye—Linton appeared as
if he could not venture to stir or raise his head, and

Catherine could not move on his account—" because that lad yonder seems determined to beat me, and I'd thank his uncle to be quick and go before him. Hullo! has the whelp been playing that game long? I *did* give him some lessons about snivelling. Is he pretty lively with Miss Linton generally?"

"Lively? No; he has shown the greatest distress," I answered. "To see him, I should say that, instead of rambling with his sweetheart on the hills, he ought to be in bed, under the hands of a doctor."

"He shall be in a day or two," muttered Heath-cliff. "But first—— Get up, Linton! get up!" he shouted. "Don't grovel on the ground there. Up, this moment!"

Linton had sunk prostrate again in another paroxysm of helpless fear. He made several efforts to obey, but his little strength was annihilated for the time, and he fell back again with a moan. Mr. Heathcliff advanced, and lifted him to lean against a ridge of turf.

"Now," said he, with curbed ferocity, "I'm getting angry, and if you don't command that paltry spirit of yours—— *Damn* you! get up directly!"

"I will, father," he panted. "Only let me alone, or I shall faint. I've done as you wished, I'm sure. Catherine will tell you that I—that I—have been cheerful.—Ah! keep by me, Catherine. Give me your hand."

"Take mine," said his father. "Stand on your feet. There now; she'll lend you her arm. That's right; look at *her*—— You would imagine I was the devil himself, Miss Linton, to excite such horror. Be so kind as to walk home with him, will you? He shudders if I touch him."

"Linton, dear!" whispered Catherine, "I can't go to Wuthering Heights; papa has forbidden me. He'll not harm you. Why are you so afraid?"

" I can never re-enter that house," he answered. " I'm *not* to re-enter it without you."

" Stop ! " cried his father. " We'll respect Catherine's filial scruples.—Nelly, take him in, and I'll follow your advice concerning the doctor without delay."

" You'll do well," replied I. " But I must remain with my mistress; to mind your son is not my business."

" You are very stiff," said Heathcliff—" I know that; but you'll force me to pinch the baby and make it scream before it moves your charity.—Come, then, my hero. Are you willing to return, escorted by me ? "

He approached once more, and made as if he would seize the fragile being; but, shrinking back, Linton clung to his cousin, and implored her to accompany him, with a frantic importunity that admitted no denial. However I disapproved, I couldn't hinder her. Indeed, how could she have refused him herself ? What was filling him with dread we had no means of discerning; but there he was, powerless under its gripe, and any addition seemed capable of shocking him into idiocy. We reached the threshold. Catherine walked in, and I stood waiting till she had conducted the invalid to a chair, expecting her out immediately, when Mr. Heathcliff, pushing me forward, exclaimed—

" My house is not stricken with the plague, Nelly, and I have a mind to be hospitable today. Sit down, and allow me to shut the door."

He shut and locked it also.

" You shall have tea before you go home," he added. " I am by myself. Hareton is gone with some cattle to the Lees, and Zillah and Joseph are off on a journey of pleasure; and though I'm used to being alone, I'd rather have some interesting company, if I can get it.—Miss Linton, take your seat by *him*. I give you what I have; the present is hardly worth accepting, but I have nothing else to offer. It is Linton I mean. How she does stare ! It's odd what a savage feeling I have to anything that seems afraid of me."

" I'm not afraid of you ! " exclaimed Catherine. She stepped close up, her black eyes flashing with passion and resolution. " Give me that key. I will have it ! " she said. " I wouldn't eat or drink here if I were starving."

Heathcliff had the key in his hand that remained on the table. He looked up, seized with a sort of surprise at her boldness, or possibly reminded by her voice and glance of the person from whom she had inherited it. She snatched at the instrument, and half succeeded in getting it out of his loosened fingers; but her action recalled him to the present—he recovered it speedily.

" Now, Catherine Linton," he said, " stand off, or I shall knock you down, and that will make Mrs. Dean mad."

Regardless of this warning, she captured his closed hand and its contents again. " We *will* go ! " she repeated, exerting her utmost efforts to cause the iron muscles to relax; and finding that her nails made no impression, she applied her teeth pretty sharply. Heathcliff glanced at me a glance that kept me from interfering a moment. Catherine was too intent on his fingers to notice his face. He opened them suddenly, and resigned the object of dispute; but ere she had well secured it, he seized her with the liberated hand, and pulling her on his knee, administered with the other a shower of terrific slaps on both sides of the head, each sufficient to have fulfilled his threat, had she been able to fall.

At this diabolical violence I rushed on him furiously. " You villain ! " I began to cry, " you villain ! " A touch on the chest silenced me. I am stout, and soon put out of breath; and what with that and the rage, I staggered dizzily back, and felt ready to suffocate or to burst a blood-vessel. The scene was over in two minutes.

Catherine, released, put her two hands to her temples, and looked just as if she were not sure whether her ears were off or on. She trembled like a reed, poor thing, and leant against the table perfectly bewildered.

" I know how to chastise children, you see," said the scoundrel grimly, as he stooped to repossess himself of the key, which had dropped to the floor. " Go to Linton now, as I told you, and cry at your ease. I shall be your father tomorrow—all the father you'll have in a few days— and you shall have plenty of that. You can bear plenty; you're no weakling. You shall have a daily taste, if I catch such a devil of a temper in your eyes again ! "

Cathy ran to me instead of Linton, and knelt down and put her burning cheek on my lap, weeping aloud. Her cousin had shrunk into a corner of the settle, as quiet as a mouse, congratulating himself, I dare say, that the correction had lighted on another than him. Mr. Heath-cliff, perceiving us all confounded, rose, and expeditiously made the tea himself. The cups and saucers were laid ready. He poured it out, and handed me a cup.

" Wash away your spleen," he said. " And help your own naughty pet and mine. It is not poisoned, though I prepared it. I'm going out to seek your horses."

Our first thought, on his departure, was to force an exit somewhere. We tried the kitchen door, but that was fastened outside. We looked at the windows; they were too narrow for even Cathy's little figure.

" Master Linton," I cried, seeing we were regularly imprisoned, " you know what your diabolical father is after, and you shall tell us, or I'll box your ears, as he has done your cousin's."

" Yes, Linton, you must tell," said Catherine. " It was for your sake I came, and it will be wickedly ungrateful if you refuse."

" Give me some tea—I'm thirsty—and then I'll tell

you," he answered.—" Mrs. Dean, go away. I don't like you standing over me.—Now, Catherine, you are letting your tears fall into my cup. I won't drink that. Give me another."

Catherine pushed another to him, and wiped her face. I felt disgusted at the little wretch's composure, since he was no longer in terror for himself. The anguish he had exhibited on the moor subsided as soon as ever he entered Wuthering Heights, so I guessed he had been menaced with an awful visitation of wrath, if he failed in decoying us there; and that accomplished, he had no further immediate fears.

" Papa wants us to be married," he continued, after sipping some of the liquid. " And he knows your papa wouldn't let us marry now, and he's afraid of my dying if we wait; so we are to be married in the morning, and you are to stay here all night; and if you do as he wishes, you shall return home next day, and take me with you."

" Take you with her, pitiful changeling ! " I exclaimed. " *You* marry ! Why, the man is mad, or he thinks us fools, every one. And do you imagine that beautiful young lady, that healthy, hearty girl, will tie herself to a little perishing monkey like you ? Are you cherishing the notion that *anybody*, let alone Miss Catherine Linton, would have you for a husband ? You want whipping for bringing us in here at all, with your dastardly tricks; and—don't look so silly now ! I've a very good mind to shake you severely for your contemptible treachery ! "

I did give him a slight shaking, but it brought on the cough, and he took to his ordinary resource of moaning and weeping, and Catherine rebuked me.

" Stay all night ? No," she said, looking slowly round. " Ellen, I'll burn that door down, but I'll get out."

And she would have commenced the execution of her

threat directly, but Linton was up in alarm for his dear self again. He clasped her in his two feeble arms, sobbing—

"Won't you have me, and save me?—not let me come to the Grange? Oh, darling Catherine, you mustn't go and leave, after all! You *must* obey my father—you *must*!"

"I must obey my own," she replied, "and relieve him from this cruel suspense. The whole night! What would he think? He'll be distressed already. I'll either break or burn a way out of the house. Be quiet! You're in no danger. But if you hinder me—Linton, I love papa better than you!"

The mortal terror he felt of Mr. Heathcliff's anger restored to the boy his coward's eloquence. Catherine was near distraught; still she persisted that she must go home, and tried in her turn to subdue his selfish agony. While they were thus occupied, our gaoler re-entered.

"Your beasts have trotted off," he said. "Stop snivelling, Linton, and get to bed. Once in your room, I'll not come near you. You needn't fear. By chance you've managed tolerably. I'll look to the rest."

Linton slunk out. The lock was re-secured. Heath-cliff approached the fire, where my mistress and I sat silent. Catherine instinctively raised her hand to her cheek.

"Oh! you are not afraid of me?" he sneered. "Your courage is well disguised. You seem damnably afraid."

"I am afraid of you now," she replied, "because, if I stay, papa will be miserable; and how can I endure making him miserable when he—when he—— Mr. Heathcliff, *let* me go home. I promise to marry Linton. Why should you wish to force me to do what I'll willingly do of myself?"

"Take it," he said standing in the doorway, and trusting it into my hands.

"Stay a minute," I began.

"Nay," he cried, and retired, regardless of any prayers I could pour forth to retain him. And there I remained enclosed four days and five nights, seeing no one but Hareton, once every morning, when he brought me food.

CHAPTER XVIII

ON the fifth morning, or rather afternoon, a lighter step approached my prison. It was Zillah, donned in her scarlet shawl, with a black silk bonnet on her head, and a willow basket swung on her arm.

"Eh, dear, Mrs. Dean!" she exclaimed. "Well, there's such a talk about you at Gimmerton. I never thought but you were sunk in the Blackhorse marsh, and missy with you, till master told me you'd been found, and he'd lodged you here. How long were you in the hole? Did master save you?"

"Your master is a true scoundrel," I replied. "But he shall answer for it. He needn't have raised that tale. It shall all be laid bare."

"What do you mean?" asked Zillah. "It's not his tale. They tell it in the village, about your being lost in the marsh, and I calls to Hareton Earnshaw when I come in, 'Eh, they's queer things, Mr. Hareton, happened since I went off. It's a sad pity of that likely young lass, and cant Nelly Dean.' He stared. I thought he had not heard aright, so I told him the rumour. The master listened, and he just smiled to himself and said, 'If they have been in the marsh, they are out now, Zillah. Nelly Dean is lodged at this minute in your room. Here's the key. You can bid her go to the Grange at once, if she is able, and carry a message from me that her young lady will follow in time to attend the squire's funeral.' "

" Mr. Edgar is not dead? " I gasped. " Oh, Zillah, Zillah ! "

" No, no. He's not dead. Dr. Kenneth thinks he may last another day. I met him on the road and asked."

I snatched my outdoor things and hastened below, for the way was free. Linton lay alone on the settle, apathetically sucking a stick of sugar-candy. " Where is Miss Catherine? " I demanded. " Is she gone? "

" No," he replied; " she's upstairs. She's not to go; we won't let her."

" You won't let her, little idiot ! " I exclaimed. " Direct me to her room immediately, or I'll make you sing out sharply."

" Papa would make you sing out if you attempted to get there," he answered. " Catherine's my wife now. She may cry and be sick as much as she pleases, but she shan't be allowed to leave. Papa says it's shameful she wants to leave me."

" Is Mr. Heathcliff out," I inquired, perceiving the wretched creature had no power to sympathise with his cousin's mental tortures.

" He's in the court," he replied, " talking to Dr. Kenneth, who says uncle is dying truly at last. I'm glad, for I shall be master of the Grange after him. Catherine always spoke of it as *her* house. It isn't hers. It's mine. Papa says everything she has is mine."

I considered it best to depart without seeing Mr. Heathcliff, and bring a rescue for my young lady from the Grange. On reaching it, the astonishment and joy of my fellow-servants at seeing me was intense. And when they heard that my little mistress was safe also, two or three were about to hurry up and shout the news at Mr. Edgar's door; but I bespoke the announcement of it myself. How changed I found him in those few days! He lay an image of sadness and resignation, awaiting death.

He half rose up, looked eagerly round the apartment, and then sank back in a swoon. As soon as he had recovered, I related our compulsory visit and detention, but told him it was Heathcliff who had forced us into the house. I uttered as little as possible against Linton, nor did I describe his father's brutal conduct. I did not wish to add needless bitterness to his already overflowing cup.

He divined that one of his enemy's purposes was to secure the personal property, as well as the estate, to his son, or rather himself; yet why he did not wait till his decease was a puzzle to my master, because ignorant how nearly he and his nephew would quit the world together. However, he felt that his will had better be altered. Instead of leaving Catherine's personal fortune at her own disposal, he determined to put it in the hands of trustees for her use during life, and for her children, after her, if she had any. By that means it could not fall to Mr. Heathcliff, should Linton die.

Having received his orders, I dispatched a man to fetch the attorney, and four more, provided with serviceable weapons, to demand my young lady's release. Both parties were delayed very late. Mr. Green sent word that he had other business in the village, and could not be at the Grange till the next morning. The four men came back unaccompanied also. They brought back word that Catherine was ill—too ill to leave her room. I scolded the stupid fellows for listening to the tale, which I would not carry to my master, resolving to take a whole bevy to the

Heights at daylight, and storm it literally, unless the prisoner were quietly surrendered.

Happily I was spared the journey and the trouble. At three in the morning I had gone downstairs to fetch a jug of water, when a sharp knock at the front door made me jump. I went to open it, and there was my little mistress. She threw herself on my neck, sobbing.

" Ellen ! Ellen ! is papa alive ? "

" Yes ! " I cried. " Yes, my angel, he is ! God be thanked, you are safe with us again ! "

She wanted to run, breathless as she was, upstairs to her father's room; but I compelled her to sit down on a chair, and made her drink, and chafed her pale face with my apron till a faint colour came into it. Then I said I must go first and tell of her arrival, imploring her to say she would be happy with young Linton. Soon understanding why I counselled her to utter this falsehood, she assured me she would not complain.

I couldn't abide to be present at their meeting. I stood outside for a quarter of an hour before re-entering. All was composed, however. Catherine's despair was as silent as her father's joy.

He died blissfully, Mr. Lockwood; he died so. Kissing her cheek, he murmured—

" I am going to her—to your mother, darling child; and you shall come to us."

He never stirred nor spoke again, but kept his radiant gaze fixed on her face till his pulse imperceptibly stopped and his soul departed. None could have noticed the exact minute of his death, it was so entirely without a struggle. Catherine sat on beside the deathbed, and it was not till noon that we persuaded her to come away and take some repose. It was well I succeeded in removing her, for at dinner time Mr. Green, the lawyer appeared, having first called at Wuthering Heights to get his instructions how to behave. He had sold himself to Mr. Heathcliff; that was the cause of his delay in obeying my master's summons.

Mr. Green took it upon himself to order everything and everybody about the place. He gave all the servants notice to quit. Catherine was suffered to remain at the Grange till her father's corpse had quitted it.—She told me that she had owed her escape on the morning of her father's death to Linton, who had at last been spurred by her anguish to take the risk of releasing her.

§

The evening after the funeral my young lady and I were seated in the library, musing mournfully over our loss, and conjecturing as to the gloomy future. We had just agreed that the best destiny which could await Catherine would be a permission to continue resident at the Grange—at least during Linton's life—he being allowed to join her there, and I to remain as housekeeper—when a servant (one of the discarded ones) but not yet departed—rushed hastily in. He told us "That devil Heathcliff" was coming through the court; should he fasten the door in his face?

But before we had time to reply, Heathcliff entered. He was the master now, and availed himself of the master's privilege to walk straight in without saying a word. It was the same room into which he had been ushered as a guest, eighteen years before. Catherine rose, with an impulse to dash out, when she saw him.

"Stop!" he said, arresting her by the arm. "No more runnings away! I'm come to fetch you home, and I hope you will be a dutiful daughter, and not encourage my son to further disobedience—or it'll be the worse for both of you."

"Why not let Catherine continue here," I pleaded,

" and send Master Linton to her?   As you hate them both, you'd not miss them."

" I'm seeking a tenant for the Grange," he answered, " and I want my children about me, to be sure.   Besides, that lass owes me her service for her bread.   I'm not going to nurture her in luxury and idleness after Linton has gone.   Make haste and get ready now, and don't oblige me to compel you."

" I shall," said Catherine.   " Linton is all I have to love in the world, and though you have done what you could to make him hateful to me, and me to him, you *cannot* make us hate each other.   I defy you to hurt him when I am by, and I defy you to frighten me."

" You are a boastful champion," replied Heathcliff. " But don't expect thanks for your noble devotion.   He is as bitter as gall for your desertion.   I heard him draw a pleasant picture to Zillah of what he would do if he were stronger."

" I know he has a bad nature," said Catherine; " he's your son.   But I'm glad I've a better, to forgive it; and I know he loves me, and for that reason I love him.   Mr. Heathcliff, *you* have *nobody* to love you; and however miserable you make us, we shall still have the revenge that your cruelty arises from your greater misery.   You *are* miserable, are you not?   Lonely like the devil, and envious like him.   *Nobody* will cry for you when you die. I wouldn't be you."

Catherine spoke with a kind of dreary triumph.   She seemed to have made up her mind to enter into the spirit of her future family, and draw pleasure from the griefs of her enemies.

" You shall be sorry for yourself presently," said her father-in-law, " if you stand there another minute. Begone, witch, and get your things."

She scornfully withdrew.   In her absence I began to

beg for Zillah's place at the Heights, offering to resign
mine to her; but he would not suffer it on any account.
He bade me be silent; and then, for the first time,
allowed himself a glance round the room, and a look at
the pictures. Having studied Mrs. Linton's he said—

"I shall have that home—not because I need it,
but——" He turned abruptly to the fire, and continued,
with what, for lack of a better word, I must call a smile.—
"I'll tell you what I did yesterday. I got the sexton,
who was digging Linton's grave, to remove the earth off
her coffin lid, and I opened it. I thought, once, I would
have stayed there. When I saw her face again—it is
hers yet—he had hard work to stir me; but he said it
would change if the air blew on it; so I struck one side
of the coffin loose, and covered it up—not Linton's side,
damn him! I wish he had been soldered in lead. And I
bribed the sexton to pull it away when I'm laid there, and
slide mine out too. I'll have it made so. And then, by
the time Linton gets to us, he'll not know which is which."

"You are very wicked, Mr. Heathcliff," I exclaimed.
"Were you not ashamed to disturb the dead?"

"I disturbed nobody, Nelly," he replied, "and, I
gave some ease to myself. I shall be a great deal more
comfortable now, and you'll have a better chance of
keeping me underground when I get there. Disturbed
her! No! she has disturbed me, night and day, through
eighteen years, incessantly, remorselessly, till yesternight;
and yesternight I was tranquil. I dreamt I was sleeping
the last sleep by that sleeper, with my heart stopped and
my cheek frozen against hers."

"And if she had been dissolved into earth, or worse,
what would you have dreamt of then?" I said.

"Of dissolving with her, and being more happy still,"
he answered. "Do you suppose I dread any change of
that sort? I expected such a transformation on raising

the lid, but I'm better pleased that it should not commence till I share it. Besides, unless I had received a distinct impression of her passionless features, that strange feeling would hardly have been removed. It began oddly. You know I was wild after she died, and eternally, from dawn to dawn, praying her to return to me her spirit. I have a strong faith in ghosts; I have a conviction that they can and do exist among us. The day she was buried there came a fall of snow. In the evening I went to the church-yard. It blew bleak as winter; all round was solitary. I didn't fear that her fool of a husband would wander up the den so late, and no one else had business to bring them there. Being alone, and conscious two yards of loose earth was the sole barrier between us, I said to myself, ' I'll have her in my arms again! If she be cold, I'll think it is this north wind that chills *me*; if she be motion-less, it is sleep.' I got a spade from the toolhouse, and began to delve with all my might. It scraped the coffin. I fell to work with my hands. The wood commenced cracking about the screws. I was on the point of attaining my object, when it seemed that I heard a sigh from some-one above, close at the edge of the grave, and bending down. ' If I can only get this off,' I muttered, ' I wish they may shovel in the earth over us both!' and I wrenched at it more desperately still. There was another sigh close at my ear. I appeared to feel the warm breath of it displacing the sleet-laden wind. I knew no living thing in flesh and blood was by; but as certainly as you perceive the approach to some substantial body in the dark, though it cannot be discerned, so certainly I felt that Cathy was there—not under me, but on the earth. A sudden sense of relief flowed from my heart through every limb. I relinquished my labour of agony, and turned consoled at once, unspeakably consoled. Her presence was with me; it remained while I refilled the grave, and led me home. You may laugh if you will, but I was sure I should see her there. I was sure she was with me, and I could not help talking to her. Having reached the Heights, I rushed eagerly to the door. It was fastened, and, I remember, that accursed Earnshaw and my wife opposed my entrance. I remember stopping to kick the breath out of him, and then hurrying upstairs to my room and hers. I looked round impatiently; I felt her by me; I could *almost* see her, and yet I *could not*! I ought to have sweat blood then, from the anguish of my yearning, from the fervour of my supplications to have but one glimpse. I had not one. She showed herself, as she often was in life, a devil to me! And since then, sometimes more and sometimes less, I've been the sport of that intolerable torture—infernal! keeping my nerves at such a stretch that, if they had not resembled catgut, they would long ago have relaxed to the feebleness of Linton's. When I sat in the house with Hareton it seemed that on going out I should meet her; when I walked on the moors I should meet her coming in; when I went from home I hastened to return. She *must* be somewhere at the Heights, I was certain. And when I slept in her chamber, I was beaten out of that. I couldn't lie there, for the moment I closed my eyes she was either outside the window, or sliding back the panels, or entering the room, or even resting her darling head on the same pillow as she did when a child, and I must open my eyes to see. And so I opened and closed them a hundred times a night, to be always disappointed. It racked me. I've often groaned aloud, till that old rascal Joseph no doubt believed that my conscience was playing fiend inside me. Now, since I've seen her, I'm pacified—a little. It was a strange way of killing—not by inches, but by fractions of hair-breadths—to beguile me with the spectre of a hope through eighteen years!"

Mr. Heathcliff paused and wiped his forehead. His hair clung to it, wet with perspiration; his eyes were fixed on the red embers of the fire, the brows not contracted, but raised next the temples, diminishing the grim aspect of his countenance, but imparting a peculiar look of trouble and a painful appearance of mental tension towards one absorbing subject. He only half addressed me, and I maintained silence. I didn't like to hear him talk. After a short period he resumed his meditation on the picture, took it down and leant it against the sofa to contemplate it at better advantage; and while he was so occupied Catherine entered, announcing that she was ready, when her pony should be saddled.

"Send that over tomorrow," said Heathcliff to me; then, turning to her, he added, "You may do without your pony. It is a fine evening, and you'll need no ponies at Wuthering Heights, for what journeys you take your own feet will serve you. Come along."

"Good-bye, Ellen!" whispered my dear little mistress. As she kissed me, her lips felt like ice. "Come and see me, Ellen; don't forget."

"Take care you do no such thing, Mrs. Dean!" said her new father. "When I wish to speak to you I'll come here. I want none of your prying at my house."

He signed her to precede him, and casting back a look that cut my heart, she obeyed. I watched them from the window walk down the garden. Heathcliff fixed Catherine's arm under his, though she disputed the act at first evidently, and with rapid strides he hurried her into the alley, whose trees concealed them.

CHAPTER XIX

I HAVE paid a visit to the Heights, but I have not seen her since she left. Joseph held the door in his hand when I called to ask after her, and wouldn't let me pass. He said Mrs. Linton was " thrang ", and the master was not in. Zillah has told me something of the way they go on, otherwise I should hardly know who was dead and who living. She thinks Catherine haughty, and does not like her, I can guess by her talk. My young lady asked some aid of her when she first came, but Mr. Heathcliff told her to follow her own business and let his daughter-in-law look after herself; and Zillah willingly acquiesced, being a narrow-minded, selfish woman. Catherine evinced a child's annoyance at this neglect, repaid it with contempt, and thus enlisted my informant among her enemies as securely as if she had done her some great wrong. I had a talk with Zillah about six weeks ago, a little before you came, one day when we foregathered on the moor; and this is what she told me.

" The first thing Mrs. Linton did," she said, " on her arrival at the Heights, was to run upstairs, without wishing good-evening to me and Joseph; she shut herself into Linton's room, and remained till morning. Then, while the master and Earnshaw were at breakfast, she entered the house and asked, all in a quiver, if the doctor might be sent for; her cousin was very ill.

" ' We know that,' answered Heathcliff; ' but his life is not worth a farthing, and I won't spend a farthing on him.'

" ' But I cannot tell how to do,' she said; ' and if nobody will help me, he'll die.'

" ' Walk out of the room,' cried the master, ' and let me never hear a word more about him. None here care what becomes of him.   If you do, act the nurse; if you do not, lock him up and leave him.'

" Then she began to bother me, and I said I'd had enough plague with the tiresome thing.   We each had our tasks, and hers was to wait on Linton; Mr. Heathcliff bade me leave that labour to her.

" How they managed together I can't tell.   I fancy he fretted a great deal, and moaned hisseln night and day and she had precious little rest, one could guess by her white face and heavy eyes.   She sometimes came in to the kitchen all wildered like, and looked as if she would fain beg assistance.   But I was not going to disobey the master—I never dare disobey him, Mrs. Dean; and though I thought it wrong that Kenneth should not be sent for, it was no concern of mine either to advise or complain, and I always refused to meddle.   Once or twice, after we had gone to bed, I've happened to open my door again and seen her sitting crying on the stairs' top; and then I've shut myself in quick, for fear of being moved to interfere. I did pity her then, I'm sure; still I didn't wish to lose my place, you know.

" At last, one night she came boldly into my chamber, and frightened me out of my wits by saying—

" ' Tell Mr. Heathcliff that his son is dying.   I'm sure he is, this time.   Get up instantly, and tell him.'

" Having uttered this speech, she vanished again.   I lay a quarter of an hour listening and trembling.   Nothing stirred—the house was quiet.

" ' She's mistaken,' I said to myself.   ' He's got over it.   I needn't disturb them.'   And I began to doze.   But my sleep was marred a second time by a sharp ringing of the bell—the only bell we have, put up on purpose for Linton; and the master called to me to see what was the matter, and inform them that he wouldn't have the noise repeated.

" I delivered Catherine's message.   He cursed to himself, and in a few minutes came out with a lighted candle, and proceeded to their room.   I followed.   Mrs. Heathcliff was seated by the bedside with her hands folded on her knees.   Her father-in-law went up, held the light to Linton's face, looked at him, and touched him.   Afterwards he turned to her.

" ' Now, Catherine,' he said, ' how do you feel? '

" She was dumb.

" ' How do you feel, Catherine? ' he repeated.

" ' He's safe, and I'm free,' she answered.   ' I should feel well, but,' she continued, with a bitterness she couldn't conceal, ' you have left me so long to struggle against death alone that I feel and see only death.   I feel like death.'

" And she looked like it too.   I gave her a little wine. Hareton and Joseph, who had been wakened by the ringing and the sound of feet, and heard our talk from outside, now entered.   Joseph was fain, I believe, of the lad's removal; Hareton seemed a thought bothered, though he was more taken up with staring at Catherine than thinking of Linton.   But the master bade him get off to bed again; we didn't want his help.   He afterwards made Joseph remove the body to his chamber, and told me to return to mine, and Mrs. Heathcliff remained by herself.

" In the morning he sent me to tell her she must come down to breakfast.   She had undressed, and appeared going to sleep, and said she was ill, at which I hardly wondered.   I informed Mr. Heathcliff, and he replied—

" ' Well, let her be till after the funeral, and go up now and then to get her what is needful; and as soon as she seems better, tell me.' "

Cathy stayed upstairs a fortnight, according to Zillah, who visited her twice a day, and would have been rather more friendly, but her attempts at kindness were proudly and promptly repelled.

Heathcliff went up once to show her Linton's will. He had bequeathed the whole of his and what had been her movable property to his father. The poor creature was threatened or coaxed into that act during her week's absence when his uncle died. The lands, being a minor, he could not meddle with. However, Mr. Heathcliff has claimed and kept them in his wife's right and his also—I suppose legally. At any rate, Catherine, destitute of money and friends, cannot disturb his possession.

" Nobody," said Zillah, " ever approached her door, except that once, but I ; and nobody asked anything about her. The first occasion of her coming down into the house was on a Sunday afternoon. She had cried out, when I carried up her dinner, that she couldn't bear any longer being in the cold ; and I told her the master was going to Thrushcross Grange, and Earnshaw and I needn't hinder her from descending. So, as soon as she heard Heathcliff's horse trot off, she made her appearance, donned in black, and her yellow curls combed back behind her ears as plain as a Quaker. She couldn't comb them out.

" Joseph and I generally go to chapel on Sundays." The kirk, you know, has no minister now, explained Mrs. Dean, and they call the Methodists' or Baptists' place (I can't say which it is) at Gimmerton a chapel. " Joseph has gone," she continued, " but I thought proper to bide at home. Young folks are always the better for an elder's overlooking ; and Hareton, with all his bashfulness, isn't a model of nice behaviour. I let him know that his cousin would very likely sit with us, and she had been always used to see the Sabbath respected, so he had as good leave his guns and bits of indoor work alone while she stayed. He coloured up at the news, and cast his eyes over his hands and clothes. The train-oil and gun-powder were shoved out of sight in a minute. I saw he meant to give her his company, and I guessed by his way he wanted to be presentable; so, laughing as I durst not laugh when the master is by, I offered to help him, if he would, and joked at his confusion. He grew sullen, and began to swear.

"Now, Mrs. Dean," Zillah went on, seeing me not pleased by her manner, "you happen think your young lady too fine for Mr. Hareton, and happen you're right, but I own I should love well to bring her pride a peg lower. And what will all her learning and daintiness do for her now? She's as poor as you or I—poorer, I'll be bound. You're saving, and I'm doing my little all that road."

Hareton allowed Zillah to give him her aid, and she flattered him into a good humour. So, when Catherine came, half forgetting her former insults, he tried to make himself agreeable, by the housekeeper's account.

"Missis walked in," she said, "as chill as an icicle, and as high as a princess. I got up and offered her my seat in the armchair. No, she turned up her nose at my civility. Earnshaw rose too and bade her come to the settle and sit close by the fire; he was sure she was starved.

"'I've been starved a month and more,' she answered, resting on the word as scornful as she could.

"And she got a chair for herself, and placed it at a distance from both of us. Having sat till she was warm, she began to look round, and discovered a number of books in the dresser. She was instantly upon her feet again, stretching to reach them; but they were too high up. Her cousin, after watching her endeavours a while, at last summoned courage to help her. She held her frock, and he filled it with the first that came to hand.

"That was a great advance for the lad. She didn't

thank him, still he felt gratified that she had accepted his assistance, and ventured to stand behind as she examined them, and even to stoop and point out what struck his fancy in certain old pictures which they contained. Nor was he daunted by the saucy style in which she jerked the page from his finger. He contented himself with going a bit farther back, and looking at her instead of the book. She continued reading, or seeking for something to read. His attention became, by degrees, quite centred in the study of her thick, silky curls. Her face he couldn't see, and she couldn't see him. And, perhaps not quite awake to what he did, but attracted like a child to a candle, at last he proceeded from staring to touching. He put out his hand and stroked one curl, as gently as if it were a bird. He might have stuck a knife into her neck, she started round in such a taking.

" ' Get away this moment! How dare you touch me! Why are you stopping there? ' she cried in a tone of disgust. ' I can't endure you! I'll go upstairs again if you come near me.'

" Mr. Hareton recoiled, looking as foolish as he could do. He sat down in the settle very quiet, and she continued turning her volumes another half-hour. Finally Earnshaw crossed over and whispered to me—

" ' Will you ask her to read to us, Zillah? I'm stalled of doing naught; and I do like—I could like to hear her. Dunnot say I wanted it, but ask of yourseln.'

" ' Mr. Hareton wishes you would read to us, ma'am,' I said immediately. ' He'd take it very kind—he'd be much obliged.'

" She frowned, and looking up, answered—

" ' Mr. Hareton and the whole set of you will be good enough to understand that I reject any pretence at kindness you have the hypocrisy to offer! I despise you, and will have nothing to say to any of you! When I would have given my life for one kind word, you all kept off. But I won't complain to you. I'm driven down here by the cold, not either to amuse you or enjoy your society.'

"' What could I ha' done? ' began Earnshaw. ' How was I to blame? '

"' Oh, you are an exception,' answered Mrs. Heathcliff. ' I never missed such a concern as you.'

"' But I offered more than once, and asked,' he said, kindling up at her pertness—' I asked Mr. Heathcliff to let me wake for you—— '

"' Be silent! I'll go out of doors, or anywhere, rather than have your disagreeable voice in my ear,' said my lady.

" Hareton muttered she might go to hell, for him, and unslinging his gun, restrained himself from his usual Sunday occupation no longer. He talked now freely enough, and she presently saw fit to retreat to her solitude; but the frost had set in, and in spite of her pride, she was forced to condescend to our company more and more. However, I took care there should be no further scorning at my good nature. Ever since I've been as stiff as herself, and she has no lover or liker among us; and she does not deserve one, for, let them say the least word to her, and she'll curl back without respect of any one. She'll snap at the master himself, and as good as dares him to thrash her; and the more hurt she gets, the more venomous she grows."

At first, on hearing this account from Zillah, I determined to leave my situation, take a cottage, and get Catherine to come and live with me; but Mr. Heathcliff would as soon permit that as he would set up Hareton in an independent house, and I can see no remedy at present, unless she could marry again, and that scheme it does not come within my province to arrange.

.   .   .   .   .

Thus ended Mrs. Dean's story. Notwithstanding the doctor's prophecy, I am rapidly recovering strength; and though it be only the second week in January, I propose getting out on horseback in a day or two, and riding over to Wuthering Heights to inform my landlord that I shall spend the next six months in London; and, if he likes, he may look out for another tenant to take the place after October. I would not pass another winter here for much.

CHAPTER XX

YESTERDAY was bright, calm and frosty. I went to the Heights as I proposed. My housekeeper entreated me to bear a little note from her to her young lady, and I did not refuse, for the worthy woman was not conscious of anything odd in her request. The front door stood open, but the jealous gate was fastened, as at my last visit. I knocked, and invoked Earnshaw from among the garden beds. He unchained it, and I entered. The fellow is as handsome a rustic as need be seen. I took particular notice of him this time; but then he does his best, apparently, to make the least of his advantages.

I asked if Mr. Heathcliff were at home. He answered, No, but he would be in at dinner-time. It was eleven o'clock, and I announced my intention of going in and waiting for him, at which he immediately flung down his tools and accompanied me, in the office of watchdog, not as substitute for the host.

We entered together. Catherine was seated near the window. She looked more sulky and less spirited than when I had seen her first. She hardly raised her eyes to notice me, and never returned my bow and good-morning by the slightest acknowledgment. But after a minute I approached her, and pretending to desire a view of the garden, adroitly dropped Mrs. Dean's note on her knee, unnoticed by Hareton. But she asked aloud, " What is that ? " and chucked it off.

" A letter from your old acquaintance, Mrs. Dean," I answered, annoyed at her exposing my kind deed, and fearful lest it should be imagined a missive of my own.

She would gladly have gathered it up at this information, but Hareton was too quick for her. He seized it and put it in his waistcoat, saying Mr. Heathcliff should look at it first. Thereat Catherine silently turned her face from us, and stealthily drew out her handkerchief and applied it to her eyes; and her cousin, after struggling for a while to keep down his softer feelings, pulled out the letter and flung it on the floor beside her. Catherine caught and perused it eagerly; then she put a few questions to me concerning the inmates of her former home; and gazing towards the hills, murmured in soliloquy—

" I should like to be riding Minny down there ! I should like to be climbing up there ! Oh, I'm tired—I'm *stalled*, Hareton ! " And she leant her pretty head back against the sill, and lapsed into an aspect of abstracted sadness.

" Mrs. Heathcliff," I said, after sitting some time mute, " may I not take back some message to Mrs. Dean? You are constantly in her thoughts. She'll be greatly disappointed if I return with no news of you, except that you received her letter and said nothing."

" You must tell her," said she, " that I would answer her letter, but I have no materials for writing—not even a book from which I might tear a leaf."

" No books ! " I exclaimed. " How do you contrive to

live here without them ! I'm frequently dull enough at the Grange, though provided with a large library."

" Mr. Heathcliff destroyed all I had," said Catherine, " except for a secret stock of them which Hareton has appropriated and hidden away from me—from mere love of stealing, I suppose, for they can be of no possible use to *him*."

Earnshaw blushed crimson, and stammered an indignant denial of this accusation.

" Mr. Hareton is desirous of increasing his amount of knowledge," said I, coming to his rescue. " He'll be a clever scholar in a few years."

" And he wants me to sink into a dunce meantime," answered Catherine. " Yes, I hear him trying to spell and read to himself, and pretty blunders he makes.—I wish you would repeat ' Cherry Chase ', as I heard you yesterday, Hareton. It was extremely funny."

The young man evidently thought it too bad that he should be laughed at for his ignorance, and then laughed at for trying to remove it. I had a similar notion, and observed—

" But, Mrs. Heathcliff, we have each had a commencement. And had our teachers scorned instead of aiding us, we should stumble and totter in our reading yet."

" Oh ! " she replied, " I don't wish to limit his acquirements. Still he has no right to take what is mine. Those books, both prose and verse, are consecrated to me by other associations, and I hate to have my favourite pieces debased and profaned by his vile mistakes and mispronunciations."

Hareton's chest heaved a minute in mortification and wrath. Then, rising, he hurried from the room—to reappear a minute later with half a dozen volumes, which he threw into Catherine's lap, exclaiming—

" Take them ! I never want to hear, or read, or think about them again."

" I won't have them now," she answered. " I shall connect you with them, and hate them." And, opening one of them, she began to read a portion in the drawling tone of a beginner. But this was too much for Hareton's control. To spare his feelings, I crossed to the doorway. But his self-love would endure no further torment. He seized the volume from her hand, gathered the rest from her lap, and hurled all of them into the fire.

" Yes, that's all the good a brute such as you can get from them ! " cried Catherine, scornfully watching the conflagration.

" Hold your tongue," he answered fiercely. His agitation precluded further speech. He advanced hastily to the entrance; I drew aside to let him pass; but ere he had crossed the door-stones, Mr. Heathcliff, coming up the causeway, encountered him, and laying hold of his shoulder, asked—

" What's to do now, my lad ? "

" Naught, naught," he said, and broke away to enjoy his grief and anger in solitude.

Heathcliff gazed after him and sighed.

" It will be odd if I thwart myself," he muttered, unconscious that I was behind him. " But when I look for his father in his face, I find *her* every day more. How the devil is he so like ? I can hardly bear to see him."

He bent his eyes to the ground and walked moodily in. There was a restless, anxious expression in his face I had never remarked there before, and he looked thinner. Catherine, perceiving him, immediately escaped into the kitchen, so I remained alone.

" Ah, Mr. Lockwood," he said, in reply to my greeting. " What brings *you* here ? "

H

"I have come," said I, "to inform you that I am leaving for London next week. I have no disposition to remain at Thrushcross Grange any longer."

"Oh! So you've tired of being banished from the world, have you?" he replied. "But I would remind you that you have taken the Grange for twelve months. If you have come to plead off paying for a place you won't occupy, your journey is useless. I never relent in exacting my due from anyone."

"I'm coming to plead off nothing about it," I exclaimed, considerably irritated. "Should you wish it, I'll settle with you now." And I drew my notebook from my pocket.

"No, no," he replied coolly; "you'll pay what you owe as it becomes due, I've no doubt. I'm not in such a hurry. Sit down and take your dinner with us. A guest that is safe from repeating his visit can generally be made welcome.—Catherine, bring the things in. Where are you?"

Catherine reappeared, bearing a tray of knives and forks.

"You may get your dinner with Joseph," muttered Heathcliff aside, "and remain in the kitchen till Mr. Lockwood is gone."

She obeyed his directions very punctually; perhaps she had no temptation to transgress.—With Mr. Heathcliff, grim and saturnine, on the one hand, and Hareton, absolutely dumb, on the other, I made a cheerless meal, and bade adieu early. I would have departed by the back way, to get a last glimpse of Catherine and old Joseph, but my host himself escorted me to the door, so I could not fulfil my wish.

"How dreary life gets over in that house!" I reflected, while riding down the road. "What a realisation of something more romantic than a fairy tale it would have been for Mrs. Linton Heathcliff had she and I struck up an attachment, as her good nurse desired, and migrated together to the stirring atmosphere of the town ! ''

CHAPTER XXI

1802.—This September I was invited to devastate the moors of a friend in the north, and on my journey to his abode came within fifteen miles of Gimmerton.   A sudden impulse seized me to visit Thrushcross Grange.   I conceived that I might as well pass a night under my own roof as in an inn.

I reached the Grange before sunset, and knocked for admittance.   I rode into the court.   Under the porch a girl of nine or ten sat knitting, and an old woman reclined on the house-steps, smoking a meditative pipe.

" Is Mrs. Dean within ? '' I demanded of the dame.

"Mistress Dean?   Nay !   Shoo's up at th' Heights. Aw keep the house now.''

" Well, I'm Mr. Lockwood, the master.   I wish to stay the night.''

" T' maister ! '' she cried in astonishment.   " Yah sad ha' sent word.   They's nowt dry nor mensful abaht t' place nowt there isn't.''

Soon perceiving that I had almost upset her wits by my unexpected apparition, I bade her to be composed. I would go for a walk, and meanwhile she must try to prepare a corner of a sitting-room for me to sup in, and a bedroom to sleep in.   No sweeping and dusting—only fires and dry sheets were necessary.—And having thus reassured her, I set forth.

Wuthering Heights was the goal of my proposed excursion. Before I arrived in sight of it, all that remained of the day was a beamless amber light along the west; but the moon was rising and brightening, and by its light I could see every pebble on the path, and every blade of grass. I had neither to climb the gate nor to knock. That's an improvement, I thought. And I noticed another by the aid of my nostrils—a fragrance of stocks and wallflowers wafted on the air from amongst the friendly trees.

Both doors and lattices were open, and a fine red fire illumined the chimney. But the occupants of the house had stationed themselves away from its influence, not far from one of the windows. I could both see and hear them before I entered, and looked and listened in consequence, being moved thereto by a mingled sense of curiosity and envy that grew as I listened.

"Con-*trary*!" said a voice as sweet as a silver bell. "That for the third time, you dunce! I'm not going to tell you again. Recollect, or I'll pull your hair."

"Contrary, then," answered the other, in deep but softened tones. "And now, kiss me for minding so well."

"No; read it over first correctly, without a single mistake."

The male speaker began to read. He was a young man, respectably dressed, and seated at a table, having a book before him. His handsome features glowed with pleasure, and his eyes kept impatiently wandering from the page to a small white hand over his shoulder. Its owner stood behind, her light, shining ringlets blending at intervals with his locks, as she bent to superintend his studies; and her face—it was lucky he could not see her face, or he would never have been so steady. I could, and I bit my lip in spite at having thrown away the chance I might have had of doing something besides staring at its smiting beauty.

The task was done—not free from further blunders; but the pupil claimed a reward, and received at least five kisses, which, however, he generously returned. They then came to the door, and from their conversation I judged they were about to issue out for a walk on the moors. Judging that my appearance at this juncture would hardly be welcome to them, I skulked round to the kitchen. Here, in the doorway, I found my old friend Nelly Dean, sewing, and singing as she sewed. She recognised me instantly, and jumped to her feet, crying—

"Why, bless you, Mr. Lockwood! how could you think of returning in this way? All's shut up at Thrushcross Grange. You should have given us notice."

"I'm staying only one night," I answered; "and all is arranged. I depart again tomorrow. And how are you transplanted here, Mrs. Dean? Tell me that."

"Zillah left, and Mr. Heathcliff wished me to come, soon after you went to London. But step in, pray. Have you walked from Gimmerton this evening?"

"From the Grange," I replied. "I want to finish my business with your master, because I don't think of having another opportunity in a hurry."

"What business, sir?" said Nelly, conducting me into the house. "He's gone out at present, and won't return soon."

"About the rent," I answered.

"Oh! then it is with Mrs. Heathcliff you must settle," she observed, "or rather, with me. She has not learned to manage her affairs yet, and I act for her; there's nobody else."

I looked surprised.

"Ah! you have not heard of Heathcliff's death, I see," she continued.

" Heathcliff dead ! " I exclaimed, astonished. " How long ago ? "

" Three months since. But sit down, and I'll tell you all about it. Stop; you have had nothing to eat, have you ? "

" I want nothing; I have ordered supper at home. You sit down too. I never dreamt of his dying. Let me hear how it came to pass."

" At least have a drink of our old ale; it will do you good; you seem weary."

She hastened to fetch it before I could refuse, and while I drank it she furnished me with a sequel of Heathcliff's history. He had a " queer " end, as she expressed it.

I was summoned to Wuthering Heights within a fortnight of your leaving us (she said), and I obeyed joyfully, for Catherine's sake. My first interview with her grieved and shocked me—she had altered so much since our separation. Mr. Heathcliff did not explain his reasons for taking a new mind about my coming here; he only told me he was tired of seeing Catherine. I must make the little parlour my sitting-room, and keep her with me. She seemed pleased at this arrangement; and by degrees I smuggled over a great number of books and other articles that had formed her amusement at the Grange. But Catherine, contented at first, in a brief space grew irritable and restless. I was forced to quit her frequently, and she complained of loneliness. She preferred quarrelling with Joseph in the kitchen to sitting at peace in her solitude. I did not mind their skirmishes; but Hareton was often obliged to seek the kitchen also when the master wanted to have the house to himself; and though in the beginning she either left it at his approach, or quietly joined in my occupations, and shunned remarking or addressing him, after a while she changed her behaviour and became incapable of letting him alone; talking at him, commenting on his stupidity and idleness, expressing her wonder how he could endure the life he lived, how he could sit a whole evening staring into the fire and dozing.

" He's just like a dog, is he not, Ellen? " she once observed, " or a cart-horse? He does his work, eats his food, and sleeps eternally. What a blank, dreary mind he must have !—Do you ever dream, Hareton? And if you do, what is it about? But you can't speak to me ! "

Then she looked at him, but he would neither open his mouth nor look again.

" He's perhaps dreaming now," she continued. " Ask him, Ellen."

" Mr. Hareton will ask the master to send you upstairs, if you don't behave," I said. He had not only twitched his shoulders, but clenched his fist, as if tempted to use it.

" I know why Hareton never speaks when I am in the kitchen," she exclaimed on another occasion. " He is afraid I shall laugh at him. Ellen, what do you think? He began to teach himself to read once, and because I laughed he burned his books and dropped it. Was he not a fool? "

" Were not you naughty? " I said. " Answer me that."

" Perhaps I was," she went on, " but I did not expect him to be so silly.—Hareton, if I gave you a book, would you take it now? I'll try."

She placed one she had been perusing on his hand. He flung it off, and muttered that if she did not give over he would break her neck.

" Well, I shall put it here," she said—" in the table drawer; and I'm going to bed."

Then she whispered to me to watch whether he touched it, and departed. But he would not come near it; and so I informed her in the morning, to her great disappointment. Her conscience reproved her for frightening him

off improving himself. But her ingenuity was at work
to remedy the injury. While I ironed or pursued other
such stationary employments, she would bring some
pleasant volume and read it aloud to me. When Hareton
was there she generally paused in an interesting part
and left the book lying about ; but he was as obstinate as a
mule, and, instead of snatching at her bait, in wet weather
he took to smoking with Joseph ; and they sat like auto-
matons, one on each side of the fire. On fine evenings
Hareton went out and Catherine yawned and sighed, and
said she was tired of living—her life was useless.

Mr. Heathcliff, who grew more and more disinclined to
society, had almost banished Earnshaw from his apartment.

One rainy evening I was busy getting up linen in the
kitchen. Earnshaw sat, morose as usual, at the chimney
corner, and my little mistress was beguiling an idle hour
with drawing pictures on the window-panes, varying her
amusement by smothered bursts of songs, and whispered
ejaculations, and quick glances of annoyance and im-
patience in the direction of her cousin, who steadfastly
smoked, and looked into the grate. At a notice that I
could do with her no longer intercepting my light, she
removed to the hearthstone. And presently I heard her
begin—

" I've found out, Hareton, that I want—that I'm glad—
that I should like you to be my cousin now, if you had not
grown so cross to me and so rough."

Hareton returned no answer.

" Hareton, Hareton, Hareton ! do you hear ? " she
continued.

" Get off wi'ye ! " he growled, with uncompromising
gruffness.

" No," she persisted, " I won't. When I call you
stupid, I don't mean anything. I don't mean that I

despise you. Come, you shall take notice of me, Hareton. You are my cousin, and you shall own me."

" I shall have naught to do wi' you, and your mucky pride ! " he answered. " I'll go to hell, body and soul, before I look sideways after you again."

Catherine frowned and retreated to the window-seat, chewing her lip, and endeavouring, by humming an eccentric tune, to conceal a growing tendency to sob.

" You should be friends with your cousin, Mr. Hareton," I interrupted, " since she repents of her sauciness. It would make another man of you to have her for a companion."

" A companion ! " he cried, " when she hates me, and does not think me fit to wipe her shoon ! "

" It is not I who hate you; it is you who hate me ! " wept Cathy, no longer disguising her trouble. " You hate me as much as Mr. Heathcliff does."

" You're a damned liar," began Earnshaw. " Why have I made him angry by taking your part, then, a hundred times, and that when you sneered at and despised me ? "

" I didn't know you took my part," she answered, drying her eyes, " and I was miserable and bitter at everybody; but now I thank you, and beg you to forgive me. What can I do besides ? "

She returned to the hearth, and frankly extended her hand. He blackened and scowled like a thundercloud, and kept his fists resolutely clenched, and his gaze fixed on the ground. Catherine, by instinct, must have divined it was obdurate perversity, and not dislike, that prompted this dogged conduct, for, after remaining an instant undecided, she stooped and impressed on his cheek a gentle kiss. Then, drawing back, she took her former station by the window.

Whether the kiss convinced Hareton I cannot tell. He

was very careful, for some minutes, that his face should not be seen; and when he did raise it, he was sadly puzzled where to turn his eyes.

Catherine employed herself in wrapping a handsome book neatly in white paper, and having tied it with a bit of ribbon, and addressed it to " Mr. Hareton Earnshaw," she desired me to be her ambassadress, and convey the present to its destined recipient.

" And tell him if he'll take it I'll come and teach him to read it right," she said; " and if he refuse it I'll go upstairs and never tease him again."

I carried it, and repeated the message, anxiously watched by my employer. Hareton would not open his fingers, so I laid it on his knee. I returned to my work. Catherine leaned her head and arms on the table, till she heard the slight rustle of the covering being removed; then she stole away and quietly seated herself beside her cousin. He trembled, and his face glowed; all his rudeness and all his surly harshness had deserted him.

" Say you forgive me, Hareton, do. You can make me so happy by speaking that little word."

He muttered something inaudible.

" And you'll be my friend? " added Catherine interrogatively.

" Nay, you'll be ashamed of me every day of your life," he answered, " and the more ashamed the more you know me; and I cannot bide it."

" So you won't be my friend? " she said, smiling as sweet as honey, and creeping close up.

I overheard no further distinguishable talk, but, on looking round again, I perceived two such radiant countenances bent over the page of the accepted book that I did not doubt the treaty had been ratified on both sides, and the enemies were thenceforth sworn allies.

The intimacy thus commenced grew rapidly, though it

encountered temporary interruptions. Earnshaw was not to be civilized with a wish, and my young lady was no philosopher and no paragon of patience; but both their minds tending to the same point—one loving and desiring to esteem, and the other loving and desiring to be esteemed —they contrived in the end to reach it.

You see, Mr. Lockwood, it was easy enough to win Mrs. Heathcliff's heart. But now I'm glad you did not try. The crown of all my wishes will be the union of those two. I shall envy no one on their wedding day. There won't be a happier woman than myself in England.

CHAPTER XXII

On the morrow I speedily found it would be impracticable to retain my charge beside me as heretofore (Mrs. Dean continued). She got downstairs before me, and out into the garden, where she had seen her cousin at work; and when I went to bid them come to breakfast, I saw she had persuaded him to clear a large space of ground from currant and gooseberry bushes, and they were busy planning together an importation of plants from the Grange.

I was terrified at the devastation which had been accomplished in a brief half-hour. The black-currant trees were the apple of Joseph's eye, and she had just fixed her choice of a flower-bed in the midst of them.

We always ate our meals with Mr. Heathcliff. I held the mistress's post in making tea and carving, so I was indispensable at table. Catherine usually sat by me, but today she stole nearer to Hareton, and I presently saw she would have no more discretion in her friendship than she had in her hostility.

"Now, mind you don't talk with and notice your cousin too much," were my whispered instructions as we entered the room. "It will certainly annoy Mr. Heathcliff; he'll be mad at you both."

"I'm not going to," she answered.

The minute after she had sidled up to him, and was sticking primroses in his plate of porridge.

He dared not speak to her there—he dared hardly look; and yet she went on teasing till at last he uttered a smothered laugh. Mr. Heathcliff started from the gloomy reverie in which he had been sunk; his eye rapidly surveyed our faces. Catherine met it with her accustomed look of nervousness and yet defiance, which he abhorred.

"It is well that you are out of my reach," he exclaimed. "What fiend possesses you to stare back at me continually with those infernal eyes? Down with them! I thought I had cured you of laughing."

"It was me," muttered Hareton.

"What do you say?" demanded the master.

Hareton looked at his plate, and did not repeat the confession. Mr. Heathcliff looked at him a bit, and then silently resumed his breakfast, and his interrupted musing. We had nearly finished, and the two young people prudently shifted wider asunder, when Joseph appeared at the door, revealing by his quivering lip and furious eyes that the outrage committed on his precious shrubs was detected. He must have seen Cathy and her cousin about the spot before he examined it, for he began at once to complain to his master of this havoc Hareton had wrought, and to ascribe it all to Catherine's influence.

"Is the fool drunk?" asked Mr. Heathcliff—finding it

hard to follow the old man's whinings, " Hareton, is it you he's finding fault with ? "

" I've pulled up two or three bushes," replied the young man, " but I'm going to set 'em again."

" And why have you pulled them up ? " said the master.

" We wanted to plant some flowers there," Catherine cried. " I'm the only person to blame, for I wished him to do it."

" And who the devil gave *you* leave to touch a stick about the place ? " demanded her father-in-law, much surprised.—" And who ordered *you* to obey her ? " he added, turning to Hareton.

The latter was speechless. His cousin replied—

" You shouldn't grudge a few yards of earth for me to ornament, when you have taken all my land ! "

" Your land, insolent slut ! You never had any," said Heathcliff.

" And my money," she continued, returning his angry glare, and meantime biting a piece of crust, the remnant of her breakfast.

" Silence ! " he exclaimed. " Get down, and begone ! "

" And Hareton's land, and his money," pursued the reckless thing. " Hareton and I are friends now, and I shall tell him all about you."

The master seemed confounded a moment. He grew pale and rose up, eyeing her all the while with an expression of mortal hate.

" If you strike me, Hareton will strike you," she said, " so you may as well sit down."

" If Hareton does not turn you out of the room I'll strike him to hell," thundered Heathcliff. " Damnable witch ! dare you pretend to rouse him against me ?— Off with her ! Do you hear ? Fling her into the kitchen! —I'll kill her, Ellen Dean, if you let her come into my sight again ! "

Hareton tried, under his breath, to persuade her to go.

"Drag her away!" he cried savagely. "Are you staying to talk?" And he approached to execute his own command.

"He'll not obey you, wicked man, any more," said Catherine, "and he'll soon detest you as much as I do."

"Whisht! whisht!" muttered the young man reproachfully. "I will not hear you speak so to him. Have done."

"But you won't let him strike me?" she cried.

"Come, then," he whispered earnestly.

It was too late. Heathcliff had caught hold of her.

"Now, *you* go!" he said to Earnshaw. "Accursed witch! This time she has provoked me when I could not bear it, and I'll make her repent it for ever!"

He had his hand in her hair. Hareton attempted to release her locks, entreating him not to hurt her that once. Heathcliff's black eyes flashed—he seemed ready to tear Catherine in pieces; and I was just worked up to risk coming to the rescue, when of a sudden his fingers relaxed; he shifted his grasp from her head to her arm, and gazed intently into her face. Then he drew his hand over his eyes, stood a moment to collect himself apparently, and turning anew to Catherine, said with assumed calmness, "You must learn to avoid putting me in a passion, or I shall really murder you some time! Go with Mrs. Dean, and keep with her, and confine your insolence to her ears. As to Hareton Earnshaw, if I see him listen to you I'll send him seeking his bread where he can get it. Your love will make him an outcast and a beggar.—Nelly, take her; and leave me, all of you!—leave me!"

I led my young lady out. She was too glad of her escape to resist. The other followed, and Mr. Heathcliff had the room to himself till dinner. I had counselled Catherine to dine upstairs, but as soon as he perceived her vacant seat he sent me to call her. He spoke to none of us, ate very little, and went out directly afterwards, intimating that he should not return before evening.

The two new friends established themselves in the house during his absence, when I heard Hareton sternly check his cousin on her offering a revelation of her father-in-law's conduct to his father. He said he wouldn't suffer a word to be uttered in his disparagement. Catherine was waxing cross at this, but he found means to make her hold her tongue by asking how she would like *him* to speak ill of her father. Then she comprehended that Earnshaw took the master's reputation home to himself, and was attached by ties stronger than reason could break—chains forged by habit, which it would be cruel to attempt to loosen. She showed a good heart, thenceforth, in avoiding both complaints and expressions of antipathy concerning Heathcliff, and I don't believe she has ever breathed a syllable against him in Hareton's hearing since.

When this slight disagreement was over they were friends again, and as busy as possible in their several occupations of pupil and teacher. I came in to sit with them after I had done my work, and I felt so soothed and comforted to watch them that I did not notice how time got on. You know they both appeared in a measure my children. I had long been proud of one, and now I was sure the other would be a source of equal satisfaction. His honest, warm and intelligent nature shook off rapidly the clouds of ignorance and degradation in which it had been bred, and Catherine's sincere commendations acted as a spur to his industry. His brightening mind brightened his features, and added spirit and nobility to their aspect. I could hardly fancy it the same individual I had beheld on the day I discovered my little lady at Wuthering Heights, after her expedition to the Crags. While I admired and they laboured, dusk drew on, and with it returned the master. He came upon us quite unexpectedly, entering by the front way, and had a full view of the whole three ere we could raise our heads to glance at him. Well, I reflected, there was never a pleasanter or more harmless sight, and it will be a burning shame to scold them. The red firelight glowed on their two bonny heads, and revealed their faces animated with the eager interest of children.

They lifted their eyes together, to encounter Mr. Heathcliff. Perhaps you have never remarked that their eyes are precisely similar, and they are those of Catherine Earnshaw. The present Catherine has no other likeness to her, except a breadth of forehead and a certain arch of nostril that makes her appear rather haughty, whether she will or not. With Hareton the resemblance is carried further. It is singular at all times; *then* it was particularly striking, because his senses were alert, wakened to unwonted activity. I suppose this resemblance disarmed Mr. Heathcliff. He walked to the hearth in evident agitation; but it quickly subsided as he looked at the young man—or, I should say, altered its character, for it was there yet. He took the book from his hand and glanced at the open page, then returned it without observation, merely signing Catherine away. Her companion lingered very little behind her; and I was about to depart also, but he bade me sit still.

" It is a poor conclusion, is it not ? " he observed, having brooded a while on the scene he had just witnessed—" an absurd termination to my violent exertions ? I get levers and mattocks to demolish the two houses, and train myself to be capable of working like Hercules, and when everything is ready and in my power, I find the will to lift a slate of either roof has vanished ! I can't take the trouble to raise my hand. I have lost the faculty of enjoying their destruction, and I am too idle to destroy for nothing.

"Nelly, there is a strange change approaching; I'm in its shadow at present. I take so little interest in my daily life that I hardly remember to eat and drink. Those two who have left the room are the only objects which retain a distinct material appearance to me, and that appearance causes me pain, amounting to agony. About *her* I won't speak, and I don't desire to think, but I earnestly wish she were invisible. *He* moves me differently; and yet if I could do it without seeming insane, I'd never see him again. You'll perhaps think me rather inclined to become so," he added, making an effort to smile, "if I try to describe the thousand forms of past associations and ideas he awakens or embodies. But you'll not talk of what I tell you; and my mind is so eternally secluded in itself, it is tempting at last to turn it out to another.

"Five minutes ago Hareton seemed a personification of my youth, not a human being. I felt to him in such a variety of ways that it would have been impossible to have accosted him rationally. In the first place, his startling likeness to Catherine connected him fearfully with her. That, however, which you may suppose the most potent to arrest my imagination, is actually the least; for what is not connected with her to me? and what does not recall her? I cannot look down to this floor but her features are shaped in the flags. In every cloud, in every tree—filling the air by night, and caught by glimpses in every object by day—I am surrounded with her image. The entire world is a dreadful collection of memoranda that she did exist, and that I have lost her. Well, Hareton's aspect was the ghost of my immortal love, of my wild endeavours to hold my right, my degradation, my pride, my happiness, and my anguish—

"But it is frenzy to repeat these thoughts to you;

only it will let you know why, with a reluctance to be always alone, his society is no benefit, rather an aggravation of the constant torment I suffer; and it partly contributes to render me regardless how he and his cousin go on together. I can give them no attention any more."

"But what do you mean by a *change*, Mr. Heathcliff?" I said, alarmed at his manner, though he was neither in danger of losing his senses, nor dying, according to my judgment. He was quite strong and healthy; and as to his reason, he might have had a monomania on the subject of his departed idol, but on every other point his wits were as sound as mine.

"I shall not know that till it comes," he said. "I'm only half conscious of it now."

"You have no feeling of illness, have you?" I asked.

"No, Nelly, I have not," he answered.

"Then you are not afraid of death?" I pursued.

"Afraid? No!" he replied. "I have neither a fear, nor a presentiment, nor a hope of death. Why should I? With my hard constitution, and temperate mode of living, I shall probably remain above ground till there is scarcely a black hair on my head. And yet I cannot continue in this condition. I have to remind myself to breathe, almost to remind my heart to beat. It is by compulsion that I do the slightest act not prompted by one thought, and by compulsion that I notice anything alive or dead which is not associated with one universal idea. I have a single wish, and my whole being and faculties are yearning to attain it. They have yearned towards it so long and so unwaveringly that I'm convinced it *will* be reached—and *soon*—because it has devoured my existence. I am swallowed up in the anticipation of its fulfilment. My confessions have not relieved me, but they may account for some otherwise unaccountable phases of humour which I show.—O God! it is a long fight, I wish it were over!"

He began to pace the room, muttering terrible things to himself, till I was inclined to believe, as he said Joseph did, that conscience had turned his heart to an earthly hell. I wondered greatly how it would end. Though he seldom before had revealed his state of mind, even by looks, it was his habitual mood, I had no doubt. He asserted it himself; but not a soul, from his general bearing, would have conjectured the fact.

CHAPTER XXIII

FOR some days after that evening Mr. Heathcliff shunned meeting us at meals, yet he would not consent formally to exclude Hareton and Cathy. He had an aversion to yielding so completely to his feelings, choosing rather to absent himself; and eating once in twenty-four hours seemed sufficient sustenance for him.

One night, after the family were in bed, I heard him go downstairs and out at the front door. I did not hear him re-enter, and in the morning I found he was still away. We were in April then. The weather was sweet and warm. After breakfast Catherine insisted on my bringing my chair, and sitting with my work under the fir-trees at the end of the house; and she beguiled Hareton to dig and arrange her little garden, which was shifted to that corner by the influence of Joseph's complaint. I was comfortably revelling in the spring fragrance around, when my young lady, who had run down near the gate to procure some primrose roots for a border, returned only half laden, and informed us that Mr. Heathcliff was coming in.

" And he spoke to me," she added, with a perplexed countenance.

" What did he say ? " asked Hareton.

" He told me to begone as fast I could," she answered. " But he looked so different from his usual look that I stopped a moment to stare at him."

" How ? " he inquired.

" Why, almost bright and cheerful. No, *almost* nothing —*very much* excited, and wild and glad ! " she replied.

" Night-walking amuses him, then," I remarked, affecting a careless manner—in reality as surprised as she was. I framed an excuse to go in. Heathcliff stood in the open door. He was pale, and he trembled; yet certainly he had a strange, joyful glitter in his eyes that altered the aspect of his whole face.

" Will you have some breakfast ? " I said. " You must be hungry rambling about all night."

I wanted to discover where he had been, but I did not like to ask directly.

" No, I'm not hungry," he answered, averting his head and speaking rather contemptuously, as if he guessed I was trying to divine the occasion of his good humour.

" I don't think it right to wander out of doors," I observed, " instead of being in bed. It is not wise."

That noon he sat down to dinner with us, and received a heaped-up plate from my hands, as if he intended to make amends for previous fasting.

He took knife and fork, and was going to commence eating, when the inclination appeared to become suddenly extinct. He laid them on the table, looked eagerly towards the window, then rose and went out. We saw him walking to and fro in the garden while we concluded our meal.

I set his plate to keep warm on the fender, and after an hour or two he re-entered, when the room was clear, in no degree calmer—the same unnatural appearance of joy under his black brows; the same bloodless hue, and his teeth visible, now and then, in a kind of smile; his frame shivering—not as one shivers with chill or weakness, but as a tight-stretched cord vibrates—a strong thrilling rather than trembling.

I will ask what is the matter, I thought; or who should? And I exclaimed—

"Have you heard any good news, Mr. Heathcliff? You look uncommonly animated."

"Where should good news come from to me?" he said. "I'm animated with hunger, and seemingly I must not eat."

"Your dinner is here," I returned; "why won't you get it?"

"I don't want it now," he muttered hastily. "I'll wait till supper. And, Nelly, let me beg you to warn Hareton and the other away from me. I wish to be troubled by nobody."

"Is there some new reason for this banishment?" I inquired. "Tell me why you are so queer, Mr. Heathcliff. Where were you last night?"

"Last night I was on the threshold of hell. Today I am within sight of my heaven. I have my eyes on it—hardly three feet to sever me. And now you'd better go. You'll neither see nor hear anything to frighten you if you refrain from prying."

He did not quit the house again that afternoon, and no one intruded on his solitude, till, at eight o'clock, I deemed it proper to carry a candle and his supper to him. He was leaning against the ledge of an open lattice, but not looking out; his face was turned to the interior gloom. The fire had smouldered to ashes; the room was filled with the damp, mild air of the cloudy evening. I uttered an ejaculation of discontent at seeing the dismal grate, and commenced shutting the casements, one after another, until I came to his.

" Must I close this ? " I asked, in order to rouse him, for he did not stir.

The light flashed on his features as I spoke. Oh, Mr. Lockwood, I cannot express what a terrible start I got by that momentary view—those deep black eyes, that smile, and ghastly paleness ! It appeared to me, not Mr. Heathcliff, but a goblin; and in my terror I let the candle bend towards the wall, and it left me in darkness.

" Yes, close it," he replied, in his familiar voice. " There, that is pure awkwardness ! Why did you hold the candle horizontally ? Be quick, and bring another."

I hurried out in a foolish state of dread, and said to Joseph—

" The master wishes you to take him a light and re-kindle the fire." For I dared not go in myself again just then.

Joseph rattled some fire into the shovel, and went; but he brought it back immediately, with the supper-tray in his other hand, explaining that Mr. Heathcliff was going to bed, and he wanted nothing to eat till morning. We heard him mount the stairs directly. He did not proceed to his ordinary chamber, but turned into that with the panelled bed. Its window, as I mentioned before, is wide enough for anybody to get through; and it struck me that he plotted another midnight excursion, of which he had rather we had no suspicion.

I rose at dawn and went into the garden as soon as I could see, to ascertain if there were any footmarks under his window. There were none. " He has stayed at home," I thought, " and he'll be all right today." I pre-pared breakfast for the household, as was my usual custom, but told Hareton and Catherine to get theirs ere the master came down, for he lay late. They preferred taking it out of doors, under the trees, and I set a little table to accommodate them.

On my re-entering I found Mr. Heathcliff below. His countenance had the same eager, excited expression, even more exaggerated. He took his seat in the place he generally chose, and I put a basin of coffee before him. He drew it nearer, and then rested his arms on the table and looked at the opposite wall, as I supposed, surveying one particular portion, up and down, with glittering, restless eyes.

" Come now," I exclaimed, " eat and drink while it is hot."

He didn't notice me, and yet he smiled. I'd rather have seen him gnash his teeth than smile so.

" Mr. Heathcliff ! master ! " I cried, " don't, for God's sake, stare as if you saw an unearthly vision."

" Don't, for God's sake, shout so loud," he replied. " Turn round and tell me—are we by ourselves ? "

" Of course," was my answer—" of course we are."

Still I involuntarily obeyed him, as if I was not quite sure. With a sweep of his hand he cleared a vacant space in front among the breakfast things, and leant forward to gaze more at his ease.

Now I perceived he was not looking at the wall, for when I regarded him alone it seemed exactly that he gazed at something within two yards' distance. And whatever it was, it communicated apparently both pleasure and pain in exquisite extremes—at least the anguished yet raptured expression of his countenance suggested that idea. The fancied object was not fixed either : his eyes pursued it with unwearied diligence, and, even in speaking to me, were never weaned away.

I sat, a model of patience, trying to attract his absorbed attention from its engrossing speculation and induce him to eat, until he grew irritable, and got up, asking why I

would not allow him to have his own time in taking his
meals, and saying that on the next occasion I needn't
wait—I might set the things down and go. Having
uttered these words he left the house, slowly sauntered
down the garden path, and disappeared through the gate.

The hours crept anxiously by; another evening came.
I did not retire to rest till late, and when I did I could not
sleep. He returned after midnight, and instead of going to
bed, shut himself into the room beneath. I listened and
tossed about, and finally dressed and descended. It was
too irksome to lie there harassing my brain with a hundred
idle misgivings.

I distinguished Mr. Heathcliff's step restlessly measuring
the floor, and he frequently broke the silence by a deep
inspiration resembling a groan. He muttered detached
words also. The only one I caught was the name of
Catherine, coupled with some wild term of endearment or
suffering, and spoken as one would speak to a person
present—low and earnest, and wrung from the depth of his
soul. I had not courage to walk straight into the apartment, but I desired to divert him from his reverie, and
therefore fell foul of the kitchen fire; stirred it, and
began to scrape the cinders. It drew him forth sooner
than I expected. He opened the door immediately, and
said—

" Nelly, come here. Is it morning? Come in with
your light."

" It is striking four," I answered. " You want a candle
to take upstairs."

" No, I don't wish to go upstairs," he said. " Come in
and kindle *me* a fire."

I proceeded to do this. He roamed to and fro, meantime, in a state approaching distraction, his heavy sighs
succeeding each other so thick as to leave no space for
common breathing between.

"When day breaks I'll send for Green," he said. "I wish to make some legal inquiries of him. I have not written my will yet, and how to leave my property I cannot determine. I wish I could annihilate it from the face of the earth."

"I would not talk so, Mr. Heathcliff," I interposed. "Let your will be for a while; you'll be spared to repent of your many injustices yet. Do take some food and some repose. You need only look at yourself in the glass to see how you require both."

"It is not my fault that I cannot eat or rest," he replied. "I assure you it is through no settled designs. I'll do both as soon as I possibly can. But you might as well bid a man struggling in the water to rest within arm's length of the shore! I must reach it first, and then I'll rest. Well, never mind Mr. Green. As to repenting of my injustices, I've done no injustice, and I repent of nothing. I'm too happy; and yet I'm not happy enough. My soul's bliss kills my body, but does not satisfy itself."

"Happy, master?" I cried. "Strange happiness! If you would hear me without being angry, I might offer some advice that would make you happier."

"What is that?" he asked. "Give it."

"You are aware, Mr. Heathcliff," I said, "that from the time you were thirteen years old you have lived a selfish, unchristian life. Could it be hurtful to send for some one (a minister of any denomination) and show you how greatly you have erred, and how unfit you will be for heaven, unless a change takes place before you die?"

"I'm rather obliged than angry, Nelly," he said, "for you remind me of the manner in which I desire to be buried. It is to be carried to the churchyard in the evening. You and Hareton may, if you please, accompany me; and mind particularly to notice that the sexton obeys my directions concerning the two coffins. No minister need come, nor need anything be said over me. I tell you I have nearly attained *my* heaven, and that of others is altogether unvalued and uncoveted by me."

As soon as he heard the other members of the family stirring he retired to his den, and I breathed freer. But in the afternoon, while Joseph and Hareton were at their work, he came into the kitchen again, and with a wild look bade me come and sit in the house; he wanted somebody with him. I declined, telling him plainly that his strange talk and manner frightened me, and I had neither the nerve nor the will to be his companion alone.

" I believe you think me a fiend," he said, with his dismal laugh—" something too horrible to live under a decent roof." Then turning to Catherine, who was there, and who drew behind me at his approach, he added, half sneeringly, " Will *you* come, chuck? I'll not hurt you. No! To you I've made myself worse than the devil. Well, there is *one* who won't shrink from my company. By God, she's relentless! Oh, damn it! It's unutterably too much for flesh and blood to bear—even mine."

He solicited the society of no one more. At dusk he went into his chamber. Through the whole night, and far into the morning, we heard him groaning and murmuring to himself. Hareton was anxious to enter, but I bade him fetch Mr. Kenneth, and he should go in and see him. When Kenneth came, and I requested admittance and tried to open the door, I found it locked, and Heathcliff bade us be damned. He was better, and would be left alone; so the doctor went away.

The following evening was very wet—indeed it poured down till day-dawn; and as I took my morning walk round the house I observed the master's window swinging open, and the rain driving straight in. " He cannot be in bed," I thought; "those showers would drench him through. He must either be up or out. But I'll make no more ado; I'll go boldly and look."

Having succeeded in obtaining entrance with another key, I ran to unclose the panels, for the chamber was vacant. Quickly pushing them aside, I peeped in. Mr. Heathcliff was there, laid on his back. His eyes met mine so keen and fierce, I started; and then he seemed to smile. I could not think him dead; but his face and throat were washed with rain, the bedclothes dripped, and he was perfectly still. The lattice, flapping to and fro, had grazed one hand that rested on the sill. No blood trickled from the broken skin, and when I put my fingers to it I could doubt no more—he was dead and stark !

I hasped the window; I combed his black long hair from his forehead; I tried to close his eyes—to extinguish, if possible, that frightful, life-like gaze of exultation before anyone else beheld it. They would not shut—they seemed to sneer at my attempts; and his parted lips and sharp white teeth sneered too. Taken with another fit of cowardice, I cried out for Joseph. Joseph shuffled up and made a noise, but resolutely refused to meddle with him.

" Th' divil's harried off his soul," he cried, " and he may hev his carcass int' t' bargain for aught I care ! "

I thought he intended to cut a caper round the bed; but suddenly composing himself, he fell on his knees, and raised his hands, and returned thanks that the lawful master and the ancient stock were restored to their rights.

I felt stunned by the awful event, and my memory unavoidably recurred to former times with a sort of oppressive sadness. But poor Hareton, the most wronged, was the only one who really suffered much. He sat by the corpse all night, weeping in bitter earnest. He pressed its hand, and kissed the sarcastic, savage face that everyone else shrank from contemplating and bemoaned him with that strong grief which springs from a generous heart, though it be tough as tempered steel.

We buried him, to the scandal of the whole neighbourhood, as he wished. Earnshaw and I, the sexton, and six men to carry the coffin, comprehended the whole attendance. The six men departed when they had let it down into the grave. We stayed to see it covered. Hareton, with a streaming face, dug green sods and laid them over the brown mould himself. At present it is as smooth and verdant as its companion mounds, and I hope its tenant sleeps as soundly. But the country folks, if you ask them, would swear on the Bible that he *walks*. There are those who speak to having met him near the church, and on the moor, and even within this house. Idle tales you'll say, and so say I. Yet, still I don't like myself being out in the dark now, and I don't like being left by myself in this grim house. I shall be glad when they leave it and shift to the Grange.

" They are going to the Grange, then ? " I said.

" Yes," answered Mrs. Dean, " as soon as they are married, and that will be on New Year's day."

" And who will live here then ? "

" Why, Joseph will take care of the house, and perhaps a lad to keep him company. They will live in the kitchen, and the rest will be shut up."

" For the use of such ghosts as choose to inhabit it," I observed.

" No, Mr. Lockwood," said Nelly, shaking her head. " I believe the dead are at peace, but it is not right to speak of them with levity."

At that moment the garden gate swung to ; the ramblers were returning.

" *They* are afraid of nothing," I grumbled, watching

their approach through the window. " Together they would brave Satan and all his legions."

As they stepped on to the door-stones, and halted to take a last look at the moon—or, more correctly, at each other by her light—I felt irresistibly impelled to escape them again; and pressing a remembrance into the hand of Mrs. Dean, and disregarding her expostulations at my rudeness, I vanished through the kitchen as they opened the house-door.

My walk home was lengthened by a diversion in the direction of the kirk. When beneath its walls I perceived decay had made its progress, even in seven months. Many a window showed black gaps deprived of glass, and slates jutted off here and there beyond the right line of the roof, to be gradually worked off in coming autumn storms.

I sought and soon discovered the three headstones on the slope next the moor—the middle one gray, and half buried in heath; Edgar Linton's only harmonized by the turf and moss creeping up its foot; Heathcliff's still bare.

I lingered round them under that benign sky, watched the moths fluttering among the heath and harebells, listened to the soft wind breathing through the grass, and wondered how any one could ever imagine unquiet slumbers for the sleepers in that quiet earth.

THE END